Make Mine
SWEET

GENNY CARRICK

Cover design and illustration by Melody Jeffries

Edited by Cindy Ray Hale

ISBN (ebook): 978-1-957745-18-3

ISBN (paperback): 978-1-957745-19-0

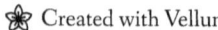 Created with Vellum

For those searching for a safe harbor. May you find someone to sail through storms at your side.

If they growl at you like a pirate, so much the better.

WHAT TO EXPECT

This book includes a grumpy-sunshine scenario, past parental abandonment, past romantic abandonment, vivid memories of a vehicle accident, discussion of limb loss, an unexpected animal encounter, and extensive pirate imagery.

ONE
IAN

I REALLY NEED a *Go away* sign.

The doorbell's cheery chime rings through my apartment for the third time. I've been lying on the couch pretending I'm not home in the hope my uninvited visitor would go away, but they haven't taken the hint. Since I only ever get the one visitor, it was a pointless hope. My aunt's allergic to the word *No*.

The chime rings again, quicker this time, and I groan, rolling up to a sitting position. My blinds are closed, but I still squint against the harsh summer sunshine like a vampire awoken too early from his slumber. Might even hiss, but that's more from my aching back than the sunlight burning my skin. This couch wasn't built for naps.

My dog's got his nose practically pressed to the front door, whining and wagging his tail. Yep. It's my aunt Amy waiting on the other side.

Can't expect anyone else when she's the only person I know here in Sunshine. That was the whole point in coming to a small town in central Oregon—the isolation. But Amy and I haven't seen eye to eye on that. Case in point: her unpredictable social calls. It's like the woman doesn't know what "holing up so I can lick my wounds in peace" means.

I push up my sweatpants leg and re-secure my prosthesis. I don't sleep with it on, and I'd been expecting a longer nap than the one I got.

Raking my fingers through my long hair, I groan again at how far I've fallen. Taking afternoon naps like an old man in a nursing home. If only the readers of *Crux Monthly* could see me now. Those fifteen minutes of fame sure disappear fast.

The moment I throw the door open, Amy accosts me with her grin. "Ian. I was starting to think you were out on a hike."

She doesn't mean anything by it. Still feels like a dig. The closest I get to hiking anymore is walking the two-mile trail that starts behind the duplex. I used to climb dangerous mountain peaks for a living. Now, I have to hype myself up to tackle the kiddie hill.

She bends down to greet my dog, Dutch, who tries to lick her face. But Amy's familiar with his tactics and steers clear of his whip-fast tongue.

"I was just—" I gesture vaguely around the apartment. *Avoiding humanity and staring into the abyss.* "You caught me at an awkward time."

She straightens, searing me with a fiery look. "That implies there's a good time to catch you."

I can't help the laugh that gusts out of me. She's not wrong. I haven't been at my best for...well. A solid two years now. "If I'd known you were coming, I might have..."

Her eyebrows lift, waiting for me to finish that sentence. What would I have done? Cleaned the apartment? Showered? Not lain motionless for ten minutes hoping she would give up and drive away?

None of the above.

She just laughs. "Don't strain yourself on my account."

Amy and I are closer in age than a typical aunt/nephew pair. She's only ten years older than I am, just a step above my oldest brother. Most of the time, she's more like an overly familiar cousin than a matronly aunt.

I shudder. If she had any idea I even *thought* the word "matronly" in connection with her, she'd skin me alive.

I step back from the doorway and motion her to come inside, even though it puts me on edge. I have enough sense left to know I should do something about the mess. Just don't have the motivation.

Amy walks into the middle of the living room as though she doesn't see the granola bar wrappers, dirty plates, and empty coffee mugs on every flat surface. But Dutch licks at a crumb on a spoon as he passes the coffee table, calling me out on my shoddy housekeeping. *Thanks, man's best friend.*

"Jodi wanted to send a burger and fries over, but I told her if she did, it'd be even longer before she sees you again." She smiles, making the comment more affectionate than it deserves to be.

It also twists something in my gut. Shame, probably. Amy and her wife, Jodi, run a local diner and own several rental properties around town. They offered me this apartment to "recuperate" for a while, and I've showed my gratitude by stopping in to visit them a handful of times in three months.

The thing is, Delish is a popular place. Not that long ago, I would have reveled in the crowds, but now, they make my skin crawl. I'm out of the habit of being around that many people. I don't know how to carry myself anymore. And that's just trying to grab a bite to eat.

"I'll drop by this week," I tell her. Near closing, when the place is almost empty.

"Good. She misses your face." Amy hitches a shoulder. "Such as it is."

I scrape a hand over my beard. "It's not that bad."

Her "Oh, really?" look could melt glass. "That beard's somewhere between 'Hagrid' and 'Gandalf.'"

I consider the two options. "Which one's worse?"

"That's not the question you should be asking."

Maybe not. What I look like isn't high on my priority list anymore. Nothing really is.

"What brings you by?" I try to put some friendliness in it, but it comes out an accusation. Typical of Amy, she ignores my caustic tone.

"I was talking with Mitchell Choi yesterday. I told you about his business, Horizon Hikes. He said they're looking to hire more guides."

I make not a single sound. Even a grunt of acknowledgement would encourage her to keep talking. She knows I haven't led anyone on so much as a walk around my back yard since I lost my left leg two years ago.

She waits, her eye contact too pointed to miss. "Seems like an opportunity you would want to know about."

I cross my arms and stare her down. "I'm out of that business."

She knows that, too, since it's why I came to Oregon. I couldn't keep haunting the successful guiding company my brothers and I had built in Colorado, always present but unable to do anything meaningful. I haven't been any more useful here, but at least my brothers and employees don't give me cheerful smiles to cover up their pity twenty times a day.

Losing my leg took an adjustment, but I learned to adapt. It's just meat. But losing my career? My reputation? Everything that made me who I was? I haven't figured out how to adjust to that.

She doesn't flinch away from my glare. "There's always that

wilderness camp for kids. They're hiring counselors ages seventeen and up. Pretty sure you qualify."

I snort. "I don't think I'm real suited to taking care of kids."

"Join a book club at the library."

"I'm not an official resident."

She sighs all the air from her lungs. "Explore the town. It'd be good for you to have a break from this apartment now and then."

"Dutch is offended."

She points a finger at me. "That right there. You need more company than that dog."

I look to where my trusty companion made himself comfortable on the couch. He's a big, brown mutt with strangely perceptive eyes and the dopiest doggie grin. He slurps his tongue into his mouth, unbothered by Amy's slights.

"Agree to disagree."

Dutch only judges me when I don't share my food with him. But people? They're full of pointed questions, sorrowful gazes that follow me everywhere I go, and whispered gossip about everything I've lost. I'll stick with my dog, thanks.

Something out the window behind me catches her eye. The tiniest smirk hits her mouth before she chases it away again. "Well. You know best. Come meet your new neighbors."

She moves past me to the front door, but I freeze. "My new *what*?"

"Neighbors." She says the word nice and slow so I don't miss a syllable. "They're moving in today."

Today? "But you said..."

She arches that eyebrow at me again, refuting everything I thought we'd discussed. "I said we had no plans to let the unit next door as a short-term rental anymore. I never said we wouldn't rent it out long-term."

She walks outside, leaving me standing here with my mouth open. A long-term renter? I pull a hand down my face, searching for calm. Beggars can't be choosers, but I've had a real good set up here.

I like that the duplex sits at the end of a long lane few people have a reason to drive up. I like that it rests at the edge of the foothills near a short hiking path—I appreciate the views, even if I don't often use the trail. I especially like that the unit next door has been empty for the last three months.

I step out onto the front porch next to Amy, Dutch following close behind. A blue station wagon sits a space away from my SUV. I stare at the wagon, but sunlight glare prevents me from seeing who's inside.

"I'm not real sociable lately," I mutter under my breath.

Amy laughs. "I've noticed."

"I like my privacy."

"If by 'privacy' you mean 'turning into a recluse,' I've noticed that, too."

"If you expect me to—" The rest of my idle threat dies out as I swallow my tongue.

The woman who gets out of the station wagon is drop-dead gorgeous. Blond, in a red-and-white striped shirt and jeans shorts that show off curves out of my dreams, she shoots a grin Amy's direction and waves.

Like an idiot, I lift my hand to wave back. I have enough sense to redirect and rake my fingers through my hair. That "Gandalf or Hagrid?" debate roars back to life in my head. Hair past my shoulders, beard several inches beyond my chin, my shirt creeping into its third day of rotation—I could pass for a cave man if I had a couple of rocks to bang together.

The only saving grace is that I put on sweatpants this morning and never changed out of them. I've come to terms with my prosthetic leg in most ways, but there's not a world in which I want this woman to look at me with pity in her eyes the moment I meet her. Give her a chance to get to know me, at least.

Then she can pity me for entirely different reasons.

Amy steps off the porch and greets her as the woman opens the rear passenger door. A little boy with pale blond hair jumps out and slips his hand into hers.

Something beneath my ribcage shifts. Whatever useless hope flared to life in there dies back down. No doubt a man will appear any minute now to round out their family unit. Probably some clean-shaven suit who doesn't use the sniff-test on his clothes every morning.

I cross my arms back over my chest.

"Tess and August, meet my nephew, Ian." Amy gestures over at me. "Ian, these are two of the best people in Sunshine you'll ever know."

The woman—Tess—smiles brightly at me. That stupid hope tries to flutter back into existence, but I squash the life out of it. It's nothing personal. Just the last shreds of my self-preservation.

"It's nice to meet you, Ian."

I don't react, but her smile doesn't budge. She's either a nurse or works retail to be this unfazed by me ignoring her kindness. Maybe a teacher.

"Mister, can I pet your dog?" The little boy's practically dancing next to his mother—I might be assuming too much, but they look too alike for them to be anything else.

I nod. The dog hasn't had a whole lot of practice, but he's been good with kids so far. Tess lets go of the boy's hand, and he steps up onto the low porch both duplexes share. He holds a hand out, and Dutch sniffs it. Next second, he licks it, and the kid starts petting him in long strokes down his back. Dutch leans so hard against him, the kid almost falls over.

At least one of us is happy to have neighbors.

TWO
TESS

I KNEW my apartment came with a reclusive neighbor attached, but I didn't anticipate this much scowling. Or facial hair.

Seriously, that is a Dude Thor-level beard.

But I promised Amy I would try to befriend her nephew, and while she never explicitly said my efforts are in exchange for the phenomenally cheap rent she offered me, I'm not stupid. Although, with the way the man's glaring at me, it's fair to say my optimism butts up against naiveté.

As if I didn't know that already.

I go on smiling at Ian. In my experience, a little sweetness goes a long way. Whether in my family's bakery when the line is long and customers get twitchy or when August is grumpy and doesn't want to do his blood sugar tests, a warm smile and cheerful attitude can be infectious.

Ian's scowl is a sweetness-repelling shield. He's giving strong "Keep Out, No Trespassing" vibes. Which is awkward, considering we'll be sharing a duplex for the foreseeable future.

Scowls or not, I need this apartment. I'm thirty-two—it's long past time I create some space for August and me. And maybe get out from under my mother's increasingly smothering wings in the process.

"I don't have much time today." Amy hands me my house keys and reminds me of a few last details about the rental. Before I know it, she's at her car again, ready to leave. "Ian, why don't you help Tess and August carry their things inside? That'd be neighborly of you."

She winks at him, hops into her car, and drives away. Leaving me with the least neighborly guy I can imagine.

I side-eye my new lumberjack-looking companion. When Amy offered me this apartment, I'd been too focused on the steeply discounted rent to ask much about the solitary nephew she'd mentioned. Now, I've got nothing but questions. Like:

Does he ever smile?

Is he trying to zap me into oblivion with his ice-blue eyes?

How long does he plan on giving us the silent treatment?

"What's your dog's name, Mister?" August asks. He hasn't stopped petting the dog since he got permission. We probably have five minutes before he declares it his new best friend.

At least the dog is friendly. The man's more likely to growl at us than that dog is.

Ian's gaze drops down to where August's sitting on the porch, the dog right next to him exulting in his pets and scratches. The big dog practically vibrates from joy as August strokes its fluffy, mottled brown fur. It's also got a tongue approximately two feet long and an urge to taste-test anywhere on August he can reach.

"His name's Dutch." Ian's voice comes out gravelly, like he doesn't use it often.

August lights up. "Like Double Dutch!"

"Or like Arnold Schwarzenegger in *Predator*," Ian mutters. He must not appreciate his dog being linked with a kid's jump rope game instead of a muscled-out action movie hero.

"I haven't seen that one," I say.

His gaze hits mine. "Probably not for everybody."

I've never been one for violent, blood-and-guts movies, and I'm pretty sure that one qualifies. "The one where he plays a Kindergarten teacher is probably more my speed."

I'm guessing. I haven't actually seen that one, either.

Ian only blinks at that information. All right, moving on.

"I hope Amy didn't spring us on you." My awkward laugh grows more shrill when Ian goes on staring blankly. He's throwing off the opposite of warm fuzzies. Cold pricklies are definitely a thing.

He ticks his head to the side. "It's her house."

Yeah. That's an "I'm not happy about having new neighbors" if I ever heard one. I want to say something reassuring about how we're all going to get along great...but even I'm not that naive.

"Come on, August." I can't spend all day on the porch working up anxiety about the man next door I promised to try to befriend. "Help bring your things inside."

I unlock the front door and push it open. It's a simple two-bedroom apartment filled with comfortable furniture. We're lucky to get it—grumpy neighbor and all.

I send August off to his new room, his excitement echoing around the house, and go back out to my station wagon. I open the hatch, and my heart jumps straight into my throat when Ian appears at my side like a lumbering bear.

I do *not* scream. I do, however, make a strangled sound I deeply regret.

His eyes rake over me almost like he's used to startling people. "Amy said I should help."

Oh. I kind of figured he would ignore that bit of advice. I'm grateful, though—we brought a lot of stuff, and I'm already sweating even though the late-May day isn't all that hot. "Thanks. Do you mind getting the biggest luggage?"

He hefts the giant bag out of the back as if it's empty. My bear assessment was pretty spot on.

I grab a couple of smaller pieces of luggage and go into the house. My bedroom is cozy but bright, the orange and blue in the bedspread and rug making it cheery. It's got a big window that lets in plenty of light. This will be a good place for us.

I refuse to let it be anything else.

I set my bags by the dresser, and Ian does the same with the bigger one. He's almost comically out of place in the feminine room. If it weren't for Amy's vehement reassurance she trusts him implicitly, I might be uncomfortable sharing such a small space with this man.

Might be. A tremor of unease skates through my stomach, despite my friend vouching for him. He's just so imposing. He's probably only got a couple of inches on my five-eight frame, but his broad shoulders and bulging biceps are impossible to miss. Not to mention his long red hair and beard and that furrowed brow telegraphing his displeasure.

"Is your apartment decorated pretty much the same?" Amy and Jodi used to let both units out as short-term rentals, which is why they're fully furnished. It's hard to imagine him in an equally colorful room. Pretty sure he favors things like Storm-cloud Gray and Bleak Black.

His gaze cuts my way, skating over me as though he's trying not to acknowledge my presence. "No."

He shuffles out again. Okay. This is going...not great. But I can do this. I'm the go-to for dealing with grumpy customers at the bakery. Mostly because if my sister, Wren, has to handle them, she grouses back. Someone has to grin and bear it in retail.

I go out to the car for the next round, passing August, who's given up on his unloading duties. He's snuggling with Dutch on the porch, no doubt getting covered in dog hair and slobber. But he's distracted, so I'll take it.

Ian's already at the back of my car like he's waiting for instructions, so I try again.

"This is a great place out here. Do you do a lot of hiking on the trail?" A path starts just past the duplex's back yard. I'm not huge on hiking myself, but it seems like a safe enough topic.

"No."

I refuse to sigh. I shouldn't have expected more conversation from a man Amy described as living in a "self-imposed hermitude," but I'd hoped he would at least be responsive to small talk. This is fine, though. I'll just keep trying.

Ian drags a big box to the edge of the hatch, but I stop him.

"That one's a beast." It's got my extremely expensive, extremely precious, extremely heavy mixer in it.

He cuts me a look like he and his giant biceps don't appreciate the warning. He scoops it up without a struggle. With those arms, I'm not sure a washing machine would be a struggle.

I grab a much lighter box and follow him into the house.

"Where do you want this?" he asks over his shoulder.

"Just on the kitchen counter, thanks." I tuck the box of August's toys into his room and join Ian. "Amy says you haven't been in town very long. Where did you live before?"

"Colorado."

I wait for more, but he doesn't offer more. "How do you like Sunshine?"

Apparently, my only goal in life is to smother this man with smiles and get him to talk to me in more than single sentences. I'm probably doing too much for the first day, but I can't stop myself. We don't have to become BFFs, but I have to hope we can reach some level of non-glaring social interactions one day. Otherwise, guilt over my too-cheap rent will crush me down to a powder.

"It's changed since I was here last."

"When was that?" I don't remember ever seeing this man before. You'd think a guy who looks like he'd fit right in on a Viking longboat heading off to plunder a village would stick out more in my memory.

"About fifteen years ago. I worked as a rafting guide one summer."

My triumph over him saying two sentences together pauses. Freezes. Crumbles away entirely.

Ian Vaughn. My heart somehow speeds up, slows down, and sinks into the crawl space beneath the duplex all in one go.

Amy never told me his last name, but now that I've connected the dots, it has to be him. The red hair should have made it obvious, but he's just so *different* in every possible way. Back then, he'd been all breathtaking boyish good looks and handed out wide smiles to everyone. I'd been instantly charmed. He'd effortlessly turned the summer before my senior year of high school into a twisted knot of unrequited infatuation.

My hands go clammy, and my stomach floods with anxious moths. My stab at independence relies on me befriending my old crush who's become some bizarro-world version of himself?

Cool. Cool, cool, cool.

August runs into the kitchen. "Mister, can Dutch come inside to play in my room?"

"His name is Ian." *And your mom was hopelessly obsessed with him when she was a teen.*

"Ian," August says solemnly, "can Dutch come inside?"

Ian gives him another cautious look. I get the feeling he hasn't been around children very much. "Probably not a good idea, kid."

August's smile only slips for a moment. "Can I give him some of my snack?"

"I don't think dogs like apple slices," I tell him.

He thinks for a second, his five-year-old brain working over-time. "Can I eat my snack on the porch with Dutch if I don't give him a single bite? Not even one?"

I look to Ian, who shrugs indifference.

"Sure, buddy," I tell my son. "Can you get your snack out of my bag?"

"I know where it is!" He scrambles into the living room where I left my purse and the bag with his extra snacks, juice boxes, and insulin kit.

Ian and I stare at each other for a moment in the quiet kitchen. I've never been this close to him before, even all those years ago. His glower seems harsher now that I know who he is. Or who he used to be. I'm struggling to merge those memories with the man standing in front of me.

My mind scrambles over possible explanations for the divide between the two versions of him. Amy said he's been through a rough patch and needs to be "pulled out of his doom and gloom." She thought I'd be an ideal candidate for the job. Thinking mostly of the money I'll save and not how many glares I can endure in one lifetime, I'd agreed.

It's that optimism/naïveté again.

"Well," I say, shoving away my old, cringe-inducing memo-ries. "Hopefully, Sunshine has changed for the better."

There goes that indifferent shoulder again. "It's all right."

I'm going to tell my friend, Lila, to put that on the town's new tourism website she's working on. *Sunshine, Oregon: It's all right.*

It's hard to believe this is the same guy who had all the women for miles around swooning whenever he made an appearance in town. He'd had a healthy share of admirers back then, and I'd been jealous of everyone brave enough to actually speak to him. I'd never risked it, too afraid I'd say something silly and ruin my chance for a good first impression.

Now? I'm not sure it's possible to make a good impression on him.

I go outside and crawl into the back of my wagon to pull a few boxes toward the hatch, only to swallow down another shriek when I discover Ian at my side once more when I climb back out.

"How are you so quiet?" I lay a hand over my racing heart.

"Didn't think I was."

The front drive is gravel—he couldn't have been completely silent. My thoughts must have been too caught up in the past to pay attention.

"Maybe I'm just used to a little boy who makes the noise of five people everywhere he goes." I stand straighter. "Not that we're going to be obnoxious neighbors. We'll keep the volume reasonable."

August's high-pitched laughter carries to us, shining a bright spotlight of doubt on my assurances. It also makes me suspect he's trying to share his snack with the dog, after all, but one thing at a time.

"We'll be quiet as a mouse. You won't even know we're here." Seems like a lot to promise when I have no experience living in a duplex like this—the walls could be tissue thin. For all I know, Ian will be able to hear every cough and toilet flush.

He moves to grab one of the boxes I slid closer. "Three people usually aren't quiet as a mouse."

"Two people, and we'll do our best. Within reason." I'll make sure August isn't a wild man at night, but it's not practical to expect him to be quiet during the day. If Ian works nights and needs to sleep when we're home, we could run into trouble.

His gaze hits mine. "It's just the two of you moving in?"

I can feel my customer service smile strain at the edges. "Just us."

This is where people usually ask questions. Divorced?

Widowed? Nobody knows what to say when they find out I was never married. Then come all the questions they want to ask but don't. Isn't the dad in the picture? Can't you hold onto a man? Where's your sense of decency?

Typically, women pry more than men do, but I've had my share of strange men put me on the spot about being a single mom. I don't know Ian well enough to get into any of the answers.

But his gaze just travels briefly over me, his head dips in a quick nod, and he hefts the big box out of the back of my car.

Huh. A win for the indifferent hermit.

THREE

IAN

I GO on carting Tess's boxes and bags into her house, shutting down every stupid thought trying to creep into my brain.

This doesn't change anything. It *can't*.

These thoughts are reflexive, that's all. I've barely spoken with a woman who wasn't a relative or a nurse in the last two years. The most naturally beautiful woman I've seen in possibly my entire life moves in next door, thoughts are going to crop up.

Just have to find a way to ignore them. Somehow.

"That one goes in the kitchen, too," Tess calls from behind me.

I set the box on the counter and read *Cake pans, sheet pans* written neatly on top.

She catches me inspecting it. "My family owns the bakery in town."

That explains all the extra stuff in the kitchen. Amy has the places pretty well outfitted, but you'd never know it from the assortment of fresh boxes Tess brought along.

"I don't think I've seen you in there." Her smile threatens to knock the air out of my lungs, and I have to look away.

It's a hint at a question I should just ignore. Finish this task

Amy gave me and go on with my day. But since up until half an hour ago my day entirely consisted of throwing a stick for my dog and taking a nap, I respond.

"I don't go into town much."

Back in Durango, I couldn't even go to the grocery store without running into someone I knew. Someone who would give me too-cheerful encouragement or thinly-masked sympathy about my accident. Usually both. There are only so many times someone can tell me I'm a "fighter" before I crack. Eventually, I stopped going out. Didn't see any reason to change when I moved here.

Tess doesn't seem deterred. "Well, next time you do, you should stop in. I'll give you a cupcake on the house."

Of course it would be cupcakes. I've been around her less than an hour, and it's clear the woman is sweetness personified. It could be an act, but I used to be able to read people pretty well. From her interactions with her son, me, even the dog, she's been nothing but gentle and warm-hearted.

For the first time in a long while, a twinge of regret hits me for how sour I've become. But instead of shifting gears, I dig in my heels. Things will be easier for everyone if I stay the course.

"I'm watching my figure."

Her gaze darts down to my chest and slips over my arms before popping back up to meet my eyes. My skin warms from her quick glance, even though her expression gives nothing away.

It's not like I care what she thinks of my body. If I had shorts on, she'd only notice my prosthesis, anyway.

A hint of what she thinks wouldn't hurt.

"When you have a cheat day, then."

My impulse is to reject the offer. I've refused nearly every request Amy's made of me since I got here. I don't go into town,

I don't browse the shops, and I don't chit chat with gorgeous, impossibly soft-looking women.

"Maybe," comes out of my mouth anyway.

She beams as though I delivered her a solemn promise.

We walk back out to her car to get the last of their things. For starting out packed to the gills, they didn't bring much beyond clothes, some toys, and baking supplies. Then again, neither did I, but I don't need much. Seems like a family would have a whole lot more with them.

Makes me wonder if she's getting out of a bad situation. A hot spike of protectiveness runs through me, but I tell it to calm down with the heroics. I'm proof looks don't count for anything, but nothing about her makes it seem like she's running from something. The only thing I can see causing her any anxiety is me.

The way her gaze keeps darting to me like she's waiting for me to do or say something crazy has got me rethinking my Neanderthal-chic look.

"Is this it?" I ask, arms full of reusable tote bags loaded with stuffed animals and soft blankets.

"For now." She pulls the last bag from the rear section not occupied by a booster seat. "If we forgot anything we need, I can always drive across town and get it later."

"Flexible landlord." Pretty sure most expect you to move out everything you own when you leave. Mine did. Although he was more upset about me breaking my lease than anything I might have left behind.

"Oh no, we lived with—" She flinches, and her answer fades into strained laughter.

That spike goes through me again, but this time it's colored with jealousy. Completely inappropriate, but here all the same, flashing bright green.

"Your ex-husband?" I suggest in a flat voice. I'm not asking for details. Don't need them.

She cringes. "No. Definitely not."

I shrug. "Ex-boyfriend, then."

She lifts the hand not holding the bag. "No. It's nothing like that. We just, uh..."

After the interrogations complete strangers have seen fit to impose on me when they catch a glimpse of my leg, I try not to ask too many questions. I don't want to be that guy nosing into sensitive topics. But Tess's reluctance to give a straight answer about where she used to live piques my curiosity.

She piques my curiosity, something I'm actively trying to ignore. Failing horribly, but trying.

"Are you escaping some kind of cult situation?"

The sound that bursts out of her is half gasp, half laugh. "No! Gosh! We lived with my mother and sister, okay? Nothing as exciting as a cult."

Her cheeks grow pink, but there has to be more to it than that. If she had any idea how many climbers I knew well into their thirties and forties who funded their lifestyle by living with their parents, she wouldn't be half so embarrassed.

But I don't say any of that. I just nod and carry her bags into the house.

"Thank you for all your help," she says as soon as I've set down her things. "It went so much quicker than if I'd been working alone."

"It's fine."

"I'd offer you something cold to drink, but I don't have any food yet. We're going to the grocery store as soon as we finish up here. I could bring you something by after we get back."

"Don't worry about it." I start to move closer to the door. I don't need this many thanks for lugging a few things inside for her. Especially not when it's taking all my focus to keep my eyes off her.

"If you ever want suggestions of places to go in town or outdoorsy activities around—"

"I don't." My "outdoorsy activities" days are long gone.

Her smile falters, and I regret my sharp tone. But I don't need another person trying to convince me how great life can be if I just get back out there and give it a try. I'd rather stick to socializing exclusively with my dog.

"Right. Because of when you were here before."

Her cheeks go pink again, but I can't connect why. Must be the warm day—temperature's creeping up, and on a clear day like this it feels hotter than it really is. Almost makes me wish I wasn't wearing sweatpants. But I'm not that much of a masochist.

I step out onto the porch and find Dutch cuddled up with her kid. You'd think I ignore the poor dog all day, the way he's eating up the attention.

"I love your dog, Mister." The kid gazes up at me, his eyes the same bright blue as his mom's.

"His name is *Ian*," Tess says from behind me. "And it's time for Dutch to go home."

"Dutch is my new best friend."

Tess's laugh rings out, tempting me to turn around to witness it. I want to see her wide smile and the crinkles around her eyes. But I keep my focus on my front door. Stay the course.

"I saw that coming," she says. "You make best friends everywhere."

Her voice is threaded with so much love, everything inside me itches to tilt toward her like a sunflower. Makes sense she'd live in a town called Sunshine. She's made of the stuff.

It's got to be the isolation making me think these ridiculous thoughts. Her softness and sweetness are a novelty, nothing more. She's not directing that affection toward me.

If she did, though, I'd be worse than Dutch, eagerly eating up her crumbs.

I push open my front door and whistle for my dog. He stands, and the little boy gives him one last hug before he trots over.

"See you later, boy!" August calls.

"Go wash your hands so we can go to the grocery store," Tess tells him. As soon as he runs inside their half of the duplex, she turns her attention to me. "Thank you again for helping me with all the—"

"It's not a problem." But it will be if she thanks me again.

She purses her lips, and we have a brief stare down. Too bad for her, I have a lot of practice with out-staring people these days.

Finally, she takes a step backward into her apartment. I won —but can't celebrate.

"We'll see you around, Ian."

Almost sounds like a threat.

FOUR
TESS

FIVE-YEAR-OLDS ARE FUN. Sometimes, they don't pay attention to significant events—like, say, a big move—and carry on as though nothing in their life has changed. Other times, they fixate obsessively on one small detail and refuse to let it go.

Tonight, it's the fixation.

"Did you see how much Dutch likes me?" August asks as he slips into bed.

I've tried to keep to our usual routine, despite the new location. We ate one of his favorite dinners—tomato and basil pasta salad, carrot sticks, and green grapes—unpacked our clothes, and read through at least twenty of his most-loved picture books.

I keep waiting for him to say something about missing his Nana and Aunt Wren, but the dog he met today is taking up too much space in his brain.

Kind of the way the dog's owner is in mine. Not like he did when I was a teen, of course. My days of getting caught up in charming men who do dangerous things for a living are long over. Apparently, so are Ian's days of being charming, so I guess we're good there.

Mostly, I'm thinking about how ridiculous I was to jump

into this "befriend Amy's nephew" situation without learning a few more pieces of information about the nephew.

"You were so good to pet Dutch so gently. I'm sure he liked that." I double check the continuous glucose monitor and insulin pump on the backs of August's arms, but they're still on tight. We did his nightly finger prick before he brushed his teeth, and his numbers are looking good for the evening. "Your super shields are all set."

How do you explain to a little child what insulin does or that we need his blood sugar levels to stay in a certain range or he'll get sick? I told him about the two medical devices in broad euphemisms when he first got them a couple of years ago, settling on "super shields." He mostly understands what they do for him now, but I haven't let go of the cute nicknames.

He is my little superhero, after all.

"I like the guy, too." August's l-sounds come out sounding like a y. He *yikes* the guy.

"His name is Ian," I remind him. Names don't stick well in his head. He needs a lot of gentle encouragement not to call everyone new he meets "guy" and "lady."

"Yeah, him. He's funny."

"Mmm." I didn't see much evidence of Ian's sense of humor. He used to have one, years ago. But if I start remembering how great his laugh was or how a glimpse of his smile could make my whole day, this situation will get even trickier than it already is. Best to accept Ian exactly how he is now, with no illusions about *Past Ian* or the expectation of seeing any smiles.

"I want a big beard when I grow up, too." August pats an imaginary beard about six inches below his chin.

I smooth his pale blond hair over his forehead, not remotely in the mindset to think of him as anything other than my tiny little boy. "One day."

He settles against his pillow, his eyelids drooping. "He asked me to take him on walks sometimes."

"Ian asked you to walk his dog?" It's obvious he hasn't been around kids much, but I didn't think the man was obtuse enough to request pet care from a five-year-old.

"Dutch asked me to walk him." August flashes a sleepy smile, showing off his missing tooth.

"Oh. For now, let's just be happy when we get to pet him, okay?"

"Okay." He cuddles his favorite stuffed ostrich closer. "Can I pet him again tomorrow?"

"We'll see." I'm sure the dog would be willing. It's convincing his owner I'm less certain about. I kiss August on the forehead. "Goodnight, sweetie."

"Night, Mama."

I switch off the bedside lamp and leave his room by the glow of the duck nightlight we brought. Another little touch of home, like the plush dinosaur blanket on top of his bed and his favorite cups in the kitchen. I brought as much as I reasonably could to make this space feel comfortable and familiar. I leave his door ajar and step out into the decidedly unfamiliar apartment.

The rooms have a faint, lemon-fresh scent, but they're cozy. It's weird to be in them at all. I haven't been on my own since before August was born, and that attempt didn't last long. For most of my life, I've lived right down the hall from my mom and sister.

The apartment is unbelievably quiet, my solitary footsteps strangely lonely. I sought out this small separation from my family, but now, I kind of wish I'd brought a fuzzy blanket to snuggle up in, too.

I get comfortable on the couch and do the next best thing. I call my sister.

Wren picks up right away. "I was wondering when I'd hear from you. Are you all unpacked? Do you miss us yet?"

"We've only been gone a few hours." No need to admit the reason for the call.

"I already took over your drawers in the bathroom. I'm used to this lifestyle now, so if you're thinking about trying to come right back, you'll be out of luck on the storage situation."

"You move fast." We've shared that tiny bathroom since we were kids—I would have done the same thing.

"I have my priorities. How do you feel about your new place now that you're there?"

"It's different being right on the foothills practically surrounded by trees, but I like it." Our childhood home where Wren still lives with Mom is in a more traditional neighborhood, close to downtown.

She pauses, her voice growing softer. "How's our little man handling it?"

I glance at his undisturbed bedroom door. "He's too obsessed with our neighbor's dog to process the big change yet."

"Ooh, that's right. Amy's relative. What's he like?"

I drop my voice in case he really can hear me through the walls. "It's Ian Vaughn."

"You say that like I should know who that is."

"I guess you wouldn't." She was in middle school the last time he was in town. I've never been much for sharing my crazy crushes the way Wren and her friends do and certainly wouldn't have told her anything private back then. She had too many ways of learning more than I meant to tell her.

Still does, unfortunately.

"So you already know each other?"

"Not really." One-sided infatuation doesn't equal an acquaintance.

"You're driving me nuts. You need to give me more than this. Who is Ian Vaughn?"

If I don't spill at least a few beans, she'll wind up parked on my porch every day for a week until she finds out everything she wants to know about him.

"He visited town right before my senior year of high school. He was a few years older and...really cute." I grimace hearing myself say it. Cute doesn't begin to cover a guy with unbridled confidence and a killer smile, but that's all I'm willing to tell her. "I had a thing for him that whole summer."

"Oh. My. Gosh." Wren's gasp makes me roll my eyes. "This is just like Hope getting reunited with Griffin."

"It's nothing like that." I need to shut down whatever insanity's swirling in her brain before those thoughts take hold. Ian and I are not in some kind of romantic Christmas festival scenario the way our friend was last winter. "He's a totally different man now. He's a grump who didn't smile and barely talked to me this afternoon. Whatever charms he had fifteen years ago, they're gone now."

"*Charms.*" The woman actually giggles.

Clearly, she only heard me say the one word. She's as bad as August when she's fixated. "Please stop."

"Come on. It's so rare for you to pay attention to a man at all. You can at least give me a second to enjoy it."

This is exactly why I don't talk to her about things like this. She enjoys it too much. True, I haven't been interested in a man in ages. But I'm certainly not breaking that streak with Ian Vaughn.

"Any attention I pay him is for Amy's sake. That's all."

"Right," she says, dragging out the word. "It's for Amy."

I'm going to have to strangle my sister. It won't be easy at the bakery without her, but Mom and I will find a way to get by.

"Wren."

She makes a sound of irritation. "You're no fun. So what's going on with him that Amy asked you to draw him out?"

"Nothing obvious." Although I know better than most that you don't have to look sick to have a serious illness.

"Could it be PTSD? Wasn't one of Amy's relatives in the military? She has so many cousins and whatnot who've stopped through. It's hard to keep track."

"I don't know. If he was, he's abandoned the clean-cut look." I won't mention that he's already influenced my son to grow facial hair as soon as he's able. "Have you seen a guy with long red hair and a bushy beard around town?"

"No! You mean it's *him*? I've only seen him a couple of times, but...wow. Okay. I'm starting to understand why you had a crush on him."

"What? How is that your takeaway?"

"Because he's hot! In a rakish pirate kind of way."

I say nothing. I definitely don't think about how perfectly that description fits Ian. Or picture him giving orders at the helm of a ship. Looks mean nothing.

Even surprisingly good looks.

"You're safe living next door to the guy though, right?" Her voice goes hard, like she's ready to come over here and bust his head if she needs to.

"Nothing about him feels sketchy, just...off-putting." Like a prickly cactus you can't get too close to. Or those brightly colored frogs that are chock full of venom. His whole personality is a neon sign that says *Do not touch*.

"Which is why Amy wants you to befriend him."

"Exactly." I probably shouldn't have revealed so much to Wren, but she'd had a thousand questions for me when I told her I was finally moving out. I had to give her a little information or she'd burst into flames.

She's quiet for a moment. "Do you want me to come over

and spend the night? Just so it won't be as weird for you? I can bring a sleeping bag and stay on the couch."

"Aww. You don't have to do that. You're going to have your own place soon anyway. Save the sleepover for when it's *your* place."

"Ugh. Mom's going to flip when we're both gone."

"I know." After our dad left us almost twenty years ago, Mom cinched Wren and me closer to her. At first, it was comforting—we had each other's backs no matter what. But now that we're adults, that closeness is becoming a too-tight belt around us we're struggling to loosen. "How is she tonight?"

"She said a few times she hopes this isn't too much for you to handle. Sighed a lot. No tears."

Maureen Krause doesn't sob over her regrets. She throws herself into action. She doesn't agree with my choice to get a place for August and me—she thinks we need our little village to raise this child—but she hasn't interfered, either. She even offered to help us unpack after the bakery closed tonight, but I wanted to do this on my own.

"But don't worry," Wren says. "I'm sure she'll be relieved when she finds out about your hottie pirate next door."

"You're not going to tell her about that." I didn't mention Amy's reduced rent to Mom, and I sure didn't tell her about needing to be nice to a strange man as part of the package. She absolutely would have interfered if she'd known that little detail.

"No, no. Not me." Wren's gloating is limitless. "But how long until August tells her?"

I sag against the couch. Mom's definitely going to find out about the hottie pirate next door.

FIVE
IAN

MY ARM'S STARTING to ache, but I toss a tennis ball across my back yard for the thousandth time. Also for the thousandth time, Dutch tears across the grass to grab it and trots on back. He could easily do this for hours, and today, I'm indulging him.

It's my way of making it up to him for not letting him play with the kid next door.

Each evening since they moved in, August's done his own tearing around in the yard we share. Dutch has whined at the door every time, ready to abandon me for the kid in a heartbeat. But I'm not totally convinced Tess approves of her son playing with my dog, so I've avoided the situation entirely.

If that keeps me from having to speak with Tess again, so much the better. I've got a feeling any little interaction with her will stick in my head, and I don't need the distraction.

Dutch drops the slobbery tennis ball at my feet, ready for more. Yeah. It's important to keep my focus.

My phone buzzes, and I step onto the porch to check it. I get about as many phone calls as I do visitors these days, and I have a good guess who's calling. A glance at the screen proves my hunch.

I let his last two calls go to voicemail. Probably best I don't push my oldest brother any further. I don't need him tag-teaming with Amy, showing up on my doorstep to harass me in person.

"Pierce." I chuck Dutch's drool-covered ball across the yard.

"Ian. I'm pleased your schedule opened up enough to take my call." His voice is thick with sarcasm. He preferred it when I was in Durango and couldn't avoid him.

"You know how it is."

"I don't have a clue how it is. You avoid all my calls. Most of my texts are left on read."

"I'm a busy guy."

He got enough first-hand experience with how I'm doing in the year I tried to keep working at our company. Don't think he really needs a minute-by-minute update when nothing about my status has changed.

He grumbles into the phone. "I'll skip the pleasantries and cut right to the chase."

"Were you going to be pleasant?" I cut in.

"I was going to tell you about the baby, but you can forget it now."

"Man. That would have been pleasant."

Pierce is expecting his first child and absolutely losing his mind over it. He treats his wife, Bonnie, like she's a fragile little bird, had the nursery painted and furnished months ago, and it seems to physically pain him if he doesn't bring the baby into every conversation. He's an absolute beast on a mountainside, but the softest kitten when it comes to a kid who isn't even here yet.

The nonstop pregnancy updates I got when I worked in the office might have been as bad as all the "chin-up" commentary.

I toss Dutch's ball again, waiting for my brother to crack. He clearly has something to say. It takes ten seconds of silence, max.

"Bonnie decided she didn't want to wait any longer to learn the baby's sex," he finally says.

"That's nice."

He huffs another breath, and I grin to myself imagining his exasperation. He can't expect much else when he calls me. I've never been great at playing along.

"You're not even going to ask?"

Best to indulge him. If I refuse, he really might show up on my porch. "Are you having a boy or a gi—"

"It's a girl!" He sounds like he's celebrating at the summit of a mountain peak.

"Congrats." First grandchild in a family of brothers who haven't been in a rush to start families—our mom will spoil her rotten. "Try to get Bonnie to hold out until my birthday."

Pierce chuckles. "She'll throttle you if you say that to her. She's ready to deliver her now, and she's still got a few weeks left to go."

"Just tell her to relax. She always loves it when you do that."

"You're trying to get me murdered." He exhales long and low. "I can't believe the baby will be here so soon."

Pierce has climbed some of the most dangerous mountains in the world, stays calm under pressure, and knows more about business finance than I would ever care to. Strange to hear him talking about a kid like it's the new center of his whole life.

Happy for him. I just don't get it.

"Can't wait to meet her."

"Exactly why I called." His voice loses the dreamy quality and slips back into no-nonsense mode. "When are you coming home to Durango?"

My brief spark of joy for my brother fizzles out. "I have no immediate plans."

I was never the guy with the plan. Everything just came to

me. The climbing, the articles, the sponsorships, even what I achieved in our guiding business—I'd lucked into it all. Sure, there'd been a lot of hard work along the way, but even at the peak of my career, I hadn't known what was going on more than a few months ahead of time. My schedule just magically filled.

Now? I'm nowhere near the peak of my career, and all I see is a long stretch of nothing.

"We need you here."

They need the Ian I used to be, not who I am today. I'm not entirely sure who I am today. After my accident and surgeries, it took months to learn how to walk again and get my current prosthesis. Months more before I could safely travel over uneven terrain, let alone consider tackling a single-pitch climb or scaling frozen waterfalls. My brothers tried to keep me involved in our business, but it wasn't the same. Demonstrating knot tying and how to wear a harness in our beginner courses can't compete with the challenging treks I'd been known for.

So I ran off to Oregon. To regroup or...something.

"You were doing just fine when I left." Better than fine, to be honest. Vaughn Mountain Views is more successful than any of us ever dreamed it would be. We started ten years ago on a hope and a prayer, and now we're one of the best-known mountaineering companies in Colorado. They don't need me leading the easy walks to keep that momentum.

"But you *are* coming back."

"Funny how you make that sound like a command." Even when we worked together every day, he was only my boss in the loosest sense of the word.

"This is just a...sabbatical."

That's a generous term for what I'm doing here. "I have no immediate plans."

"You're impossible. Are you even doing any of that stuff you said you were going to do out there? Build up your endurance and all that?"

My gaze goes to the trail that starts just past my back yard. I've walked it a few times, but not enough to count as physical therapy. Not enough to make me think I could go back to the strenuous, often technically challenging week-long climbs I used to lead.

"I'm doing some of it."

He groans. "Please tell me you're not just wallowing out there."

"Wallowing is such a dirty word."

"What's a better one?"

I pause for a second. "Contemplating the crushing weight of existence."

"You are such a..." He seems unable to come up with the proper description. "When was the last time you went into town?"

I think back. "I had dinner with Amy and Jodi about a month ago."

And went home right after we'd finished eating. I'd said I needed to let Dutch out, but really, their homey happiness made me feel like a ghoul draining their joy. I'd left for them as much as myself.

"You need to get out more."

Dutch drops his tennis ball in front of me and lies down on the porch panting hard. Finally got him winded.

"You and Amy must be sharing notes."

"Spend some time around people again. Get involved in the community." He sounds like he's leading a business meeting, outlining a list of to-dos. "Make a friend. Meet a woman."

My thoughts careen straight to my new neighbor. Beautiful, soft, gentle. A smile that blinds you in the best way. In another life, I'd be looking for an opportunity to ask her out instead of doing my best to avoid her.

I was never the guy to avoid women before, but since she moved in, it's my new hobby.

"Not happening," I grumble.

Dutch's ears perk up, and in a flash, he's on his feet. Next second, Tess's door flies open, and August bounds out.

"Dutch is outside, Mama!" he shouts over his shoulder. "Can I play with him?"

Before he gets an answer, he leaps off the porch and into the yard. Dutch has a miraculous second wind and sprints along with him, doing laps in the grass.

"What was that?" Pierce asks.

I barely hear him. Tess steps over the threshold, watching her son. Her gaze cuts to me, and she offers a small smile before going back to keeping an eye on the excitement in the yard.

I am spectacularly bad at my new hobby.

All I can do is stare. Tess in her casual outfit, messy hair, and rosy cheeks scrambles my brain.

"Uh, that was the TV," I say into the phone after too many seconds of silence.

"It didn't sound like—"

"Gotta go." I end the call before he can finish.

Then I just stand here on my side of the porch, decked out in my worn sweatpants and a Vaughn Mountain Views T-shirt. Probably looking just as feral as I did the day we met. I sure haven't done anything to change my look.

"I didn't mean to interrupt," Tess says.

"You didn't." I would have hung up on him eventually if he'd kept going with that line of conversation.

She gestures at the chaos in the yard. "Is this okay with you?"

"Doesn't bother me." Dutch is loving it. I'm not sure which of the two is more excited. "Is it okay with you?"

She watches as they tumble in the grass. "I don't mind, as long as he doesn't bite."

I shrug. "The boy's teeth are so blunt, Dutch wouldn't even feel it."

Her eyebrows tug together. Guess my little joke didn't land.

"Dutch isn't aggressive," I tell her. "Just big."

Doesn't mean I won't watch them the whole time they're together, though. No sense being careless.

"That's good. I, um, have something for you. Don't go anywhere."

If only she knew.

Tess ducks inside her apartment, returning again with a purple box in her hands. She walks over, smile bright, and holds it out to me.

My gaze drops to the box. "What is it?"

Why would she bring me anything? We don't know each other. We've barely spoken.

The bigger question: why is my heart racing over a nondescript purple box?

"They're cupcakes. From our bakery." She lifts the box a touch higher.

Her smile cranks up, tightening something in my chest. I ignore the smile and the too-tight sensation behind my ribs.

People love to bring food after a tragedy. It's the only thing they can think to do. Your father died from a stroke at fifty-five? Here's a casserole. Your mother had a double mastectomy to combat her aggressive cancer? Here's a lasagna. You lost your leg in a stupid accident? Here's a platter of enchiladas.

I don't move to take her offering. "Why would you bring me cupcakes?"

She hesitates, putting my defenses on red alert.

"You haven't come by the bakery, so I thought I'd bring them to you instead."

This is where most people drop their gaze to my legs, giving their motivations away. Morbid curiosity always has a tell. But Tess keeps her eyes on mine. If anything, she seems amused by my reluctance.

She lifts her eyebrows. "I made them fresh this morning. They're not day-olds or anything like that."

Still feels too much like a consolation prize. *Sorry about your leg. Here's a pastry.*

My stomach tilts. I never thought to ask just how much Amy told her about me. Does she know about my accident? About the high-profile career I won and lost? About the magazine article that put me on a list of "career-ending tragedies?"

August leaps onto the porch, panting hard. "Hi, guy! We brought you cupcakes."

I keep my gaze on his mom. "I see that."

Tess still holds the purple box out to me, undeterred by my lack of enthusiasm.

The little boy ambles closer, Dutch at his side. "Mama said you need a friend. We can be your friends."

I need a friend, huh? I guess I'll have to stop by the diner and visit with my aunts, after all. Find out exactly how much they shared with my new neighbors.

"I said it's the neighborly thing to do," Tess jumps in. "And his name is Ian."

"Yeah, Ian," August repeats. "It's the neighborly thing to do."

The boy's speech impediment makes the word come out *neighboryee*. It's kind of cute.

Still. The whole situation smacks of making me out to be a charity case.

"It's neighborly to accept cupcakes when they're offered,

too." Tess's voice is gentle, her smile soft like she's teaching me a life lesson the same way she would her son.

Great. Cupcakes of mercy *and* getting treated like a child. Although...I can't deny that I need a refresher course on manners. It's been too long since I cared enough to put in the effort. What have I become that I'm side-eyeing baked goods brought to me by a pretty woman?

I take the box from her. "Thank you."

Her expression brightens even more, without dipping once to my legs. "You're welcome. I brought you two each of strawberry cream, lemon blueberry, and piña colada."

I lift the lid. "Wow."

Six fat cupcakes rest inside, topped with piped frosting flecked with strawberries, blueberries, and what must be pineapple. I catch their sweet scent and suppress a groan. My mouth immediately starts watering.

Would eating one in a single bite be neighborly, too?

"Mama makes the best cupcakes." August gives the box a longing look. "The strawberry ones are my favorite."

"I'll eat those first," I tell him.

He grins and goes back to running around with Dutch. I replace the lid on the box and go on standing around with it. If I set it down, ants or wasps will show up to inspect all that sugar.

"They'll keep in the refrigerator for two or three days," Tess says.

"You underestimate me."

She smiles up at me, apparently unfazed by my ragged appearance and unfriendly attitude. Her eyes shine in the sunlight, a dark sea-blue ringed with thick lashes. Her golden hair is tucked into a loose knot on her head, strands trailing around like a halo. Like an angel dropped down from heaven to bless me with cupcakes.

I've grown skilled at pushing people away, but she makes

me want to draw closer. And if I did? What happens when this dream woman finds out about my reality?

"I'd better put them away," I growl as I stalk past her and into my apartment.

If she is an angel, God's got a real brutal sense of humor.

SIX

TESS

WHAT ARE the odds Ian went inside and threw those cupcakes straight into the trash? I'm going with sixty-forty. At least I tried. If Amy asks, I can confidently say I'm doing my part.

Whether it'll make a difference or not is anybody's guess.

I sit on one of the patio chairs and watch August play. He's settled a bit after his initial home from daycare blitz, and he's sitting in the grass talking to the dog. Probably making all kinds of plans for what they're going to do together this summer.

I keep reminding him Dutch isn't ours, but it's not sticking.

Ian walks back outside. His presence is mildly unsetting for so many reasons—the lingering ghost of my old crush, his unfriendly demeanor, the way he glares around like he wishes August and I lived anywhere else. He crosses his arms and stands by his door, our duplex's grumpy bouncer. I half expect him to call Dutch inside for the night, just take his toys and go home, but he doesn't.

Doesn't say anything, either.

I still can't imagine what could have happened to make him change so much. Sure, it's been fifteen years, but he was outgoing and friendly, talkative and engaging. A major flirt, too, not that I ever experienced that side of him.

Frankly, the only thing I experienced of Ian Vaughn back then was admiring him from afar. But I watched him well enough to know he wasn't shy with the local girls. He'd lean in close, whip out a devastating smile, and every girl in his orbit melted.

In my more embarrassing daydreams, I was a few years older, we were a whole lot closer, and he never noticed a single one of those other girls. He only had eyes for me.

"Seems awfully optimistic," Ian grumbles behind me.

I startle out of my reminiscing, my cheeks going hot. There's no way I actually said that out loud, right?

"What is?" I squeak, my stomach flipping over.

He nods into the yard. "Dutch doesn't make a very good pony."

I follow his gaze to where August is trying to ride Dutch like a horse. Thankfully, his feet don't leave the ground as he awkwardly hovers over the dog, but he waves one hand in the air like a rodeo star. The dog doesn't seem to mind.

"Don't put any weight on him," I call.

August stops spinning his invisible lasso and waves, then goes straight back to being a cowboy.

"Dutch weighs more than the kid does," Ian says.

That's true. Maybe I'm worried about the wrong one getting hurt. But it's a gorgeous evening, warm without being overly hot like it will get in another month or so. I want August to enjoy it as much as he can. And right now, he's certainly enjoying playing with that dog.

Ian steps closer but pauses before he reaches me. The porch stretches from one side of the house to the other, set up with double of everything: two patio tables, four chairs each, two barbecue grills. We even have identical fire pits at opposite corners in the yard. His table is about twenty feet from mine, and he's hesitating like he might be inclined to walk to it.

"You can sit over here if you want." Seems kind of ridiculous for him to stay all the way over there when we're both watching the same thing. My offer is practical, that's all. It has nothing to do with those long-ago thoughts swirling through my head. I'm trying to be neighborly like I promised.

Ian nods and walks over to my table, lowering himself into the seat farthest from me, and staring out to where August is accosting his dog. Two lines form between his eyebrows as though the sight of a little boy frolicking is somehow distasteful to him. His beard is as scraggly as it was a few days ago, and I don't look at his sweatpants and T-shirt too closely. Those might be the same, too.

His long hair is different though. It's up in a bun, a style I've never really found appealing on a man. But it shows off his deep widow's peak and the streaks of gray starting to pepper his temples. Honestly, he looks more like a pirate than ever, which I will die before mentioning to Wren. The look weirdly suits him.

And matches me. I'm not sure I've ever had the same messy updo as a man five feet away from me before.

"Twins." I snap my mouth shut and turn my face to the yard. Now, that I *did* say out loud.

Lovely.

"What?" he asks.

"Nothing," I blurt. "What, um, do you do for work?"

Work is good. Work is safe. Way better than random comments on hairstyles.

His lips twitch for a few seconds before he responds. "Consulting."

That's nice and vague. Yet another thing I should have asked Amy about him. Not that it's really my business, but as long as it's nothing illegal...wait. It wouldn't even have to be illegal.

"Are you in the marijuana business?"

His eyes widen a touch, his eyebrows lifting. "The marijuana business?"

I flail a hand around. I don't know the proper terms for it, I just know it's out there. "You know. Colorado. Oregon. I thought maybe..."

I'm not really sure what I thought, but the stunned look on his face tells me I've guessed wrong.

He barks a laugh. It's more exhale than true laughter, but it's a start.

"No. I'm not in that business." He shifts in his seat, looking away from me. "The mountaineering business."

"Like actually climbing mountains?"

He nods, his gaze still on August and Dutch.

That makes sense for him. I don't know him super well—okay, at all—but before, he'd seemed fearless.

Compared to me, everyone did.

But I could see that working for Ian. The old Ian, anyway. Brash and confident, he would have made a good climber ready to forge his own path just to prove he could. He had the kind of carefree energy that matched the extreme sports enthusiasts I've known.

And probably a certain amount of *carelessness*, too. That seemed to go along with guys who sought out jobs like that. Rock climbing instructor. White water rafting guide.

Ski instructor.

I draw in a deep breath and shiver despite the warm breeze. I definitely do not need to be thinking about *him*. No point in ruining a perfectly nice evening.

"Is that why you're out here?" I ask, eager to steer my thoughts any other direction. "To climb in the Cascades?"

I've got a little too much enthusiasm in my voice, like I'm a late night host leading my guest to launch into a story to charm the audience.

He whips his head around to me, his gaze narrowing. Once again, I get the feeling my guess is all wrong.

"No," he finally says. He turns back to watch August and his dog.

This guy would be an absolute bust on a talk show.

August runs around inspecting the big, decorative rocks that ring the yard. He squats down, gazes at the ground for a while, and then moves to the next rock. Dutch follows him like they're explorers on a mission.

"What are you finding?" I call out.

"We're looking for bunnies in these holes!" he shouts back.

This kid and his animal kick. We saw a bunny at the park a few weeks ago, and he's been hoping for a repeat ever since. Every little creature delights him. Squirrels, deer, even the tiny frogs that come out near my mom's house every spring. He'd bring every last one home to live with us if I let him.

"Tell me if you find one."

"Seems more likely he'll find a rattlesnake under those rocks," Ian says.

I snap my attention to him. "Rattlesnakes?"

Do rattlesnakes live in holes under rocks like that? I'd seen August inspecting them the other day, and I'd just assumed they were caused by rain or something. Maybe insects. Not snakes.

"It's too hot for rabbits to be out, but it's perfect for a snake looking for something to..." Ian catches whatever horrified thing my face is doing and leaves off the rest of his *Wild Kingdom* commentary.

"Should I be worried about rattlesnakes?" Funnily enough, my voice comes out a low hiss. I don't want to scare August if I don't have to. But there's no scenario in which I'm prepared to deal with a snake.

Ian doesn't seem too concerned. "Dutch has been barking up a storm all afternoon. He probably scared away anything that might have been in the yard."

I guess that's one benefit to the noise they're making.

"I never thought about snakes." My mom's yard is an oasis of greenery in the middle of town—the worst we ever had were deer coming along to eat their share of her summer plants. This duplex is closer to the forest and landscaped more sparsely.

Looking at it now, those rocks are probably perfect for snakes to burrow under, or whatever they do. Slither into crevices and rattle their tails. Lie in wait for little children.

Another shiver rocks through me, and I keep my eyes stuck on the ground around August's feet, watching for signs of movement.

Ian tilts his head toward the back gate and the walking trail beyond. "I'd be more concerned about bobcats or coyotes coming down from the canyon."

"*What?*" My pulse skyrockets. "Are you serious?"

He takes in my reaction, his eyebrows twitching. "I thought you grew up here."

"Yeah, but I've never seen an actual predator before." Never once did I think about any kind of threat when I accepted this place. I thought we'd see a few more *cute* animals, not anything dangerous. "We lived in town, not right on the edge of the wilderness."

His mouth works like he might have something to say about me calling this area *wild*. I guess to a mountain guide, it's probably pretty tame. But it's not to me if he thinks bobcats might show up some day.

"Get some bear spray and you'll be fine."

A strangled sound comes out of my throat before I can stop it. "Should I be worried about bears, too?"

I look to the scrub and trees beyond the fenced yard. Yes, we're on the outskirts of town, but there are still houses everywhere. We're still safe. I think?

"Just what kind of sheltered life did you live in town?" he asks.

I snap my jaw shut, his off-hand remark pressing against an old bruise. I *was* sheltered, coddled by my mom in her protective embrace. I'd grown up naive and trusting to an unhealthy degree. When I finally ventured out into the world, I had a lot of hard lessons in store for me. The biggest one came from a charismatic ski instructor.

I push those memories away. He's not worth wasting time thinking about. And I don't entirely regret my mistakes. I never could.

I return my focus to Ian. "Do you always jump to the worst-case scenarios?"

He seems unfazed by my snappish tone. "Might be unlikely, but you don't want to be reckless out here. It is the *wilderness*."

I can't tell if he's teasing or trying to scare me, but I'm still going to buy bear spray tomorrow. Just to be on the safe side.

"You know, you're nothing like I remember you."

He goes completely still. "And how was that?"

"Recklessness was kind of your whole deal." Trust me when I say I kept my ear out for gossip about him. He was rumored to do everything from white water rafting to mountain biking to climbing Smith Rock. He would have been the last guy I'd expect to give me a rundown on all the potential dangers in my own back yard.

He watches me for long seconds. "I didn't realize we knew each other."

I will not be telling this man I ate up every scrap of information about him like a fangirl, all without ever actually speaking to him. "It was a long time ago."

Ian swallows hard, his beard wobbling over his throat. "I don't have the strongest memory of those days."

I have memories for the both of us. Cringey, cringey memories.

"You weren't the safety patrol guy. You were...fearless. Bold. Charming."

I wish I hadn't thrown in that last part, but I can't deny its truth. He'd drawn people in, and not just teenage girls with hearts in their eyes. He'd had a following around town, and everybody liked him.

He nods, watching me like he's suddenly wary of what I'll say next. Probably because it's been fifteen years, and I'm still fangirling over him.

"And we dated," he says.

I stare at him, my lungs refusing to do their job. His comment isn't quite a question, but there's a lilt to it like he needs me to confirm his conclusion. Because he doesn't know. And I can't help it—I burst into laughter.

His expression shutters and he glances away, probably wishing a bobcat would come along and drag me into the woods. Meanwhile, I can't shake my giggles. Ian Vaughn thinks it's even a possibility we dated—and he doesn't remember? Seventeen-year-old me would be mortified, but thirty-two-year-old me is hunched over from laughing so hard.

"You must have had a *good* summer," I say when I catch my breath again. "Can't keep track of all your girls."

He scowls harder than he did the day I arrived here. "I was twenty-two."

That's it. That's his whole explanation for flirting with every girl in town. It just makes me laugh more.

"The young and hot defense," I say between giggles.

His eyebrows tick up. "Hot?"

I can't even be embarrassed I said it. He obviously knows he had a way with women. Anybody who isn't entirely sure who he once dated isn't in need of a refresher on his own looks. "Hey. You were twenty-two."

"It was a lifetime ago," he grumbles.

August bounds onto the porch and straight to my side. "What's so funny, Mama?"

"Just a joke Ian told."

His little face brightens beneath the fine layer of dirt all over it. "I want to hear the joke."

Ian winces as though I might actually tell my son about our exchange. My laughing fit isn't very neighborly of me, even if his full social calendar back then strikes me as a bit ridiculous. I rearrange my features into something less outright amused by the whole conversation.

"I'll tell you a joke later. You've got a couple more minutes before we need to go inside for dinner, okay?"

"Okay." August runs back into the yard to perch on one of the bigger rocks surrounding the grass, holding court with Dutch.

The rattlesnakes Ian mentioned flit through my mind again, but I'll have to trust that he's right. Snakes would have been scared away by all of August's shouts and running around long before now. It's when you take them by surprise that bites happen. Probably.

Doesn't mean I won't think about them every time we come out here, though.

I finally relax again, and my gaze lands on Ian. He's still scowling at me, and lifts his eyebrows, waiting for my answer.

Right. I guess I'd better put the guy out of his misery.

"Sorry. I got carried away. We did *not* date. We never even spoke."

His shoulders ease back down, and I swear he sighs. Crisis averted, I guess. But I get it. Living next door to an old flame would be so much more awkward than living next to an old crush.

Although, given today's conversations, living next to a crush can still be pretty dang awkward.

"Yet you remembered me?"

My laughter dies out, probably giving way to pink cheeks. I didn't think about just how much I was admitting. "The red hair is pretty memorable."

He nods. "And charming."

Embarrassment blooms to life in my chest like I'm in high school again. Maybe I can swing the conversation back to dangerous animals.

His gaze drops over me as if he's noticing me for the first time. The open appraisal makes heat crawl up my neck, but it's not...unpleasant. I don't get noticed. Not like this, anyway.

"I wouldn't have been surprised if we had dated."

Did the grump just flirt with me? Or is his remark meant to be a reminder of how many girls he met that summer?

Much safer to assume the latter.

"If we had dated, I can tell it would have been really special."

He glowers, but his mouth tilts to one side like he's trying to fight a smile. Might be wishful thinking on my part, but I'm going to count this disastrous conversation as a step closer to friendship.

SEVEN
TESS

MOST DAYS in our family's shop, I'm grateful for short breathers between customers. Brief moments when the baking's complete, the display cases are stocked, and I can lean against the back counter and relax.

Today, those breaks mean questions from Wren. A line of cranky customers snaking out the door would be more relaxing.

She slides over next to me as soon as the bakery's empty again. "What did he say when you gave him the cupcakes?"

I don't need to ask who she's talking about. Ian's been her subject of conversation all morning.

"I already told you." In the most innocuous way possible, but I should have known she wouldn't give up her curiosity after I admitted I used to have a crush on him.

Used to is the part I've been reminding myself ever since our conversation last night.

"Yeah, but it seems like there would have been more to that." That's Wren, always digging for more.

"Nope, I pretty well covered it with his grumbled 'Thank you.'"

The rest—his inability to remember if we'd dated and the

tentative almost-smile he'd offered when I teased him about it—
will stay with me.

"You didn't say anything about his piercing blue eyes or
devilish grin."

He sure didn't give me any devilish grins, but his eyes are
just as intense as they used to be. Maybe even more so now that
I've actually had them trained on me. Wait. I didn't tell her any
of that.

Wren's looking at something on her phone, nodding in
appreciation.

"I mean, look at the guy." She spins the screen toward me.

I'm confronted with a version of Ian I've never seen before.
Somewhere between the young man I'd crushed on and my
haggard, unhappy neighbor, the picture legitimately makes me
hold my breath. His jaw is covered in the barest stubble, his dark
red hair just long enough to fall carelessly into his eyes. His face
carries the lines of the man I know today, but he's still got the
bright spark of the younger man he was years ago. He's grinning
into the camera like he knows exactly how good he looks.

He's also clinging to a rock face somewhere, shirtless and
artfully streaked with mud.

I do not take in the planes of his pecs or his insanely
muscled shoulders. I don't notice how he's holding onto the rock
with one hand, his biceps in that arm bulging impressively. I
don't pay attention to the thick dusting of freckles that move
from the tops of his shoulders down to his hands.

This image absolutely does not etch itself into my brain.

"When—" I swallow and try again. "Where did you find
that?"

"Google is my best friend." She waggles the phone at me.
"There are a lot of photos like this. Want to see more?"

"I..." Do I want to see more photos of Ian Vaughn's stunning
chest and confident grin?

Yes, please.

But no. The last thing I need is to make things any weirder between us. Looking at photos of him...like that...could only bring on more awkwardness the next time we're in the back yard together.

Not together. Just...you know. In the same place. On the lookout for rattlesnakes.

Wren smiles wider. "There are tons of articles about him, too. I didn't read them all, but it sounds like he's a pretty famous climber. Guide. Something. I wasn't that focused on the details. Want me to send the links to you?"

"No." I grab a disinfecting rag from the sink, wring it out, and start wiping down the gleaming countertops. "That's an invasion of privacy."

"I didn't hire a private investigator to tail him. This is all public information."

Still. Nothing about Ian currently makes me think he'd want me to know anything about him. He barely answered the basic questions I asked and seemed genuinely upset at the idea I remembered him from his last visit.

Although that could have been more from fearing we'd briefly dated than that I was penetrating his bubble of seclusion.

Ugh, no. Must use a different word in future.

"I'll have them ready when you want them," she says. "Or you could do like any modern woman would do to the man she's interested in and look him up online yourself."

I spin to face her. "I'm not interested in him."

My gaze darts to the open doorway that leads to our friend's gift store next door. With any luck, Hope's got a customer or two in there to keep her busy so she can't hear a word of this. I don't need anyone else asking me pointed questions and leaping to their favorite conclusions.

Wren's mouth twitches with smug satisfaction as though I said the exact opposite.

I relax my shoulders and ease the tension from my voice. I need her to understand and not turn this into something it isn't. "Whatever he was like five years ago or fifteen, he's not the same man anymore, okay? He's grouchy and doesn't want to talk to me, let alone...anything else."

"You let me know when that changes."

"I wouldn't be surprised if we had dated." My stomach tilts, even though I have no idea exactly how he meant that. Bare minimum, it's kind of a compliment. One that should not have popped into my head on repeat all night.

He as much as confirmed my suspicions he dated a bunch of girls when he was here last time around. I've been burned once by a guy like that. I promised myself I'd never repeat that mistake.

"It doesn't matter anyway because I can't date."

Even if Ian were the kind of man I'm looking for—which he very vehemently is not—it's still a non-starter. I have to put August first. Trying to have a romantic relationship would only get in the way of that.

Instead of taking my point and dropping the subject, Wren rolls her eyes. "Don't start with the *can't* nonsense. You can date. You just won't. You ignore every man who comes in here and makes eyes at you over pie."

I scoff. "Nobody makes eyes at me over pie."

"Uh, yeah. They do. You just don't register them. You haven't paid attention to a guy in forever, and now one's got you flustered."

I say nothing for fear of proving her right. She's *not* right. It'd be stupid to get worked up over a guy based on a crush over a decade old, on traits that are long gone. Almost-smiles and questionable flirtations are not a thing to obsess over.

So I keep telling myself.

"He's not my type," I say, tossing the disinfecting rag back into the sink.

Wren nods. "Okay. What is your type?"

I splay a hand, absolutely nothing coming to mind. I haven't given it serious thought in so long, I don't even know anymore. Nice? Funny? Sweet? But a guy who once dated my town's population of young twenty-something girls and who now growls more than he talks is not on the list.

"See? He's got you flustered."

Kind of wish I'd thrown the disinfecting rag in her face.

The bell over the door chimes. I turn to greet our customer, and a tiny glimmer of sisterly spite flames to life inside me. Ha. Saved by the man who flusters *Wren*.

Shepherd Callahan lopes across the bakery to us, one hand shoved in his jeans pocket, the other brushing his ear-length dark hair out of his face. Both his arms are covered in tattoos, gray work with the occasional pop of color. His T-shirt has his bike store's logo on it, a streak of dark grease marring the Get in Gear text.

Wren's delight in poking at me snuffs out, her mouth tugging down. "Hello, Callahan."

She bites the words out, greeting him against her will.

Shepherd gives her a curt nod. "Krause."

"Hi, Shepherd." I always try to be extra friendly with him to combat the "get out" vibes Wren gives off. "Good day?"

He approaches the counter in front of Wren, not me. "Busy week for rentals."

His shop next door rents, sells, and repairs bicycles of all kinds. I'm not sure what tides him over in winter, but now that warmer days are here, I'd imagine he gets a lot of business.

"I need to come in one day this summer to get a bike for August," I tell him.

"We have a few different beginner bikes that would be great for him. Training wheels and helmets too, if you want."

Shepherd doesn't look at Wren but probably knows already that she's glaring. She's had a hate-on for him for the last two years and doesn't show any sign of giving up her grudge soon.

"Nice upsell," she mutters.

"I'll be in with him to pick something out." I put on a cheery smile to make up for her snark.

He finally turns to her. "What's fresh today?"

She huffs, spreading her arms out wide. "It's all fresh every day."

"Are you sure?" His mouth ticks beneath his short, dark beard, not quite allowing himself to smile as he challenges her.

They're like children sometimes. They go through this back and forth every week, asking simple questions loaded with... honestly, I don't even know what. Loathing? Business rivalry? Repressed attraction?

Wren might strangle me if I mentioned that last one. Still. The air gets *charged* whenever they're together.

"Am I sure?" she seethes back. "Are you seriously that—"

"Wren." I don't care if she has a thousand good reasons to hate him, she can't take it out on him in our store. Positive reviews only in here.

She rests her fists on her hips in an unnecessarily aggressive stance. "I'm sure. That's what we do here. We bake pies."

Her voice has gone sugary sweet, more babyish than she'd ever speak even to August. Shepherd listens as though she's not talking to him like he's a toddler.

"I watched Tess make all the cupcakes and the peach, strawberry cream cheese, and chocolate mint pies. I made the blackberry, strawberry-rhubarb, and key lime pies. Is my first-hand account enough for you, or do you need a notarized statement of their freshness?"

"No, I'm good," he says easily. He has to know his calm attitude only irritates her more.

She purses her lips together, most certainly holding back a retort about how he is anything but *good*.

"I'll take one of the blackberry," he says.

"A slice?"

"Whole, please."

She boxes up a blackberry pie, her cheeks pink, hands trembling. She tells him the total, and he slides some cash across the counter. When she gives him his change, their fingers brush before he drops the money into the tip jar.

I don't notice to be weird, but it's happening right in front of me. My eyes have nothing better to observe.

"Always a thrill to see you, Krause." He turns and nods my way. "Tess."

I lift a hand. "See you."

Wren stays perfectly still until he's left the bakery and disappeared from view out the front windows. Once he's gone, she exhales, shaking out her hands.

I step closer to her. "Did you still want to talk about men who make eyes at us over pie?"

The strange expression on her face hardens. "Oh, please."

I wouldn't normally push about imaginary romantic relationships, but after a morning of enduring the same, I've got a little to give back.

"He comes in every week like clockwork, but only on days you're working."

Her lips flatten into a hard line. "So he can be a jerk especially to me."

"He always buys a pie you made." At first it was just a theory, but now I've got ample proof.

She looks away. "Probably so he can do something weird to it. Like spit in it just to spite me."

"How would that spite you?"

"Just stop. You know how I feel about him."

Right now, when her face is flushed from talking with him, and a minute ago she shivered because their fingers brushed against each other? No, actually. I'm not sure how she feels about him.

"He stole our investor." She returns to her favorite complaint. "He lied to me, lied to him, and ruined my relationship."

We have very different opinions on how that all played out, but she refuses to see it my way. "You don't know any of that."

"It's the only explanation for what happened."

More accurately, the only explanation she'll accept.

"You weren't really seeing the guy," I remind her gently.

She huffs, redirecting her frustration from Shepherd to me. "We'd only just started to get to know each other, but it could have been...the point is, I hate him."

I'm not entirely sure this is hate.

"And we never needed that investor," I add.

Mom would have rejected the idea outright if she'd ever heard of it, but Wren won't give up her dislike for Shepherd. He's the town villain in her mind, and that's that.

"It's the principle," she says, crossing her arms over her purple Blackbird's Bakery apron that matches mine. "He can't be trusted. I hate his stupid, handsome face."

Yeah. Not entirely hate.

She scowls harder at me as though that slip was my fault.

The chimes over the door ring again. I greet our new customers and lean in close to whisper into Wren's ear.

"Maybe you should Google him."

———

In the spirit of keeping things as normal for August as possible, we're trying to have family dinners at Mom's at least once a week. I was worried he would struggle with being in his old home and want to stay put, but I should have been more concerned about sneak attacks from my mother.

"I just wish you'd waited until you and August could find a place closer," she says. "It's hard having you so far from us."

"They're only ten minutes away." Wren steals my answer before I can voice it.

Mom sends an affectionate look at August, who's seated next to her and devouring the barbecue chicken salad she made. "Feels like more."

I slump lower in my seat, the criminal who stole her grandson away. Wren nudges my shin under the table and gives me a bracing look.

I hate that I feel this guilty over something so perfectly natural. Wren's twenty-eight, I'm a mom in my thirties—we're grown-ups. Moving across town shouldn't make us feel like we're breaking the family apart.

"They couldn't live here forever." Wren's defense isn't just for August and me. As soon as she finds a place of her own, she won't live here, either.

Mom makes a vague sound, all but admitting she doesn't mind the idea of us living together forever. I'm sure it works for some families, but Wren and I have reached our limit.

"It's so far out of town," she says, even though the duplex is still within Sunshine proper. "I don't like you being all alone out there. What if there's an emergency?"

"We're not alone," August pipes up. He pauses long enough to lick his lips clean of barbecue-ranch dressing. He's carefully eaten only the chicken and cucumbers out of his plate of lettuce and vegetables. "We live with Dutch and Ian!"

Mom's gaze slowly tracks to me. "Is that right?"

"They're our neighbors," I explain before she can take August at his word. "They live in the other half of Amy and Jodi's duplex."

"You live next door to two men?"

August giggles. "Dutch is a dog."

This clarification doesn't seem to make things better in Mom's eyes. "Tell me about Ian then."

"He's funny. He has a big beard and red hair, and he likes Mama and he can throw a stick really far."

Thank you, precious child, for that unnecessary commentary.

"You hit all the important points, buddy," Wren tells him with a grin.

Mom's blond eyebrows lift practically to her hairline, and I can tell she's got a hundred questions dancing on the tip of her tongue.

"He's Amy's nephew, and she vouched for his character. He's pretty new to town and doesn't know anybody here. We've had a couple of conversations in the back yard while August plays with the dog. That's it."

Best for everyone at this table to hear me loud and clear. Including me.

"I'm not sure I've met him." Mom's still watching me as though waiting for a big confession.

"You've probably seen him, though. He's the guy with long red hair and a big red beard who looks like a Viking warrior."

Wren's ever so helpful. It's my turn to nudge *her* shin under the table, but I add more zest to it than she did. She sticks her tongue out at me in return.

Because we're grown ups.

"You said he looks like a pirate," I mutter.

"Oh, he definitely looks like both."

Mom's gaze darkens as though she's figured out who Wren

means. "I don't know how I feel about you living so close to...him."

Her inflection makes me weirdly defensive. After our father left us when we were young, and later, when I came home pregnant on my own, our family battled countless whispers in this town. People judged us based on what little information they saw or heard. They filled in blanks from their own imagination, without ever knowing the real story. I wouldn't have expected Mom to join that crowd based solely on someone's appearance.

It took me a long time to hold my head high and refuse to let nosy townsfolk get the best of me. Whatever else Ian's going through, judgmental stares and critical commentary are one more reason for him to avoid coming into town. People probably whisper about him, or even avoid him. All because his hair's a little scruffy and he doesn't hand out smiles like he's running for mayor? Now more than ever, I see what Amy meant when she told me about him last month—he needs a friend. And I intend to be that for him.

He can fight my efforts, but I'm still going to try.

"Ian's perfectly safe," I tell her. "If anything, you should be happy we have a man living next door in case there's an emergency."

Even if I suspect Ian would ignore my screams for help, thinking of his eventual peace when a bear drags me off into the wilderness.

EIGHT

IAN

I SHOULD HAVE JUST HAD my groceries delivered. My quick trip into town is taking twice as long as I thought it would. This late in the day, I'm tired of wearing my prosthesis and just want to go home and take it off. But this store isn't laid out like I expect, and I have to hunt for every blessed item on my list.

I shuffle my cart forward another foot, rolling my eyes at myself. Am I actually complaining about grocery store layouts? I just need to yell at some kids to get off my lawn and my transformation into a grumpy old man will be complete.

I frown at the rows of cereal boxes. I haven't been much of anything else to my new neighbors. Questioning Tess's motives when she brought me a gift and talking about rattlesnakes for some unknown reason. That was the best I could do in the face of her generosity. Grind out warnings about snakes and bears, oh my.

Not sure it's entirely my fault. She throws me off at every turn. Her kindness has to be for show—nobody's that cheerful twenty-four-seven. And does she have to smell so sweet? It's like she's been rolled in fruit and brown sugar, and I hate myself for wanting a taste.

"You're nothing like I remember you."
Join the club.

I shake my head as though I can clear it of Tess. That task has proved impossible since she moved in, but I keep up the good fight. I pull out my phone, take a pic of the empty grocery store aisle, and send it to Pierce.

> Ian: Do I get my gold star?

I toss a box of cereal into my cart and pick up the pace. I've got enough basics to get me through the week. It's not an impressive menu, but it'll do. Next week: start deliveries again.

My phone buzzes with a reply.

> Pierce: Who's the woman?

I stop in the middle of the aisle and double check that I sent the right photo. Not that there's a woman anywhere in my recent camera roll, but I still check.

> Ian: There's no woman in this picture

> Pierce: Only a woman would get you out of your funk and wandering town

> Pierce: You sure don't take my advice

> Pierce: So? Who is she?

A sound of disgust groans out of me. Should have left well enough alone. I push the cart more forcefully than I need to, leaning on the handle and furiously typing with my free thumb.

> Ian: There's no—

My cart slams into another with a resounding clang, and I drop my phone. I start to swear, but the sound dies out when I realize who's piloting the cart I crashed into. *Tess.*

Is she the only woman in this town? Are we in one of my daydreams? Admittedly, this would be one of the more pathetic ones, but I would accept that explanation. How is she here?

And why does she have to look so effortlessly stunning? She's in a T-shirt and shorts, nothing special, but the sight of her makes my mouth go dry anyway. I feel stupidly out of place confronted with her. Possibly because I look like a slob who gave up on himself years ago, and she looks like a golden goddess. Might be that.

"I'm so sorry," Tess says, even though I'm the one who ran into her. "Is your phone okay?"

"I'm sure it's fine." I bend down to grab my phone off the cement floor. It looks to be all in one piece, but I swipe my fingers over the screen to double check. I peer at the camera lenses, but I'm not sure I'd be able to tell at a glance if they were broken. "I shouldn't have been texting and driving."

The soft sound of her laughter eases some of the tension from my shoulders.

"You're dangerous behind the wheel of a shopping cart."

"You should see me on a motorcycle." I wince at my own dark humor. *Too soon.*

"I'll be sure to watch out."

I shift my weight on my feet, my mind blank. Are we flirting, or…? Am I this far gone I can't remember how to do it? It was reflexive back in the day. Would she even want me to flirt with her?

I've been trying to forget she called me both hot and charming twenty-four hours ago. I was a lot of things back then that I'm sure not now. Her laughter when I suggested we'd once dated still echoes in my ears. It'd seemed like the right conclusion—she's exactly my type, and I sure hadn't been shy when I came to town last. Most of my dates back then had been innocent enough, just flirting and having a good time, but she seemed to think I was some kind of Casanova.

Most likely, she doesn't care at all. I sure haven't given her reason to. She hasn't pushed past me yet, though, so I should at least say something. In the spirit of being neighborly...

"You're safe with—"

"Ian?" A tiny, distant voice calls my name.

I look around, then stare down at the phone in my hand. The screen is lit up with Pierce's name, the time clock steadily tracking seconds. I squeeze my eyes shut. I must have hit *Call* when I picked it up off the floor.

I'm really on a roll making things more difficult for myself. I lift the phone to my ear.

"Pierce?" As though I'd be lucky enough for it to be anyone else.

His laughter tells me he heard our entire awkward exchange. "Is that the woman?"

My gaze locks on Tess, who's still watching me two cart lengths away with a tentative smile. Not sure if it means "This guy's okay" or "This guy's crazy."

Maybe it just means "What is the minimum acceptable time I have to be in this guy's presence before I can make my escape?"

"I didn't mean to call you," I say to Pierce. I sure wouldn't have told him about Tess willingly.

"I'm glad you did. You need some coaching in the flirtation department."

That's great. Just wonderful. Now he'll tell Steven, and I'll never hear the end of this. Probably serves me right for all the ways I made jokes at my brothers' expense before they found their wives. Actually, I was worse after they found them. But this thing between Tess and me...it's not the same.

"Goodbye, Pierce."

"Take another picture—"

I make absolutely certain the call is ended and the screen is locked before I stuff the phone in my back pocket.

"Sorry," I grumble to Tess. "My oldest brother. Guess I hit the wrong button."

"I've done that, too. Accidentally called my sister on my way to August's daycare. She got an earful of us singing Taylor Swift at the top of our lungs."

Not sure why Tess and August bopping along to pop music is something I'd like to see. "Probably wasn't that bad."

She gives me a sly look that makes my stomach twist.

"We murdered *all* the high notes. It wasn't pretty."

Still bet it was.

"Where is the kid anyway?" It's a little strange to see her without him. Half expect him to appear at the end of the aisle to ask me if he can play with my dog.

"He's at my mom's watching a movie. It's easier to get my grocery shopping done when I don't have August 'helping' me pick out all his favorite things."

"I left Dutch at home for the same reason."

She fights a smile, like she's not quite sure if this is a joke to laugh at or an eccentricity she should indulge. Just proves my theory I don't know what I'm doing with women anymore. Sure don't know what I'm doing with *her*.

Her gaze drops to my cart, and her eyebrows lift.

"I'm not finished shopping yet." It's my best defense for the haphazard mix of items in there.

"I didn't say anything." Her gaze snaps back up to mine.

"You want to, though."

I wait, and I'm rewarded when she cracks another smile.

"I mean...it is a lot of meat."

"Red *and* white."

She exhales a laugh. "There's the variety. Very healthy."

I know we're only talking about groceries, but I don't mind Tess teasing me. At all.

"I have vegetables on my list."

"I'm sure." She nods, but her mouth takes a skeptical slant as if she knows I don't have a list. I'm not the list guy. I'm the figure-it-out-as-I-go guy. Except, apparently, when it comes to her.

"I'm on my way over there, but I don't know where anything is." Nobody tells you that once you're in your thirties, you start to care a lot about how grocery stores are laid out. Why is the produce nowhere near the meat department in this store? Make it make sense.

Her expression shifts to something more sympathetic. "Is this your first time in the store?"

Yeah. Shouldn't have said that. There's more than one grocery store in town, but her question isn't entirely a casual one. Like she knows just how much of an effort it took for me to come down here in the first place.

So much gentleness layers her voice, I'm tempted to admit everything. Share with her how I've been avoiding town, avoiding people because without my career, I don't know who I am anymore. Beg her to tell me where on earth the fresh fruit is located in this place. But this softness is too close to pity. That's the last thing I want from her. I shake off this...whatever she's doing to me. No point in looking at it too closely. Just need it gone.

"I should get back to it." I brace my hands on my cart, reminding myself this urge to stand right here with her until the store closes *talking* is foolish and one-sided.

"Oh. Sure." Her smile slips away, and she maneuvers her cart to the side.

A cold sensation creeps over me. It's not the first time I've felt that way when I've shut down on people these last two years...but it's the first time I want to fix it.

Pretty sure anything I tried would only make it worse. Mostly for me. Doesn't stop the urge, though.

Just before she passes me, she pauses. "It's good to see you, Ian."

This angel must really be a devil in disguise. Does she have any idea how my name on her lips tangles my stomach into a hitch knot? She can't possibly know how that one soft word unravels my impulse to sneak out of this grocery store and make sure we never cross paths again.

Just as she starts to move away, I manage to find my voice. "Thank you again for the cupcakes."

It comes out a mere step up from a growl and it's nothing I haven't already said, but I still say the words.

She stops again, directly in front of me. Looking at me with those big, blue eyes. A trace of a smile touches her mouth, and suddenly, I need to experience the whole, vibrant thing.

"They were the best I've ever had."

More like mouthwatering, but I'm not fool enough to use that descriptor in front of her. I've already got *jerk* covered, I don't need to add *creep* to the list. Still, I'd savored those cupcakes and mourned when I finished the last crumbs from the box.

She relaxes into a wide grin that hits me square in the gut. Maybe higher. All I know is, she's knocked my feet out from under me with her open smile. Even as I'm falling, bracing myself for impact, I want more.

NINE
TESS

NEVER LET a five-year-old give you exercise advice. They don't know what they're talking about. They're only five.

"You can do it, Mama." August's about fifteen feet ahead of me on the trail, cheering me on like I'm ready to cross the finish line of the Boston Marathon instead of less than a mile into a short walking path.

In my defense, it's impossible to keep up with him on flat surfaces, let alone on the side of a hill. His energy is always cranked to an eleven. I like to top out at about a seven—enough to keep from being a couch potato, but not so much I'm signing up for five-day hikes like my friend Lila did.

Actually, she doesn't especially like to be active, either. I wonder how that hike's going.

"You're so good, Mama! Almost there!"

I laugh, but the more he encourages me on, the more I want to sit down in the dirt. Just for a minute or five.

I made a specialty cake today, which always gives me an extra thrill, even if it means extra work. A group of nurses at the medical center requested a cake for their head nurse's birthday celebration. A two-layer chocolate cake with mint ganache filling and mint buttercream frosting. It'd been a joy to make, despite Mom side-eying me every time she walked into the kitchen.

She thinks our pie bakery should stick to baking pies, even if cakes are the love of my life. I convinced her to let me add our cupcake offerings to the case last year, but we don't have cakes on our website or even on our menu board in the store. They're an insider thing only, by special request.

Is it so wrong I want everyone to know about my cakes?

August runs over, loops around behind me, then runs back to where he was a second ago.

"How do you have so much energy?"

He lifts his arms in the air like he's flexing them. "It's my super shields!"

It's probably just good, old-fashioned, childhood exuberance. I trudge along, sweat running down my spine and a stitch forming in my side, feeling every bit a thirty-something.

Does the sun have to be this bright? I should have grabbed sunglasses and sun hats for both of us, but I didn't think a short hike could be this grueling.

"Mama," August whispers. "Come look."

He's stopped at the edge of the path on the side that slopes down—it's not especially steep, but I don't like him so close to it. I gently take his shoulder and encourage him to take a step back.

"What do you see?"

"Shh!" He crouches, duck-walking closer to the edge. "Down there."

I follow his pointing finger, but I don't see anything. My hand goes to my belt, where I clipped a brand-new canister of bear repellent, my brain flooding with images of bobcats and snakes, bears and cougars. I never thought I'd have to be vigilant about predators this close to my own back yard.

Thank you for that, Ian Vaughn.

My caution is crowded out by the memory of Ian's tentative smile the other night in the grocery store when he'd thanked me again for the cupcakes. It wasn't much—the barest lift at the corners of his mouth—but I'm counting it.

My heart certainly had. It'd sped up and fluttered and generally behaved like it thinks we're seventeen again.

I'd told him it was no problem, and we'd gone our separate ways. Or as separate as you can get in a smallish grocery store. We'd crossed paths three more times before I reached the checkout aisle, but we hadn't stopped again to talk.

He hadn't smiled again, either, but I'm not taking it personally. I don't think he's trying to be a jerk. I suspect he's just out of practice with people. It's kind of sweet, even though nothing about that should be endearing. Serial killers probably get out of practice with people, too. But those moments where he shows a glimpse of uncertainty behind his gruff exterior make me want to befriend him even more.

Befriend, Tess. And only befriend.

"Do you see it?" August whispers.

I stare into the sparse trees and shrubs below us. "What do you see?"

He points harder, which is less helpful than he thinks. At last, I spot it—a tiny gray bunny.

I release a huge exhale. "Thank goodness."

"Can we get him, Mama?" He puts a sinister edge to his voice, like we're experienced kidnappers lining up our next mark.

"He'd hop away before we ever reached him." Plus, I'd never let August scale the side of this mountain, so there's that.

He makes a small sound of acceptance. "I don't have a bag, either."

Because *that's* the real question when he sees a wild animal —does he have a bag big enough to nab it?

The bunny freezes for a second, then leaps away, disappearing into the scrub brush.

August slumps lower into his crouch now that his quarry's gone. "Aww."

"Sorry, buddy." In a "sorry, not sorry" way.

We stand, but the sound of gravel crunching has me turning to look up the trail. It curves around a switchback just past us, and I can't see who's coming.

Or *what*. Footsteps land in quick succession, spiking my heart rate. People don't run like that. What do bears sound like when they run? I step in front of August, touching the canister on my belt again. Should I take it out? Get the safety off? Maybe I should have done a practice spray in the yard. I never thought I'd actually have to use it, let alone the first day I had it.

I brace myself, ready for anything. Except for the big, brown animal that appears, running full tilt. My heart lurches even as I realize what it is.

"Dutch!" August moves around me and throws his arms out wide in greeting. Dutch stops short of jumping up on him, skidding to a halt so he can soak up the love. His tail wags a steady beat, his panting muzzle open in a maniacal grin. "You found us, boy!"

I put my hand on my chest, breathing hard. Thank goodness I didn't mace Ian's dog. There aren't enough cupcakes in the world to make up for that.

Speaking of...up the trail, Ian comes around the bend at a light jog. Pretty sure my heart jolts even harder than it did when I thought we were about to be attacked by a wild animal.

He's shirtless. My brain slips into shock as he comes to a stop about ten feet away.

My eyes lock on his sweaty chest, admiring in person every last feature I'd glimpsed in the picture Wren showed me. Broad shoulders. Insanely firm pecs. Biceps for days. A flat stomach that I most definitely should not be eating up with my eyes.

The sight is like Darcy coming out of the lake—unexpected and mesmerizing. Heat prickles up my neck as my fingers itch to trace the freckles that dance over waves of muscles. Totally inappropriate, but the heart wants what it wants.

My heart hasn't wanted anyone in a *very* long time.

Unbidden, my gaze tracks lower. Instead of his ubiquitous sweatpants, he's wearing athletic shorts. I suck in a breath. Where one leg is all toned muscle, the other is black plastic and metal. I take in his prosthetic leg, my mind stalling out as it shifts from silent applause to curiosity.

August's laughter as he snuggles Dutch finally breaks the spell I'm under, and I realize just how long I've been staring.

Forever. At least, that's what my heart rate says.

My attention snaps up to Ian's eyes. Twin blue flames glare back at me. His hair is up in another bun, sweaty tendrils clinging to the side of his face and beard. He's breathing hard, his chest heaving from exertion, but I refuse to let my eyes dip lower again.

I don't know how long they'd snag there this time.

Maybe he didn't notice me ogling him. There's a chance, right?

"I thought you didn't hike." It's a terrible stab at small talk when he already told me he climbs mountains for a living.

He goes on staring, utterly silent.

"Not that you can't." Even as I say it, I recognize how bad that sounds. As though I think he's *incapable.* "I'm sure you can handle it. It's a pretty easy trail. For someone like you."

Ugh, no. That came out even worse. "A professional, I mean."

I'm surprised I can speak at all, my mouth's so full of my

own feet. Ian goes on glowering as if maybe we'd both like the earth to swallow me whole.

"I haven't seen this much of you out here—I mean *much of you*. At all. I haven't seen you out here." I hate every stupid thing vomiting out of my mouth. Why don't I compliment his glistening pecs and complete my mortification?

If Ian would at least say something, that would help. But he just keeps watching me like the train wreck I am.

"It's a hot day." I fan myself like a dork. *Is it hot out here or just you?*

This is why I never spoke to Ian back when I was a teen. I would have fallen all over myself and spewed an embarrassing amount of nonsense. At least I was smart enough to realize it and kept my distance. So glad I saved that disaster for today, I guess.

Then, as if in slow motion, I look down at August at the same time he realizes Ian has joined us. It's impossible to miss the way his eyes widen as they latch onto Ian's prosthetic leg. His mouth dropping open in shock. His tiny hand lifting to point at our neighbor like he's a shiny-new exhibit in a zoo.

Angry bear. Do not feed.

"Mama, look! Ian's got a super leg! He really is a pirate like you said!"

Oh, this day is the worst.

I grab August's hand, closing over his still-pointing finger, and tug him along up the path.

"We should keep going," I say to Ian. "Need to finish up before it gets dark."

We're hours away from sunset, but I'll take any excuse to leave. If we stay, I'm afraid I'll complete this humiliation by telling him about my teenage crush.

Or my current one.

Ian says not a word. He's stood still as sculpted stone since he stopped on the trail, doing nothing but breathing hard and glaring at me. Not even a nod of acknowledgement—not that any of the moronic things I've said are worthy of his recognition.

I thought I was used to his silent glowering, but this takes it to a whole new level. I'm pretty sure he'd like to set me on fire and watch me burn down to embers. The way my chest blazes, I'm probably halfway there.

Is it my fault his body left me completely tongue-tied? I cringe because yes, it's absolutely my fault. I don't do this. I don't stare at men or flirt with them or frankly even notice them, but shirtless Ian captured my attention. To say the very least.

"We'll see you later." The smile I flash at him is fake and terrible, but I can't make my face be normal right now. Its default is *open admiration*, and I don't need that on display again.

He glares at me like I've stumbled into a funeral procession. *Here lies Tess, crushed to death by shame.*

"But, Mama," August says behind me. "What about Ian's leg?"

I shush him before he can mention I also called Ian a *viking* and keep walking. I just need a second to compose my thoughts, and I can't think straight with half-naked Ian staring at me like this. I need an escape, and the only one possible is the trail.

Or, you know, I could launch myself off the side of the mountain, but I'm not in the habit of abandoning my child. My dignity? Yes, obviously.

Dutch whines, but eventually their footsteps start up again behind us. I don't turn around. I'll either see the muscular back of my dreams or the scowl of my nightmares, and either one would absolutely ruin me.

Once we make it past the switchback and I'm sure Ian's out of sight, I finally slow down.

"Mama, you're holding my hand too tight."

I shake out of my mental spiral, releasing August's hand. "I'm sorry, baby."

"Why can't we talk to Ian? I want to know about his leg."

"I don't know if Ian wants to talk about that." Given his habit of wearing sweatpants in summer, probably not.

He definitely didn't want to talk to *me* just now. But if I'd come across a man who'd stared at me open mouthed and drooling all over himself, I wouldn't have stopped to chat, either. Might as well have wolf-whistled at him and completed the look.

"But it's like my super shields."

I sigh. My son said Ian has a "super leg." He called him a pirate to his face. And I stared like he wasn't even real. I am the worst.

"Is it gross?" August asks in a small voice.

"What?"

His shoulders sag, his eyes on the dirt at his feet. "Like when Lily said my monitor and pump are gross."

My breath holds until my lungs hurt. Maybe it's my heart aching in there. I stop in the middle of the trail, glancing back even though I can't see Ian anymore. Is that how he took my fumbled attempts at conversation—that I was thrown off by his leg? Sure, I was surprised, but that wasn't what had me tripping over my tongue.

Attraction to him knocked me flat and backed over me for good measure. But from his vantage it probably felt more like someone trying to get a better look at a car accident. For all my intentions to be a thoughtful, conscientious human, I really blew it today. I had all the tact of August's rude Kindergarten classmate.

"No, his leg isn't gross." I squat down in front of August. "And your monitors aren't gross. They're just different."

He smiles, knowing this conversation by heart. "And different is okay."

"Absolutely."

"So we can still be his friend."

If he'll let us.

"Definitely."

We stand and start walking again, more slowly than before. I need to make this right with Ian. Part of me wants to rush down the hillside this minute, but it'd be smarter to take some time to compose myself.

And compose a proper apology.

TEN

IAN

NEWS FLASH: a thick burger and salty fries don't numb the senses nearly as well as a few shots of whiskey would.

My first impulse after running into Tess on the trail was to head to the nearest dive bar and drown myself in a bottle of bourbon. But I indulged in that too often in the first year after my accident. Drinking the day away never brought back my mountaineering career or the clients who once sought me out to guide them to new heights.

My next thought was to hop on my motorcycle and peel out of Sunshine at top speed. But since I don't have a motorcycle anymore and haven't ridden one since the crash, that option was out. Rumbling out of town in my old SUV didn't sound nearly as satisfying.

So—burgers it is.

I'm sitting at the counter at Delish with a massive hamburger and tray of fries in front of me. I even ordered one of Amy's signature marionberry milkshakes, which I don't regret in the slightest.

I do regret how she's watching me. She moves around the

busy restaurant, taking orders and checking in with customers, but her gaze keeps coming back to me. Even when I'm focused on my food, I can feel it on me, prodding with unasked questions.

Maybe it's because I've rarely been in here since I came to town.

Or maybe she read more in my face when I walked in than I meant to show.

Sometimes what someone's feeling flashes like a neon sign in their expression. They can't help it. Like the horrified look that slashed across Tess's face when she caught sight of my prosthetic leg. At first, I'd thought her examination of my bare chest had some heat in it, but the longer she stared, the more it morphed into something like shock.

I'm past being horrified or depressed about my leg. Doesn't mean I expect everyone else to treat it like a normal thing. And the look on Tess's face hadn't been close to normal. From what I've seen, her default is softness and gentleness, not mild panic.

The urge to push past her and run the rest of the way home had risen up inside me, but I'd held it down and stood my ground. Might as well get her reaction over and done with as fast as possible. And by the time she continued up the hill practically dragging August behind her, *over* sure felt like the best descriptor for whatever we had going.

I told myself I didn't want any more cupcakes of mercy, right? This development should be a good thing. Even if it feels like the worst.

Amy leans on the counter across from me. "What else do you need?"

From the worried look in her eyes, I'm pretty sure she's not talking about more ketchup.

"I'm good." I don't hold eye contact with her, though. She's setting off on a deep dive into my psyche, and I don't need to do anything that would help her along.

"How are things going with Tess?"

See? She got right to the tangled, messy heart of it.

I keep my focus on my fries as I dip them in sauce. "Fine."

Except for the way Tess stared at me like she was truly seeing me for the first time. Like everything she thought or suspected or hoped about me rearranged in front of my eyes. Other than that, we're great.

She waits, but if she's holding out for more info about my neighbor, she won't get it from me.

"Have you heard from your brothers lately?"

Now that one, I can answer. "Pierce and Bonnie are having a girl."

Surprised he didn't finish his rounds with that news.

"How adorable. I'll have to call them. Should be in the next few weeks, right?"

"Something like that." I go back to my meal.

"Will you go back to Colorado to see her?"

"Trying to get rid of me already?"

Amy smiles, but I probably deserve a slap across the face. She invited me to Sunshine in the first place. I didn't know what to do with myself before she made that offer. The rent I give her doesn't come close to what she could charge for my apartment, and I repay her by being distant and cold.

"If you want me out of here, I can go. You've done plenty for me—"

She lays a hand on my arm, shutting me up. "We don't want you to move out. I just wanted to know if you're planning a trip back to meet your niece, that's all."

I know staying here is only a pitstop, but I'm not ready to figure out what to do next—and that includes visiting my brothers. They'll put the pressure on to come home and rejoin the business, and I don't know if I can do that yet.

I don't know if I want to try. Not when so much of what I used to do is quite literally out of my reach. Some people with my amputation could, no question. But I'm not there.

"I don't know," I tell her.

She nods, pats my arm, and walks away to talk to customers.

Like she heard her cue, Jodi comes out from the back. Her dark curly hair streaked with gray is pinned up into a bun like mine, her fry cook apron pristine. Her easy grin puts me on edge as much as Amy's piercing gaze does.

Her perpetual good mood just highlights how dark my own is.

"It's good to see you, honey." She talks like she was born in the south—everyone is honey or sugar or sweetheart to her.

"Good to see you."

"You coming to dinner at our place sometime soon?"

It's harder to say no to Jodi than it is with Amy. Jodi's not pressuring me to break out of my shell, she'd just genuinely like to see me at their place again. She likes my company, such as it is. Which is a pressure all of its own.

"Probably not."

"That's okay." She smiles wider. She worked at the post office here before she took over fry cook duties at the diner with Amy. I'm not sure it's possible to dampen her friendliness. "You're here now."

"Mmm." Doesn't seem like much of a consolation prize.

"Have you thought about joining us for the Fourth Fest in a few weeks? I heard the fireworks are going to be something else. We've got a new gal running the whole show. The parade's supposed to be even bigger, too."

"I don't know yet." I do know—I'm not going. But I'm not

jerk enough to say that to Jodi's face when she's only trying to draw me out.

She rests a hand on my forearm and gently squeezes. "I have to get back to it, but I wanted to tell you I'm glad you're here."

Because coming into a diner is such a big deal. For me, lately, it has been.

"Thanks, Jodi."

She nods, her gaze almost too soft as she lets me go. I think she might say something more, but she must see the futility of it, and returns to the back kitchen.

I get about three minutes with my thoughts—which are a mess, FYI—before a man sits down next to me. And I mean *right* next to me, even though there are plenty of empty barstools farther down the line. I don't look directly at him, but I don't have to. I can tell already what this guy is.

A fan.

Before the accident, my brothers and I had some popularity around Durango, and I ate up the attention I got. People could stop me in a restaurant, at my mailbox, on the street, I didn't care. The fact that I had anything remotely close to fame as a mountain guide blew me away.

To be fair, it wasn't all about climbing. Interest in me exploded after Vance Vickers hired me to guide him through one of Colorado's wilderness areas. The blockbuster actor used the two-week trek as research for some *Man vs. Nature* Oscar-contender film he had in the works. I'd seen it as a nice-paying guiding gig at the time, but it brought more recognition than I'd ever anticipated.

Ironic that I fell asleep when I tried to watch the movie. Dying alone in the snow would have been more entertaining than enduring that flick.

Even so, he'd talked me up in every interview he did for that movie. When he thanked me in his speeches for all the awards he won that year, I was suddenly on every famous actor's contact list when they wanted a vacation of roughing it in the mountains. Magazines, newspapers, and podcasts came calling. Me being me, I always answered.

But after the accident? The attention took on a different bent. Would I be willing to do an interview about disabled athletes? Could I participate in a panel on near-death experiences? Did I have any interest in being a spokesman for speed limit reforms? No thank you all around.

And fans...let's just say they have all the subtlety of the motorcycle accident that landed me here in the first place.

The man next to me clears his throat, but I don't acknowledge him. He'll either take the hint and shuffle off, or...I'll have to send him on his way.

"Ian Vaughn?" he says.

"Nope," I say before taking a big bite of my burger.

The man chuckles. "I'll leave you alone if you want—"

"Good."

His chuckle expands into a laugh. "My name's Nathan Bridger."

His hand appears in my peripheral vision, but I ignore it.

"No autographs today," I grumble. I never really was a celebrity in my own right, and I'm even less than that now.

"But a selfie's fine?"

I turn to find him grinning at me, empty hands raised as though claiming innocence. "I won't. But I wanted to talk to you for a minute if you don't mind."

I glance over Nathan, but there's nothing obviously worrisome about him. Probably a good ten years younger than I am, short dark hair, tattoos snaking down both arms, eyes bright. I wipe my mouth with a napkin and gesture for him to continue.

Might as well cap off this day with a request for a private guide I can't fulfill. Or an attempt to get Vance Vickers's personal information. Either way, Nathan's going home disappointed.

We both are, pal.

"I work for Backcountry EMT, I don't know if you've heard of it." He pauses, and I shake my head. "We provide medics for things like festivals, concerts, and remote athletic events across the state, as well as traditional emergency services."

My food sits uncomfortably in my gut. This is worse than any autograph hound.

"I don't know how long you're thinking of staying in the area," he goes on, "but if it's long-term, we'd love to have you consider joining our team."

He's recruiting me for a job? Is he serious?

"Why me?"

My curt challenge seems to invigorate him. "No reason. Only that you're a Wilderness EMT. Have AMGA certifications in alpine, ice, and rock climbing. And you have more hours on a mountainside than anybody else in this state."

It's a stretch, but the guy's done his research. Except for one small problem. "Haven't you heard? I'm not in that business anymore."

I keep saying it, but it's not entirely true. My brothers would argue I'm still very much in the business, simply on extended leave. Personally...I'm not sure what I am. But a refusal is easiest when I'm trying to finish my dinner.

His gaze drops to my leg—the wrong leg, but it tells me enough.

"I heard. That shouldn't be an issue."

"You're awfully confident."

"It's a curse." His grin says he's well aware.

I used to have the same cocky smile. Until my accident wiped it away.

"I know this is a poor way to ask if you'd ever consider

working with us, but I had to take the chance. If you're heading back to Durango, no worries, but a little birdie told me you might consider staying in town if you had the right motivation."

Of course she did. "Is that little birdie named Amy?"

"Might be."

I look around the diner until I find her hovering over a booth. She glances at me and dips her head, both confirming this is all her doing and pushing me harder toward her goal. Maybe I should be flattered she wants me to stay in town so badly, but an EMT job? Do either of them know what they're asking?

"If she's wrong, don't sweat it. If she's not..." He slides a business card over to me slick as anything. "It's something to think about."

I glance at the card, the red Backcountry EMT logo blaring up at me. I will not be thinking about it. That's not even close to what I ever did. My EMT certifications were a safety precaution, not a career path. And if he knows anything about my accident, he's already aware *safety* was a moving target for me.

"And hey, if you're ever bored some night and want to hang out and talk, I'd be down for that, too. My number's on the back. No pressure."

This guy is way too eager. I nod acknowledgement of the offer but don't so much as hint that I might take him up on it. Pretty sure I haven't *hung out* with anyone since before...well, since before.

He pats the countertop and spins on the barstool to leave, but pauses. "Seriously, it's a thrill to meet you, dude. Reading articles about you in *Crux* is part of what got me into climbing, and eventually wilderness first response. Is it too much if I say you were my hero?"

I press my lips together. "A bit."

Nathan grins wide and slips away.

In the next moment, Amy moves in front of me to gather up my plate and empty glass, subtle as a sledgehammer.

"He just called me old," I tell her.

"Out of the mouths of babes…"

I snag the last couple of fries off my plate before she can whisk it away. "You're telling people I'm looking for work now?"

"Just him." She hitches a shoulder. "And Mitchell Choi. And the volunteer Search and Rescue team lead."

This woman is relentless.

"Anybody else? Is there a dance troupe in town you gave my name to?"

She leans on the counter, chin in hand. "Don't give me ideas. I'd love to see that."

My stern look doesn't seem to affect her. "Stop meddling."

"It's small-town life. Everybody's got their fingers in everyone else's pies."

"Leave my pie alone."

Her gaze is full of sisterly affection. "I love you too much to do that."

I grumble, but I guess I knew what I was in for when I came out here. Escaped my brothers but landed on Amy's radar.

Hold up.

"Is that why you put Tess next door to me? So she can… what, assist you with your meddling?" By bringing me cupcakes and talking to me like I'm a person and smiling so hard it makes something under my ribs hurt?

Staring at me like I'm some kind of alien *thing* today probably wasn't part of the plan.

"Yes." Amy has no shame.

"You actually meant for her to keep an eye on me?" I don't need a babysitter. Worse, the thought that Tess's smiles and attempts to be *neighborly* were all just for show makes my stomach sink like I'm scrambling down a mountainside.

"Maybe I hoped you could keep an eye on each other."

I don't know why she thinks Tess needs someone looking out for her, and I can't ask. I might not have minded the job, but I don't have the heart to tell Amy her grand scheme already failed. She'll find out soon enough—probably when Tess comes to her to let her know she wants to move out.

ELEVEN

TESS

MY CHEEKS HURT from fake-smiling all day, my stomach tied into so many knots I want to double over. I can't stop thinking about every dumb thing I said to Ian yesterday. The way I shamelessly—and shamefully—stared at his body. The relentless fire in his eyes when he'd glared back at me.

His scowl stayed with me all night, a bad omen I can't shake. Whatever hopes I had of being friendly neighbors with him burnt to a crisp beneath that heavy gaze.

Any thought I might have entertained of anything more, well...those were never going to happen anyway.

"Okay, girls, do you need anything before I go?" Mom still talks to us like she's leaving us alone in the bakery for the first time instead of roughly the five thousandth. She's got her small purse looped over her shoulder, ready to head out for the afternoon.

"We've got it," Wren says next to me behind the counter. "Are you meeting friends for dinner?"

The question seems to take Mom by surprise, and she stops on her way to the door. "Yes, actually. Just a friendly get together."

"You look very pretty."

I hadn't thought about it before, but she's wearing a dress. It's not totally unusual for her, but we mostly keep it business casual in here. Now that she's slipped off her apron, the embroidered details on her navy mini dress stand out.

Mom smooths her blond hair over her shoulder. She's brushed it out of the up-do she usually wears for work, and the gentle waves suit her. "Thank you, honey. I'll see you girls at home."

It's a tiny thing, but it still sends a shard of guilt under my skin. One more reminder of how I shook things up by moving out.

She winces but smiles brighter to cover it. "I'll see you tomorrow, Tess."

Mom waves and heads out. I turn away, ready to clean. Organize. Do anything to stay occupied and keep my thoughts from spinning Ian's direction. A big goal, since they've been stuck on him all day.

Wren nudges me before I can find something productive to do. "Okay, spill. Why are you so squirrelly today?"

I've debated this all day, too—do I confide in my sister? While I don't love what I have to share, I'm not in the habit of keeping secrets from her. On the other hand, chances are high my story will lead her to a cliff perfect for jumping off into various romantic conclusions. Wren loves a good leap.

But I have to get it out. I'm too racked with regret to keep this to myself.

I sigh, sagging against the back counter. "I'm a horrible person."

"Wow, okay. Dramatic. Who'd you murder?" She clasps her hands in front of her chest. "Please say it was Callahan."

"Not murder." I slaughtered every last ounce of my pride,

but there aren't any laws against that. Self-mortification is perfectly legal.

She groans. "Is this like that time you ran a red light in Bend and freaked out for weeks because you thought you were going to get a ticket in the mail?"

I still get nervous when I find anything official-looking in the mailbox, just in case their ticketing system was delayed. By eighteen months.

"Worse."

She sidles closer. "You have to narrow it down. There's a lot of options between traffic violations and murder. I can't guess all day."

My gaze cuts to the pass-through leading to Hope's store next door. "You can't tell anybody about this."

I love Hope and trust her with my secrets, but not all of what I have to say is about me.

Instead of sobering Wren, this excites her. Of course she'd love the idea of me sharing anything secret or potentially scandalous. "I wouldn't."

I weigh her words, but if I can't trust Wren, I can't trust anyone.

"I saw Ian yesterday." I let my ominous tone convey it was more than a neighborly visit.

She grins as if she can't help herself. "Tell me more."

"We were on the trail behind the duplex, and August and I came across him finishing a run...while he was shirtless."

Her eyes widen, and I can tell she wants to combust from this news. But she manages to nod and hum agreement, my indifferent therapist mildly encouraging me to go on.

"I stared at him. A lot. Obviously and embarrassingly. I was like a cartoon character with my eyes stretching out of my head." Hopefully, my tongue stayed in my mouth, but I can't be sure.

"That picture I saw was pretty impressive. I can only imagine what it was like seeing it in person." She fans herself exactly the way I did on the trail.

"I tripped over myself trying to talk to him and sound normal, and instead I just made my stupid crush completely obvious."

My heart sinks even as Wren's face shines like a beacon. I should not have said that specific word. It's the match to the fuse for her joy explosion.

She splays her hands in the air as though any of that was worthy of celebrating. "Finally! You have a crush! Oh, I love this."

I knew she wouldn't take it as hard as I did. I'm tempted to point out she hasn't been in a rush to jump into feelings, either. Jumping into everyone else's is much easier.

"The story isn't over."

"I would hope not."

I drop my voice. "He has a prosthetic leg."

I hate that I'm even bringing it up. I want to be that person who doesn't mention differences, who's welcoming and accepting no matter what, but my behavior yesterday proved I'm not living up to it.

That, at least, makes Wren settle. "Did you know?"

"He'd never mentioned it, and I'd never seen him in shorts before." I don't know him well enough to guess whether that was intentional or not. Maybe he just likes being extra warm, even in summer. Or maybe he didn't want to invite stupid comments and open stares from weirdos.

Hi. It's me. I'm the problem.

"Does it bother you?" Wren's voice goes flat, and I can tell she's trying to hide her disapproval. I love that she can't quite conceal her disappointment, even if it casts doubt on me.

"No. I was just surprised. But the way I stared at him, and all the dumb things I said probably made him think it bothers me. August wanted to talk to Ian about it, and I practically hauled him away." The memory makes my stomach lurch all over again. "I've spent the last two years afraid people would say mean things to August about his diabetes, and then when I was faced with someone with a slight difference, I behaved like a child."

Worse than some children. August was curious and interested, but I'd escaped as quickly as I could. After, you know, blabbering about Ian tackling an easy trail, and something about wanting to see *more* of him. I don't know if I'm relieved or disappointed my shock made my memories of the conversation fuzzy.

The unexpected heat that coursed through me as I looked him over, though? *That* I remember in vivid detail. Echoes of it linger even now.

"But it wasn't really his difference that made you act that way, right? It was his..." Wren mimes massaging something in front of her. "Extremely attractive body."

I roll my eyes and slap her hands away. "It's not like I can say that, though."

"Pretty sure you could."

Maybe Wren could just go up to a man and say, "Sorry I stared, I wasn't looking at your leg, I was memorizing the muscles in your chest." Personally, I can't do that. But what I have planned doesn't feel any easier.

"I have to apologize to him." I need to prove I'm not really the kind of person I behaved like yesterday—someone who stares and says obnoxious things. First with an apology, and then by treating him exactly the same way I always have. He's not a different person just because I know about his leg, and I refuse to treat him like one.

"Yeah. I'm sure it will be okay."

I have less confidence. Nothing about that fiery glare felt very forgiving. But I still need to be a decent person and get the words out. What he does with them isn't in my control.

"Please don't say a word about his leg to anyone. I don't want to add spreading gossip to the list of ways I've offended him."

"I wouldn't say anything. Sheesh. But are we going to talk about the more important part of that story?"

I brace myself against the counter, knowing exactly what she's fixated on. "We already covered it."

She leans in close to whisper in my face. "You. Have. A. Crush."

I put my palm on her forehead and push her back a step. "Stop."

She shakes off my rejection. "This is exciting. You didn't even want to admit when you thought Thor was hot, and he's imaginary. This is a big development for you."

"I didn't want to talk about it because I knew you would mention Thor every chance you got. Which you do."

Since learning that tidbit a couple of years ago, she's plastered my bedroom in Thor posters, photoshopped me into romantic poses with him, and gave me a Thor action figure complete with hammer. I passed the action figure on to August, but the point remains: Wren doesn't let things go.

She pauses a second, thoughts swirling behind those mischievous blue eyes. "Is that what's doing it for you? The giant beard and the long hair? Is he bringing your Thor fantasies to life?"

Ignoring her, I grab napkins to refill the dispensers on the front counter. Couldn't I have explained what happened between me and Ian without mentioning my ill-advised crush?

Probably not well, since the "ogling him like a goon" part was pretty key.

Wren tails me through the bakery, grinning away. "Obviously, the muscles don't hurt."

"I envy people with no siblings," I grouse.

"Maybe it's the climber thing. You like a guy with a dangerous job."

I stiffen, but my hands keep moving, taking the top off one of the dispensers.

"Sorry," she says softly, her gloating smile gone. "I shouldn't have said that."

"It's okay." I take a fortifying breath. "It's a good point. One more reason I can't take this seriously."

I need to be Ian's friendly neighbor *only*—this interest in him isn't remotely realistic. But Wren doesn't see it the same way. She grabs my arm so I have to stop tinkering with the napkins and look at her.

"That's not a reason to write off Ian," she says gently. "*He* doesn't deserve that kind of power in your life."

He being He-who-must-not-be-named—the charismatic ski instructor I fell for during my fateful six months living outside of Sunshine. Pro tip: when a guy says he's not looking for anything serious, believe him. Me unexpectedly getting pregnant didn't turn him into a romance book hero who was suddenly invested and ready to be a dad—it made him cut all contact and run.

I've never been blocked across all possible platforms so quickly in my life.

"I'm not giving him power. But when I learn a lesson about getting burned, I'm careful to stay away from fire."

Wren flips my hand over, revealing the shimmering lines on the inside of my arm. "Says the woman covered in oven-burn scars."

A brittle laugh rattles out of me as I pull my hand away. "That's the only risk I'm willing to take."

A few burns on my hands and arms are just part of my job. I can take that kind of pain. But putting my heart on the line? That's never happening again.

TWELVE
IAN

THE DOORBELL CHIMES, reminding me I never found that *Keep out* sign I wanted. Maybe wrapping my door in bright yellow *Caution* tape would do the trick.

Wishful thinking. I'm pretty sure nothing would make a difference. It's got to be my sole visitor at the door, and I doubt she'd ever be scared away by any sign.

Amy isn't even giving me twenty-four hours before showing up again to try to drag me out of my hibernation cave. Probably with a new list of job opportunities and a selection of overeager guys for me to make friends with. Next, she'll be setting up play-dates for me at the park.

I didn't have the heart to leave Nathan Bridger's card at Delish last night to be dumped in the trash. I swiped it up just before I left. Not sure why, since a job as an EMT isn't on my horizon, and I haven't been fit for hanging out with a friend in ages. But the card sits on my entry table anyway.

A light knock sounds at the front door, nudging me. I sigh and abandon my earbuds and latest Brandon Sanderson novel I was listening to on the couch. Hauling myself up, I swipe a hand in the air, encouraging Dutch to give me space. He's sitting in front of the door, tail wagging and tongue out, ready to greet Amy.

"I told you to leave my pie alone," I grumble as I open the door. But instead of my meddling aunt, Tess stands in front of me.

The air heaves out of my lungs. After yesterday, I didn't expect to see her again unless the situation was totally unavoidable. Showing up at my door—looking soft and delectable, no less—is completely avoidable.

Her mouth quirks. "I promise not to touch your pie."

My brief laugh doesn't make a sound. Words fail me, which is probably a good thing at the rate my brain is spinning. At least I manage to stop Dutch from jumping up on her and send him back into the living room.

Tess's smile fades a touch, probably because I let my silence go on too long.

I've become good at that.

"Hi," she says.

"Hi." Our greetings sound more like questions. I get the feeling we're both testing the waters here. I know what's got me on edge, but I can't quite compute what's got her nervous.

Unless it's me.

"Do you have a minute? I won't take much of your time if you're busy."

"I'm not busy." Understatement of the year. Then again, I'd probably drop most things if she asked.

Nodding, she swallows hard and wrings her hands, fingers trembling. Her shakiness sends my heart into the depths of the abyss. I don't like that she's this nervous about whatever it is she has to say. I hate even more that it's well deserved—aside from the blip yesterday, she's been nothing but friendly to me, and I haven't given her the same kindness in return.

Why, exactly, again? So I can prove I'm mad at the world

because my career's over? The same reason I've pushed away my brothers, Amy—even Nathan Bridger last night. Seeing her this anxious about facing me has guilt churning through my stomach. Is this really the man I want to be? The one who scares everybody away?

I cross my arms, trying to relax my stance. But that just makes me look like I'm looming over her, so I uncross them again and slip my hands into the pockets of my sweatpants. Nice and casual. Or as close as I can get when she's about to say whatever she has in mind.

"I wanted to apologize for how I acted yesterday." Her words tumble out fast as if she's rehearsed this once or twice. "I was thoughtless and...well, I shouldn't have behaved like that or said those stupid things to you. I'm sorry for making you uncomfortable."

She's sorry for making *me* uncomfortable? She'd been so quick to get out of my sight, I thought it'd been the other way around. My mouth drops open—not sure what I might even say —but she continues.

"I was caught off guard, and I shouldn't have stared the way I did." Her gaze dips, but it doesn't go down to my leg. It snags on my chest and arms. In an instant, she snaps her eyes back to mine. "It was offensive, and I'm embarrassed by my behavior. I'm really sorry."

"You don't have to keep saying you're sorry." In the two years since my accident, loads of people have stared at my prosthetic leg. Said dumb things. Asked invasive questions. But the number of people who have apologized afterward is exactly zero. "I could have handled it better."

Silently staring at her, expecting her to run off the way I'd wanted to, didn't improve the situation.

She slashes a hand through the air. "That wasn't your fault at all. I was completely in the wrong. I kept ogling you and spouting off at the mouth like a schoolgirl. That was all on me."

"It wasn't—" Wait. *Wait.* "You were ogling me?"

Are we having two different conversations right now? I thought she'd stared out of shock and maybe disgust, not any sort of appreciation. This news lights a spark of pride in me—probably worse than pride, if we're being honest—that I haven't felt in years.

Her cheeks flame a delightful rose right before my eyes, her gaze shifting to the side. This confirms it even better than her words.

"The point is, I was rude, and I'm so sorry. I know what it's like to have people point and stare, and I'm ashamed I did that to you."

I want to go back to the ogling part, but a new question snares my attention. Why would anyone point and stare at Tess? Unless they're saying, "Look at that gorgeous woman who makes cupcakes that taste like the nectar of the gods," I can't come up with a good reason. But now's not the time to question her.

This is obviously taking a lot for her to admit. The fact that she's being this vulnerable with me when I've been basically an ogre the entire time we've known each other means more than she can guess.

The pleading reflected in her eyes makes me want to meet her halfway, even if it feels like a vast chasm to cross. "I thought you were staring at my leg."

It's superficial and stupid, but a lot of people can't get past it. They think a guy like me is damaged, or less than a man, or *other* in some essential way. Truthfully, on some days, that call's coming from inside the house. I'd hated to put Tess in that category, too, but maybe I got it all wrong.

She shakes her head a little. "No. It was—" One hand comes

up to gesture at my chest, but she tucks it away behind her back. "I wasn't staring at your leg. I was surprised, but I don't care about that."

Her apparent interest in my body generally and my chest specifically is taking this apology in an unexpected direction.

To be clear, I very much like the direction.

Her eyes widen, and she presses her palms to her cheeks. "I don't mean I *don't care*, it's just...that's not the most important thing about you. You know?"

I'm tempted to ask what *is* the most important thing about me, but something else from that conversation hooks in my memory. "August said you'd told him I'm a pirate."

In the moment, I'd assumed she'd made some kind of peg-leg crack to her kid. Now, it's clear she'd genuinely had no idea. So where did that description come from?

I hadn't imagined her face could get any pinker, but her skin is finding all new shades of red. The color washes from her cheeks to her temples and down her neck.

"Um, that was mostly about your hair."

"Mostly?"

"And beard. It's just so..." She reaches up almost as though she's going to touch my hair. I still, wanting that small touch. Denying me, she stops herself at the last second and closes her hand into a fist, one finger out to point at my head. "I think it's the man bun."

My hair makes me look like a pirate? I might be discouraged by this news if she wasn't so obviously embarrassed about admitting it. That blush is not the response of a disgusted woman. She's not reeling back in horror. If anything, she's leaning in.

"You don't like the man bun?" I've resorted to it out of necessity, but even when my hair was shorter, I used to tuck it up like this sometimes. Now, I'm questioning that move.

Her gaze seems to warm as she glances my hair over.

"It's definitely a rakish look for a man nearing forty."

"Ouch. Kicking me when I'm down. I'm only thirty-six." For a few more weeks. "I will take *rakish*, though."

In an instant, her face is in her hands, a sweet little groan escaping her. "I'm doing this apology all wrong. I'm so sorry."

"Please don't keep apologizing." I'm not sorry for a moment of this interaction. Pretty sure I'll be revisiting it for the foreseeable future. But I am sorry for most of the rest of my behavior these past weeks. I haven't tried to put my best foot forward with her. I haven't *tried* at all. "I'm sorry, too."

She opens her mouth, and I've got a good hunch she's about to cut me off so she can apologize some more. I wave a hand in the air to stop her. "I haven't acted like the man you—"

Deserve almost fell out of my mouth. One sincere apology—and one allusion to rakish pirates—has my imagination running wild like Dutch in the back yard. I need to maintain at least a scrap of perspective about where we really are.

"I haven't been a very good neighbor," I tell her. "I'll do better."

The relieved smile spreading across her face makes me regret that promise immediately. My thoughts aren't remotely neighborly when she looks at me this way. They're fiercely possessive, as though I have any right to her.

Note to self: you do not.

"I'll do better, too," she says.

"Unnecessary. You haven't lost any points in the good neighbor department."

"I feel like I did. I'll bring you more cupcakes tomorrow night to make up for—" She waves a hand in the air. "Yesterday."

Declarations to do better aside, I can't stop my grimace at the renewed offer of cupcakes of mercy. "You don't have to do that."

"Food is my love language." She briefly closes her eyes, shaking her head. "I didn't—that came out—"

This apology has become my favorite thing ever.

When she opens her eyes again, her mouth takes on a stern slant. "I'm doing it because it's the neighborly thing to do."

But she cracks a smile like she just won a point over me in a battle I didn't know we were waging. I do not hate it.

"If I must accept delicious cupcakes, I suppose I can live with it."

"Do you think we can start fresh?" she asks.

Start over again to create a dynamic where I don't growl at her and shut her out at every turn? Where I behave more like a man and less like a wounded animal? "I'd like that."

She manages to grin even brighter. Dipping her head in a determined nod, she holds a hand out to me. "I'm Tess. Your new neighbor."

I'm about to laugh at her eager introduction, but when my palm slides against hers so warm and perfect, my thoughts take a moment to reboot. Ten seconds ago, I would have said handshakes were nothing special, but this one changes my mind. The soft touch of her hand is like a vise grip on my ribcage. I gently press my thumb against the back of her hand, memorizing the feel of her.

"Tess." It's more caress than spoken word, but the best I can do under the circumstances.

If she notices the soft way I said her name, she doesn't show it. She just keeps on watching me with those blue eyes I want to lose myself in. The handshake goes on a couple of beats past natural before she slips free. I let her go, even though my impulse is to hold tight.

She takes half a step back. "I should check on August and make sure he isn't getting into the snacks cupboard. Or worse, Sharpies."

"Probably a good idea." It isn't. It's the worst idea. I want her to stay right here on this porch with me for hours.

Like an absolute lunatic. *Calm down, son.*

"I like his creativity to stay on paper and not the walls." Her laughter trails off as she seems to shake herself. Her smile takes on a little more uncertainty, but the outright fear she'd had at the beginning of this conversation is gone.

That's something. Not nearly enough, but it's a start.

"Well...I'll see you, Ian."

I nod and watch her disappear into her half of the duplex. I stay on my porch longer than I care to admit, watching the breeze rustle leaves down the tree-lined lane. Breathing deep. Flexing my fingers as though I can recapture the feel of her hand in mine.

I've been in a lot of delicate situations where one wrong move meant disaster, but this line I'm walking with Tess might be the most dangerous of all.

THIRTEEN
IAN

I DON'T GET NERVOUS. I've faced twenty-thousand-foot climbs, staggering snowstorms, and vertical walls of ice without ever getting jitters. So tell me why all these butterflies are careening through my stomach when I'm only wandering around town?

I intended to head straight to Tess's bakery and tell her not to restart the cupcakes of mercy. Just rip that bandage off and put a stop to her guilt-induced generosity. Instead, I veered off at the last minute. I've been walking up and down Maple Street for half an hour, neatly doing an about-face whenever I get within twenty feet of Blackbird's purple awning. It's ludicrous.

But I can't bring myself to go inside.

I want the fresh start Tess offered. Maybe I want it too much. This brand-new *want* stings like a foot that's fallen asleep and is struggling to wake up again. At the same time, its newness excites me, too, a sensation I haven't let myself experience in a long time.

But the legitimate concern I'll get everything all wrong with her—yet again—keeps me out here on the sidewalk.

In jeans. On a day that's well past seventy-five degrees. If I don't get my butt in gear soon, I'll have to head home to shower before I even consider crossing the bakery's threshold.

I'm well aware I *shouldn't* cross that threshold. It's a terrible idea, and at least two steps outside my commitment to being a better neighbor. Every interaction I've had with Tess has only made me want another. Yes, even when I thought she'd stared at my prosthetic leg out of morbid curiosity, a down-deep part of me still had a hand out, pleading for more.

I'm a grubby little beggar when it comes to that woman.

It's an unfamiliar feeling. My relationship history is patchy at best. I've wanted women before, enjoyed the thrill of the chase. But this isn't about trying to catch something shiny and new. She intrigues me. I want to solve all her mysteries. I want to carefully peel back each of her layers until she's laid bare to me.

I scrape one hand down my face, exhaling hard. That line of thought is unhelpful.

She offered to be a good neighbor, and I'm dreaming up "laid bare" scenarios. I do enjoy a challenge, but in this particular case, pretty sure I'm setting my sights too high.

As I wait to cross Maple Street on my umpteenth circuit of Sunshine's downtown district, my phone buzzes in my back pocket. I should have silenced it when Pierce started sending me a string of links to articles on how to flirt. "Become the Player, Win at the Game" isn't something I ever want to read, but the links keep coming.

This particular buzz is a phone call, not a text. I quickly check who it is. Not sure if it's better or worse that it's my middle brother, Steven.

"Hello?" If I sound wary, it's only because I know those two better than anyone should. I've got a good idea of what's coming.

"Pierce says you've got an emergency situation out there.

Patient assessment says subject doesn't know how to talk to a woman. Sounds critical."

I curse under my breath as I cross the street. I should have dumped my phone and got a new number when I moved to Oregon.

"Pierce needs to mind his own business." Along with everybody else I know.

Except Tess. She can do whatever she likes.

"You're picking up women in the grocery store now. Have I got that right? Making meaningful eye contact in the frozen food aisle?"

"I'm going to hang up."

His laughter grates on my last nerve. "How did the second half of that conversation go? You got her number, at least?"

I didn't. If I wanted to ask her out, I could take ten steps east from my apartment and knock on her door. Which I haven't and won't.

"Did you call for anything else?" I take back everything I said about deserving some of the flak I used to give out to my brothers. No way was I ever this bad.

"Come on." He puts on his peacemaking persona, as if I'm the one causing trouble. "Can't blame us for being curious. It's been a while for you."

"Thanks for the reminder."

He laughs some more. "You know what I mean."

Obviously, I do. I haven't dated since my accident. I had too much going on to consider it when I was in rehab learning how to walk again, and later...well...I haven't thought about it.

I continue to not think about it now. Mostly, I think how if I were in a dating mood, I know exactly who I'd ask. And then I think what a disaster it would be, so I don't.

"You could stand to have someone help you out with your *frozen foods*," he says.

I groan, rolling my eyes to the cloudless sky. I never should have answered his call. Finding a bench in some shade just off Maple Street, I drop onto it.

"I need you to change the subject."

"Mom's in town." Steven switches gears easily enough, but I'm not so innocent to believe he's dropped it for good. "She's waiting around for Pierce's baby to be born so she can claim first visitation rights."

"How's Mom doing?"

"You don't talk to her?"

"I do." But I wince as I say it. I don't avoid her calls, but I don't initiate many, either. "Too loving" is an absurd criticism of my mother, I know, but talking to her leaves me aching. It's like she shines a light on everything I was and should be, leaving me feeling even worse for what is. "I'm just asking how she is."

"She's good. Last I heard, she was helping Bonnie wash and ready all of the baby's reusable diapers."

"Reusable diapers?" On paper, I know diapers haven't always been disposable. In practice, I can't understand going back to the Stone Ages to care for your kid. They'll be doing laundry every day for the next three years at least.

"Better for the environment, I guess."

"What's Mom's take on that?"

"She's enthusiastic with Pierce and Bonnie. With Iris and me, she gives it two months, tops."

"I'd put my money on her prediction."

Steven laughs again. "No kidding. She was telling us about this thing called blowouts, and how the baby gets completely covered in—"

"Absolutely not. Don't say another word." I'm not prepared to even hear about another person's bodily functions, let alone be the one responsible to clean them up. I want zero details.

He chuckles. "You get my drift. This is why we're perfectly happy with our dogs."

"How is the herd?"

"Rowdy as ever. Bruce has finally stopped peeing in the house, so we're lightyears ahead of Pierce already."

My ridiculous brother and his wife named their dogs Bruce, Jeff, Dave, and Bill. Going to the dog park with them is endlessly amusing. The really strange part is every name exactly fits the dog it's attached to.

I stretch my legs in front of me, watching people walk up and down Sunshine's shopping district. I haven't been down here much, but it's not a bad little town. A surprising number of frilly shops and more new restaurants than I expected, but comfortable.

"So," Steven says. "About this woman..."

Somewhere on the other end of the line, his wife, Iris, gasps. "Does Ian have a woman?"

The situation just got worse by a factor of ten. "I don't have—"

"Iris says women like it when you ply them with produce. You should offer her an eggplant." He snickers at his little joke.

"I'm not an idiot, Steven."

The phone line goes muffled for a second before Iris comes on. "Ignore him, Ian. Now tell me about this woman."

I love Iris, I really do. She speaks her mind, and her take-charge attitude is perfect for my brother. But I'm not about to let her steamroll me into divulging information about my dating life. Not even when I have so little to tell.

"There's no woman."

"I know what you should say to her." Steven's practically shouting into the phone to make sure I hear him. "Say, 'Hey, baby, want to see what this industrial-strength leg can do?'"

I burst into laughter in spite of myself. That's one way to get Tess's attention.

"What's her name?" Iris asks. "What's she like? How did you meet?"

My mother didn't raise me to be the kind of guy who would hang up on his sister-in-law, but I'm tempted. "I'm not saying anything."

"But there *is* a woman?"

Did I just walk into a trap? How does she do this? Anything I say to them will be used against me, so I do what I do best when it comes to my personal life. Deflect. "How's the photography business going?"

"We're in the middle of peak wedding season. I'm booked every weekend. It's exhausting, but I love it. Is this your attempt to change the subject?"

"It is."

"We only ask because we care about you. You can't shut off your emotions forever." Her voice grows way too soft for my taste. "You know we're always here for you. Whatever you need."

"I know." I haven't always acted like it, but I do know it's true.

"Even though he left with barely a week's notice," Steven adds in the background.

"We want the best for you," she goes on, ignoring my brother. "Whatever that is. Maybe it's this woman you won't tell us about. Maybe it's something else. Your brothers tease you, but they're always cheering for you, too."

Why does something as simple as that make my throat stick? Pierce and Steven were there for me after my accident in every way I'd let them. They visited me in the hospital and in the physical rehabilitation center, even in the early days when I barely acknowledged their presence at my bedside. They eagerly welcomed me back to our business even though I couldn't do my old job in the same way and might never get there. The choice to leave wasn't for any lack on their part. It was all me.

"Are you still rocking that cave man look?"

That's another thing I like about Iris—she makes her point and moves on.

I twisted my hair into a bun today, but I draw my fingers through the ends of my beard. "You don't think it's rakish? Like a pirate?"

I might be too proud of that, to be honest.

"More like a guy who claims to be a wizard, but he just wanders around town wearing robes and scaring kids."

"Way to knock my ego down a peg." That's even worse than Gandalf. That's faux-Gandalf, and I would never.

"You know who Ian looks like?" Steven says in the background. "That big red-haired guy from *Game of Thrones*. The one with the crazy eyes."

I know the character they're talking about, and I don't love the comparison. This is the kind of person I remind them of now? The weirdo? He was a good fighter, too, but they didn't lead with that part. Nope. Went right for *crazy eyes*.

I'm sure there are plenty of non-unhinged, non-wizard heroes with long hair and full beards. Just can't think of any at the moment.

Iris starts laughing. "He really does."

I glare so hard an elderly woman passing in front of my bench makes a little squeak of distress and scurries away.

"Is that the look you're going for, Ian?" Steven calls out with a laugh.

I wasn't going for anything. I just haven't bothered to cut my hair or beard in a while. More accurately, I haven't cut them since I was in the hospital almost two years ago, and they were both on the long side even then.

"It's not that funny," I grumble.

Iris swallows down her laughter. "If you like how you look, that's all that matters."

Do I like how I look, though? Do I really think I look good with hair a foot past where I used to keep it and a beard that could house a whole flock of birds? Or do I like that my unkempt appearance makes people give me extra elbow room on the rare occasion I go into town?

What if I don't want people to keep their distance anymore? At least, not everyone.

Fine. One specific person.

I shift on the bench so I can catch my reflection in the shop window behind me. Dragging my free hand down my beard, I admit to myself it's not my favorite thing to deal with. It was just easier. Easier to let my hair go wild, easier to avoid talking to people, easier to scare everyone away.

When did I become the guy who looked for the easy route?

Call it fate, call it luck, call it a staple of small towns everywhere, but my gaze lands on a barbershop pole farther down the street. It's got a sandwich board out front. *Antonio's. Walk-ins welcome.*

"Iris," I say, "how would you like to see an epic set of before-and-after pictures?"

FOURTEEN

TESS

ONE OF THE best things about Blackbird's is our regulars. People who are dedicated to us and talk us up all over town. People who come in every week to check out what's on our rotating menu of pies. People who would never resort to defrosting a mass-produced frozen pie from the grocery store just because it's a couple bucks cheaper.

People like Ada and Isabel.

"How are my favorite customers?" I ask as they walk in.

The two elderly women grin adorably at that. Ada was my second-grade teacher twenty-five years ago, and Isabel used to be a nurse at the medical center. Now that they're retired, they mostly swan around town checking up on everyone as though they're vital to Sunshine's success. They probably are—they sure seem key to ours.

"We're still kicking, at least," Isabel says.

"We're providing the sweets for our book club today," Ada tells me. She's wearing a *Reading Rainbow* pin on her shirt collar that has to be vintage. I don't think she's the type to get in on a late-stage trend.

"Clara's in charge of the savory." Isabel wrinkles her nose. "I suspect we're going to have Brussels sprouts with Parmesan cheese again."

"You like Brussels sprouts," Ada shoots back.

"Not when it's the only thing she ever brings to book club."

"What kinds of books does your group read?" I've been meaning to find a group for myself but haven't gotten around to it. One of many things on my endless to-do list that gets shoved to the bottom.

A whole conversation flies back and forth in the look the two women give each other.

"Science fiction," Isabel says at the same time Ada answers, "Spy novels."

"You're reading science fiction books about spies?" Niche genre, but I don't judge what people read.

They glance at each other again without explaining further.

"You know," Wren says, sliding up to the counter beside me, "nobody's ashamed to read romance novels anymore. They're super popular right now. There are even whole bookstores devoted just to selling romances."

I would love to see a bookstore open up in Sunshine. Maybe not a romance-only store—I have a hard time suspending my disbelief for that particular brand of fiction— but I wouldn't mind sourcing my fantasy books a little closer to home.

"Well," Ada says, glancing away. "There might be a smidgen of romance in the books we read."

"But we read them for the history," Isabel puts in.

"Which history?" Wren wants to know.

"The one we just read was set in Scotland in the seventeen hundreds."

Wren's grin might as well take up the whole room. "So the hero wears a kilt?"

Ada and Isabel blush to the heavens. It's seriously the cutest thing ever. And makes me wonder just what their book club read this month.

"You're distracting us." Ada points at the display case. "We'd like a Key lime pie and a chocolate mint, please."

Wren and I box up their requests. Ada pays for the pies as I slip them into a wide bag with handles so it's easier for them to carry them off to book club.

"Will you have any special flavors for the Fourth of July?" Isabel asks.

We rotate our flavors weekly, but we have special flavors we only offer around holidays, too, like citrus-cranberry at Christmas and pumpkin at Thanksgiving.

"We'll do our usual blueberry and strawberry cream pie for a red, white, and blue theme," I tell her. "But they sell out fast."

And I'll smell like berries all week, but I don't mind that.

She blinks up at me like I missed something. "What about cakes?"

"Oh. I might do something similar with all the fresh fruit we'll have for our cupcakes that week." Since our cupcakes are more Mom indulging me than true business plan, I can do whatever I want with them.

"I'll have to special order one of those full cakes for our family get together. I've heard they're the best around." Ada nods at me like she's giving my work a gold star.

Naturally, this is when Mom slides into view. She's been doing inventory in the back, but here she is, front and center for a conversation I'd rather she didn't hear. Goodness knows, *she* doesn't want to hear about how much people love my cakes.

"I'm surprised you haven't put them up on the wall here." Isabel gestures at the chalkboard menu where we update each week's pie flavors. I haven't even put the cupcakes up there yet. "Shout it around town, drum up more business."

"The cakes aren't part of our regular offerings." I have no

idea what else to say. How do I explain that "more business" isn't part of Mom's game plan when it involves my cakes?

"They should be." Ada nods like a queen issuing a decree. "Maybe next time we bring desserts for book club, we'll bring one of your cakes instead of pie."

I'm glad I can't see my own smile. It's got to be a twisted mess of awkward pride. The last thing I want is for Mom to think I'm trying to go into competition with her, but I'll make the cake if they ask me to. "Sounds great."

Ada and Isabel wander out of the store, their work complete. I can't even look at Mom. Maybe if I let it go, she will, too. She's done a pretty good job of ignoring my random cake orders so far.

Some day—when I've had a lot of advance planning and practiced my speech—I'd intended to make my pitch to her about expanding Blackbird's offerings using spreadsheets, numbers, and solid facts. Things she would respond to a whole lot better than two regulars putting on pressure with their glowing reviews.

"We should put the cakes on the menu."

I spin to face Wren. We've danced around this with Mom for the last year—she wants to address it head-on now?

"It's too much extra work for Tess to take on." Mom's answer is calm and collected, unlike the chaos unfolding inside my chest.

"Not if we hire a couple more bakers."

I think I might be having a heart attack. I've been trying to come up with the most careful way to approach this with Mom, and Wren's going straight for the jugular, no hesitation.

"The bakery is successful as it is now." Mom's using her oh-so patient voice, but the slant to her mouth tells me how much she dislikes the idea of expanding. "We're able to live comfortably off of it. If we rush to offer more items and hire more people, we don't know what might happen."

"Yeah. It could be a wild success."

I can't relate to my sister's boldness, but I love her optimism.

"Or we could destroy our own livelihood by pushing it past its breaking point." Her smile is gentle, but her words are like a slap. "Sunshine is a small town. There's only so much success we can expect."

Wren's eagerness deflates a little. We already suspected Mom's arguments against expanding the business, but hearing them straight out like this hits different.

She steps forward to take each of us by the hand. "I love that you're so enthusiastic and dedicated to Blackbird's. But trust me on this. We don't want to do anything that would put the business in jeopardy."

My heart squeezes even harder. She means me. If I pursue my cake business, if I try to expand my specialty cake offerings or hire someone else to help me with them, my choices could ruin us. I obviously wasn't involved in Blackbird's early days, but I remember how much stress Mom was under when every day felt like a make-or-break moment. I completely get why she wants to stay in the safe cocoon of our success.

But it hurts that she can't see an outcome where my cakes could *add* to that success.

"Now." She releases us and takes a step back. "I'm going out for lunch. Will you two be okay while I'm gone?"

I used to think asking us this was just her habit, but now, I have to wonder if she really thinks Wren and I can't handle her absence for a couple of hours. Like we might run wild and eat all the pies when she's not looking or abandon the store to watch movies all afternoon.

"We've got it covered," Wren says. "You can even take a long lunch if you want."

"Oh." Mom blinks like she's never considered taking a long lunch in her life. "I might take you up on that. Thank you."

She waves, heading for the door. "Be good."

"You, too," Wren calls after her.

I turn away, Mom's parting words prickling like she thinks we're wayward children. The bell on the door rings, and I release a long exhale, my shoulders relaxing. It's way too early to go into the back and deep clean the mixers, but it might help me work off this spike of disappointment mingling with frustration.

Before I can take a step, Wren nudges me in the ribs.

I swat her arm away. "Quit it."

She dips her head toward the front window, her gaze locked tight on something out there. I turn to find whatever it is that's caught her attention so badly. Apparently, she's watching a man hug a woman who looks like Mom. Kind of weird, but I can't expect less from Wren.

Except...that woman *is* Mom. Same floral, knee-length dress, same loose blonde hair with the barest streaks of gray. The man pulls away just enough to kiss her on the cheek, one hand lingering at the small of her back. She tilts her head to the side as if she's about to swivel our way and catch us watching her, but she leads them along the sidewalk instead.

With his arm still around her, his hand resting on her hip.

I stare, taking in his salt-and-pepper hair and obvious police officer's uniform, until they disappear from sight. "What was that?"

"I think Mom has a boyfriend."

I round on Wren. "What? No, she doesn't. Since when?"

"No idea. But I've suspected for a while."

"And you didn't tell me?"

She tips her nose up. "I thought you didn't like romantic gossip."

"When it's about me, not—" I toss a hand at the front window. "That was Sheriff O'Grady, wasn't it?"

Her Cheshire Cat grin doesn't budge. "Yup. Daniel

O'Grady, Sunshine's recently elected Sheriff. He oversees patrol, corrections, and wooing our mother's heart. Apparently."

I sag against the back counter. This scenario is too unfamiliar for my brain to process. "They might just be friends."

"Did that hug look like it was just between friends?"

I swallow instead of answer. If it was a just-friends hug, they both want to be more. Nobody lingers that much over a casual acquaintance. "She hasn't dated since Dad left."

"That we know of." Wren bobs her eyebrows.

"Don't say it like that. She doesn't have some shadowy secret life she's keeping from us."

I don't think. Right now, I'm not sure any information I have about our mother is accurate.

"I'm just saying. Twenty years is a long time to wait for the right guy to come along."

When she puts it like that, I almost hope Mom *has* secretly dated other men. I don't like the idea of her being alone all this time. Logically, I know she hasn't been totally by herself—she has a tight-knit circle of friends and regularly goes out with her girl gang.

But she's never talked about romance as something she missed or wanted again. And now...

"Do you think she's been seeing him a long time?" We can only guess at the answers, but I can't help but ask.

"You think Mom would progress to the 'handsy hugging and kiss hello' stage quickly?" Wren barks a fake laugh. "That woman has 'slow burn' all over her."

"I can't think about Mom *burning* for the sheriff." I'm happy for her if this theory is true, but my brain is still stuck on her being interested in anyone at all. She's not the romantic type.

"Remember when he led all those community safety meetings for downtown businesses a couple of years ago? I bet that's when they got to know each other." She rests her elbows on the front counter, watching the window as though Mom and Sheriff O'Grady might reappear. "They became friends, and then romance blossomed at a glacial pace."

I side-eye her. "You've thought about this a lot."

"Better than pondering the nothing of *my* love life."

"I just don't understand why..." My words tumble over each other and turn into nonsense as I stare out the front window.

Wren jabs me again. "Don't be that weirdo who can't handle their single-adult parent dating again. This is good for her."

That's not what's got me frozen in place. A man is jaywalking across the street, heading straight for the bakery. I'd recognize the dark red hair and beard at twice the distance, but this isn't the man I'm used to. He pushes through the door, simultaneously pulling all the air from my lungs.

Ian Vaughn has lost the feral lumberjack look and veered straight into *heartthrob* category.

FIFTEEN

TESS

IAN'S HAD A MAKEOVER. His scraggly look gave me butterflies, but this glow-up is a herd of heart-covered elephants stomping around inside me.

His beard is neatly trimmed, still thick enough to count as a full beard but short enough to reveal the sharp jawline beneath it. His hair is shorter, too, falling just to his chin. As I watch, he rakes his fingers through it, smoothing it out of his face like a cover model.

Where did all the oxygen go? Surely, I needed that.

Wren exhales the tiniest "Oh," but my throat doesn't want to make words. Pretty sure I'll just start babbling about how handsome he is and how his new look is having a worrying effect on my heart rate if I do.

Seriously, this thudding in here isn't normal.

"Welcome to Blackbird's," Wren says when I go on staring in silence. "How can we help you?"

Ian moves closer to where I'm standing, his gaze shifting from my sister to me. "I'm in the mood for something sweet."

His gravelly voice has no right to sound so sinfully good. But then he makes it even worse—his mouth tips into the smallest of smiles that hits me like an arrow to my heart. *Bullseye.*

"You've come to the right place." Wren spreads her arms at the case in front of us. "Sweet is what we do best."

Ian nods, glancing over the pies and cupcakes before his gaze lands on me. The question there snaps me out of my dumb-struck staring. I asked for a fresh start, and now I'm being weird.

Again.

Reminding myself that a fresh start doesn't include ogling, I introduce them. "Ian, this is my sister, Wren. Wren, this is my neighbor."

"Ah, the neighbor," Wren says way too knowingly. "I've heard all about you."

My stomach lurches so hard, I think I strain something. Ian's hint of a smile sinks into his familiar scowl, closing off again. Like maybe he's wondering if I told her *all* about him. Which, unfortunately, I did. Grumpiness, leg, and all.

"You've got a big fan around here," she adds.

This creepy, floaty feeling washes over me like I just got jabbed with a shot of whole-body novocaine. I've never fainted before, but this might be my first time. I'm trying to come up with some way to recover this mess—and debating where to hide Wren's body—when she speaks up again.

"August talks about you every time I see him now."

I breathe again, but barely. Wren shoots me a sly look as if to say, "Aren't I clever?" No. She's not clever, she's the absolute worst sister I ever had, and I'm going to tell her as much in excruciating detail as soon as we're alone again.

Ian takes a step closer to the display case. "Most of his affec-tion is for the dog."

"Best dog in the world, he says."

"No argument there."

"With the softest fur and the stinkiest breath." She holds up her hands. "August's words, not mine."

"Dutch isn't skilled with a toothbrush yet."

Wren flashes a broad smile. "I have some work to get to in the back, but it's great to meet you, Ian."

With one last pointed look at me, she slips through the swinging door, leaving us alone. He just watches me, gaze so intent I have to fight to remind myself I'm trying to be normal. Polite. Neighborly.

Swooning isn't circled on that Venn diagram.

"Is this your cheat day?" I ask.

That almost-smile returns to his face. "Something like that."

"You got your hair cut." Obvious, but worthy of note.

"It was time." He rakes his fingers through it again, pulling it back until my fingers itch to do the same.

If he was Dude Thor before, now he's Bucky Barnes in *Civil War*: mysterious and possibly dangerous, but high-key gorgeous. Apparently, Marvel movies are my only reference for men's haircuts.

"Does it look okay?"

He's asking me? The woman who stared open-mouthed at him *again* not five minutes ago?

"It looks great." There. Honest without being *too* honest. What any good neighbor would say.

The teasing glint in his eyes doesn't feel neighborly in the slightest. "I didn't want to go too short and ruin the pirate look."

I can't help my laughter or the blush that surely pops onto my cheeks. "It still works."

"Good."

He looks over the pies as though that one word of praise didn't skate across my skin like a caress.

Which is wildly inappropriate. I don't think like this at

work. Or much at all, if I'm being honest, but definitely not at work.

"Are you in the mood for anything in particular today?"

His gaze never leaves the desserts. "What's your favorite flavor in here?"

"Today, I'd say strawberry-rhubarb. It's the perfect blend of sweet and tart. All the fruit is locally sourced."

"I'll take a slice of that. And one of each of the cupcake flavors."

I struggle to contain my happy smile. People order cupcakes every day, but a request has never made me light up like a glow stick quite like this. I set up the two paper boxes and get out one of the strawberry-rhubarb pies to slice.

"I told you I'd bring you cupcakes," I tell him as I press the pie slicer through the crust. "I'll give you these on the house."

"No."

That sharp word stops me mid-slice. I look up to find the vertical line between his furrowed brows has returned. Maybe neither of us is doing great at this fresh start. But as I watch, the line smooths out and his expression relaxes. He doesn't quite smile, but he doesn't look like he's about to swat an irritating fly, either.

"I want to pay for these. You can bring me some another day. If you want."

I'm about to argue that these cupcakes were supposed to be part of my apology package, but I realize that's the point. He doesn't want me bringing him something out of a sense of obligation or guilt. But the fact that he's leaving the door open for *non*-apology cupcakes another day? My hopeful little heart warms.

I tilt my head as I box up his order. "Maybe I'll bring you tester flavors some time to get your opinion. Make sure my experimental combinations don't taste like sawdust and misery."

"I will gladly be your guinea pig. But I doubt anything you make could taste anything other than decadent."

Decadent. I like that. Especially when Ian says it.

He pays for the items and drops way too much cash into the tip jar. I purse my lips at him, but he's unmoved. He gives me a quick "live with it" nod, and a lock of hair falls forward across one eye. His groan sends shivers up my spine.

"Maybe I should have gone for the buzz cut," he says.

"It's probably still long enough to go back in the man bun." Not something I ever thought I'd suggest, but I'd never seen *him* in one before.

He leans forward a touch to take the bag from the counter, staring me straight in the eye. "Arr."

The sound hums through me like a low growl. I shiver even as I have to laugh. The man just smirks.

Smirks. My heart is going through it today.

"I'll see you, Tess." He still doesn't quite smile again, but my goodness, the warmth in his parting look is more than enough.

The second Ian disappears from view out the front window, Wren reappears at my side.

"Did he just—" she starts.

"Did you have your ear pressed to the crack in the door back there?" I like to think we're past the spying stage, but what do I know? I haven't had much of anything to spy on in forever.

She lays a hand over her heart. "Sound carries in here."

Right. Not that well.

"Especially pirate-y sounds."

I glare at her, but she's never been swayed by a simple look. That sound was for *me*.

"He's definitely got the look." She keeps talking like I'm paying her to annoy me. "A pirate captain ready to swashbuckle the seas. Or whatever."

"He looks like a normal man." It'd be a lot more convincing if my voice didn't crack when I said it.

"Mmm hmm. Are you going to admit you like him now?"

Both answers spring to my lips. Saying it in words feels like overkill, but denying it? Feels too much like a lie.

Wren sighs but still manages a smile. "Just don't wait twenty years to admit it, okay?"

SIXTEEN
IAN

IT'S a little too "on the nose" to say Dutch has a Pavlovian response to August being in the yard, but the moment he starts whining at the back door, I let him out. I heard Tess's car pull up out front a few minutes ago, so I can relate. He wants the same thing I do—any time with our neighbors we can get.

August's "Hey, boy!" pierces the evening air, and they're off like a shot. I step onto the porch, my hands in my shorts' pockets. I changed out of my jeans as soon as I got home, unwilling to fight the heat and discomfort any longer. I don't like how exposed I feel in my own space, as if paparazzi might be lying in wait to snap pictures and ask questions. To be clear, nobody ever cared that much about my situation.

But Tess already knows about my prosthetic leg. And still blushed like mad when I indulged in the crazy urge to *growl* at her in her bakery.

That blush has been humming through my blood all afternoon. I want to see it again.

Tess joins me on the porch, and our eyes meet. Hold for a beat. When her lips tip up into a smile, something cracks in my ribcage. Like my heart's been encased in cement and is finally breaking free so it can beat again.

"I feel bad about commandeering your dog," she says.

"I don't," I tell her truthfully. "He's like a puppy again. I love to see it."

I haven't been as good with our walks and play time as I used to be. Knowing he's got an eager playmate makes me happier than she seems to suspect.

She sits in one of the chairs on her side of the porch and motions for me to join her. I do, enjoying the show as Dutch romps with August.

"How old is he anyway?" Tess asks.

"Just turned seven." When I took him to the vet this year, she told me he's considered a senior now. I fight down the twinge of sadness that concept brings up. I feed him well, and he clearly gets plenty of exercise. We've got a good long while together yet.

I think it again as if I can manifest that outcome. *A good long while.*

"You'd never know it. Have you had him since he was a puppy?"

I nod, my chest warming at the memory. "I'd spent the day rock climbing way out in a canyon. When I went back to my car at the end of the day, I found this tiny fluff ball curled up next to one of my tires. He was matted with mud and covered in fleas and ticks. I scooped him up, and that was it. He claimed me."

With a sloppy kiss and the most adoring eyes I'd ever seen.

"That's really sweet." She watches me like I revealed more than I meant to. All I did was get completely suckered in by a puppy in need. And fall in love in the process, but that part's obvious.

"I've never regretted it. Even when he used to dump my

kitchen trash all over the floor when he was left alone for two-point-five seconds."

She laughs. "Sounds like Dutch and August went through similar phases."

Speaking of, August runs over and stops next to my chair. "Your hair is shorter."

I don't always appreciate bluntness on my appearance these days, but I don't mind it from him. "It is. What do you think of it?"

He studies me for a minute, his little eyes narrowing. "It's okay."

"You'll keep me humble, kid."

He swivels at the hips to pet Dutch, who is of course glued to the kid's side. I spot a sticker or something on his arm, like maybe he got a little carried away at daycare.

"Kid, you've got something right here—"

I realize my mistake too late. He contorts his arm around so I can get a better look at the device my brain has just now recognized.

"That's my super shield." He beams at me like he's pointing out an award. "This one is my monitor." He twists to show me the back of his other arm. "And this one is my pump. I have diabetes."

I've suspected it before, but my heart sinks with the confirmation—I am a colossal ass. How many times have I seen him playing with Dutch in the yard and never noticed the medical devices secured to his arms? They're small, but they're not invisible. Nope, I've been too busy thinking about myself to recognize this little boy has a serious condition.

To be fair, he was doing wind sprints with my dog the other day. The small monitors would have been the only signs of that condition.

"My body needs medicine sometimes, and my super shields

give it to me like that." August claps his hands together. "I don't even feel it."

"It doesn't hurt, huh?" I've heard about these types of glucose monitors and insulin delivery systems, but I haven't met anyone who uses them.

"It's a little pinch. But sometimes Mama has to give me shots in the bottom." He laughs because of course shots in the bottom are the funniest. "Those hurt, but she's fast."

"I bet your mama takes good care of you." My gaze finds Tess, who's looking on like she expects questions. But where I typically bristle at questions, she seems as if she'd welcome them.

I have plenty. Like, how long have they been dealing with this? Is this system keeping his diabetes under control? And when she's doing everything she can to take care of her son, who's taking care of her?

But the next question doesn't come from me. It comes from August.

"Why do you have a super leg?"

I've been asked similar questions a hundred times before, but never once from someone so innocent. Never from someone who's simply curious, without any judgment.

Actually, the kid might judge me. He seems pretty discerning.

I look from him to Tess, silently asking if I have permission to answer. She nods in gentle encouragement. I take a deep breath and prepare myself to tell him something I haven't willingly spoken of since it happened.

"I crashed my motorcycle." Those four words sum up the event that threw my whole life upside down.

His blue eyes go wide. "You have a motorcycle?"

He sounds more excited about this news than I bet Tess would like.

"Not anymore." I don't think I could stand to ride one now. "I was driving too fast, and a jackrabbit crossed the road in front of me. I swerved and lost control of the bike. I landed on my left side, and my leg was too damaged to ever heal right. So the doctors amputated it, right about here."

I hitch my shorts up a few inches and gesture to where my thigh fits into the black plastic socket. I don't normally talk about my prosthetic leg, and I sure don't show it to people, but August just watches with mild curiosity. The weirdest thing is, it's kind of nice to talk about.

"Did you hit the jackrabbit?" Naturally he landed on the most important part of the story.

I tick my head to the side. "Missed him."

"I'm glad you have a super leg," he tells me. "It helps you just like my super shields help me."

Emotions flash and scramble around in my brain. I haven't been very grateful, but he's right. I should be. It takes me a second to speak through the lump in my throat. "I'm glad I have it, too."

"Can I give Dutch a bath?"

I laugh, surprised but relieved at his quick change of topic. "Maybe not today."

"Can I throw the ball?"

"Have at it."

August runs back into the yard to find one of the tennis balls scattered in the grass and starts pitching it to the dog. Dutch retrieves it and drops it gently for him, ready to go until the kid's arm gives out.

"I'm sorry about your accident," Tess says softly. "Was there really a jackrabbit?"

"I can't say why I swerved. I don't really remember the crash well." The taste of blood in my mouth and the overpowering smell of gasoline and motor oil—*that* I remember too well. "I was in the middle of nowhere—perfect opportunity for going way too fast, not as great for getting medical care in a hurry."

"You had to wait a long time?"

"It was thirty minutes before paramedics arrived. I had to do my own triage." At the crinkle of confusion between her eyebrows, I clarify. "I'm a certified EMT. The training was supposed to come in handy if I ever ran into emergencies with clients on a mountainside. Never thought I'd have to put a tourniquet on myself."

I still, remembering how I fought to stay conscious as I tightened my belt around my leg, positive if I closed my eyes I'd never open them again.

"Ian." Before I can fully process the delight of Tess whispering my name, she slips one hand around mine, giving me all new sensations to revel in. "You saved your own life?"

I never thought about it that way. "The paramedics saved me. I just made sure there was something left to save."

She squeezes my hand tighter. "You're downplaying it."

I was no hero that day. Pushing the motorcycle to its limits, buying into my own hype and thinking I was somehow invincible—I brought on all my trouble myself. The fact that I didn't die from my mistakes is more miracle than heroics.

But this conversation has already strayed into the "too much" category. I don't need to drive it home by talking any more about my ego and just how badly I screwed up. The one saving grace is that I didn't hurt anyone else when I went down.

"Anyway, now it's just me and my residual limb." I slap my empty hand down on my socket, grimacing at the term. "Stump."

Tess makes a small sound of dismay.

"You don't like those options either?" The guys in the rehabilitation center had a whole raft of terms for their remaining limbs, not all of them ones I'd want to repeat to Tess. "How about Peggy?"

She laughs, shaking her head.

"Nubbin?"

"Ew." She sounds like she just stepped in something disgusting and pulls her hand from mine. "Absolutely not. That word is an abomination. Never use it to refer to any body part ever again."

"Interesting response." Now she's blushing, which is even more interesting.

"It's, uh..." She shakes her head, hands raised. "I'm not getting into it. Just don't use it."

"Is this like the m-word?" That's Iris's big ick. Doesn't matter the context, anyone who says it gets a smack. When Tess looks at me blankly, I whisper, "Moist."

She cackles, and at least half of it is a squeal, but it might be the best sound I've ever heard. It's open and spontaneous and entirely her.

"Yes. It's exactly like that. Absolutely forbidden."

"I'll be sure to avoid it."

We both settle down again, our attention turning to the shenanigans going on in the grass. August is trying to get Dutch to fetch a stick, but he's too addicted to tennis balls to understand the intent. August goes so far as to put the stick in his own mouth to demonstrate, but Dutch remains mystified.

Tess leans forward like she's going to intervene, but relaxes again. "It probably can't do much harm, can it? How many germs can one stick have?"

I know better now than to point out we have no idea where the stick has been.

"I'm sorry about his diabetes. I didn't realize."

She lifts a shoulder. "It was scary at first, and it was a steep learning curve, but we've got it under control now. The monitor and pump were a game-changer."

"That's good." Still must be a constant source of stress for her.

"But if I never see the inside of a hospital again, I'll be a happy camper."

"Same."

"Is your accident why you came out here? To...rest and recover?"

She sounds so hopeful, even though she must suspect the truth. She's seen enough of me since she moved in to know I'm doing neither.

I came out here to avoid my problems and hope a solution magically appeared. Add in some feeling sorry for myself and a dash of wishing for a time machine, and you've just about got the whole of my three months in Sunshine.

But now...wallowing doesn't have the appeal it once did.

"I'm here for the views." I hold Tess's gaze long enough for a blush to creep over her cheeks again.

Best color I've ever seen.

SEVENTEEN

TESS

SOMETIMES YOU JUST NEED A SPONTANEOUS GIRLS' night. My friend, Lila, returned from her week-long hike this afternoon, so Wren and Hope wrangled her into an evening out to help her decompress. Get some real food in her after a week of trail mix and granola bars. But mostly, they want to hear all the juicy gossip about her new boyfriend.

Wren and I were both a little shocked when Helena Parrish, Lila and Hope's mother, came in this afternoon to casually drop that bit of info. Actually, nothing about her gossip was casual—she grinned so wide you'd think she was the one with the new man.

Mom, incidentally, stayed mum about her own new man. Typical.

The four of us slide into a booth at Delish, and Amy passes out menus, smiling over our girls' night like she has since we were teens.

She starts to leave us to consider our options—as though we don't know exactly what we're going to order—but stops next to me. "Is everything going all right over at the duplex? Ian's not giving you a hard time, is he?"

I'd meant to at least check in with her and let her know August and I are enjoying the apartment—and befriending our recluse—but I haven't found the time to stop by. And I really don't want to discuss Ian with three sets of attentive ears here to latch onto everything I might say about him.

"My nephew's been prickly lately, but if he's extending that to you, I'll talk to him." Amy's a sweetheart, but I have no doubt she would stand up for me with Ian if I asked.

A week ago, I might have answered differently, but now, I don't need her running interference.

"He was a little prickly at the beginning, but we're getting along now." I refuse to think about the way I held his hand last night, or the way he watched me like I was more beautiful than the sunset. Nope. Not on my mind. "Thank you again for renting us the apartment."

Amy waves off my thanks. "It's our pleasure to have you there."

The second she walks away, my friends lean closer to me like I'm a bug they've pinned in a display case, ready to catalogue everything about me.

"I feel like we need to hear more about your neighbor," Hope says. Newly engaged, she's probably eager to get the spotlight off her own love life. That, and Wren already made wild hints about me and Ian in front of both her and Lila.

"The guy with the dog?" Lila wants to know. I mentioned August's new canine friend earlier when she asked me about the move. Just sort of left out Dutch's owner.

"The *hot* guy with the dog." Wren isn't doing anything to make this easier on me.

"I just stopped thinking of him as a growly hermit two days ago." And in that time, my crush has exploded like a supernova, but nobody needs to hear that.

Sure, they *want* to hear it. But I'm not sharing. This whole situation is too precarious to start telling my closest friends. They'll get their hopes up and then who knows what might happen to dash them. I don't want them to be disappointed later on.

Because it's definitely *their* hopes I'm thinking about right now.

"Her exact words were 'plundering Viking.'" Wren is way too smug about this.

"We've known each other for two weeks. Could we please not jump straight into the deep end here?"

And by *we*, I absolutely mean *me*.

"Okay, but he did come into the bakery the other day, and sparks were flying all over the place."

This has Hope and Lila sporting identical grins. Maybe I should have skipped girls' night. I can hear about Lila's new boyfriend another time.

"Loads of people come into the bakery." I know it's going to be impossible to play this off as nothing, but I refuse to give up the ship this quickly. Historically, I'm not a blabber. The only issue with that is, usually I have very little interesting to blab.

Ian is plenty interesting.

"Yeah, but nobody else who looks at you like you're the only thing he wants in the whole store."

I breathe slowly, willing my face not to bloom into an incriminating shade of red. I haven't had a chance to tell Wren about the conversation I had with Ian last night, and I don't know if I will. If she knew we're actually making strides toward real friendship, she'd add two plus two, come up with eight, and jump right to declaring that he's in love with me.

That's...a strangely sobering thought. This flirtation between us is fun and exciting, but I don't even know that Ian wants a serious relationship. And more importantly—I don't know if I do.

"Even if he does—and I'm not saying he does..." I take a grounding breath. "I haven't been on a date since before August came along. I don't know how to do any of this anymore. I don't know what he expects or what I'm willing to give."

I can't do anything that would jeopardize August's happiness or stability. According to all the articles I've ever read on dating as a single parent, I'm already doing this wrong. I'm not supposed to let August get to know Ian at the same time I am. Our relationships are supposed to be completely separate, and only later merge when Ian and I are on solid ground.

Yikes. A girls' night was a *terrible* idea. I can't dream up scenarios where we're "on solid ground" some day. There's no *us*. There's only neighbors—more friendly than we were before, yes, but still just neighbors. It's absurd to assign anything romantic to that.

I've never had a neighbor *"arr"* at me and literally shiver my timbers before, but maybe some neighbors do.

"If he's the right man for you, he'll be understanding about all of that." Lila smiles sweetly at me from across the booth. She's had a crappy time of it this year, with a cheating ex who subsequently fired her from her job, but she's still optimistic about love. Meanwhile, I'm optimistic about everything *except* love. "He'll want you just as you are right now. And if he can't be patient while you sort things out, then he's not the guy. But someone else will be."

Even if I'm still uncertain, I love that she has that kind of confidence for me.

———

I guess girls' night wasn't a total bust. We spent the rest of the evening giving Lila a hard time about her new man—mostly because when her mom came into the bakery, she raved about him being some kind of a Greek god, and it's hard to let something like that go.

"I can't wait to meet this guy at Hope's engagement party," Wren says in front of Delish when we're saying goodnight. "Your mom *really* talked him up."

"She might be even more smitten than I am."

"She's got love on the brain," Hope says.

"Whose fault is that?" Lila returns.

We all point at Hope, the woman with the ring on her finger.

We say our goodbyes, and Wren and I walk around the block to where our cars are still parked behind the bakery.

"I'm not surprised Lila can go into the woods and come out with a gorgeous new boyfriend," she says. "I wish I could meet a man who's like a Greek god."

"Which one?" a deep voice asks in the parking lot.

Wren shrieks, spinning around to face Shepherd, who's standing near Get in Gear's back door. It only takes her a second to compose herself, her fear blending seamlessly into anger.

"What is the matter with you? Don't you know you're not supposed to scare women in the dark like this?"

The sun hasn't fully set yet, but that won't stop Wren from getting in a jab at him.

"Wasn't trying to scare you. Just asking which Greek god you're hoping to meet. It makes a difference."

She makes a tiny sound of irritation. "What are you talking about?"

"Ares is too hot-headed for you, that combo would never work. Apollo—he doesn't know how to be faithful, I don't recommend. Hades has a good job and loves his dog but may or may not be a kidnapper. And Zeus...you do you, but he's a creep through and through. I'd advise against it." Shepherd looks to the sky as though expecting to get zapped by a bolt of lightning.

"Someone's read *Percy Jackson*," Wren says. Pretty sure she's trying to be cutting, but it's coming across as a teensy bit impressed.

Shepherd shrugs. "I like mythology."

"Well...I was asking for a figurative Greek god, not a literal one."

He nods and finishes locking up his store. "I suggest Hephaestus. He's steady and hard-working. Peaceful and loyal. He'd be a good match for you."

Wren just watches him, her mouth slightly open, clearly at a loss for how to take that.

Shepherd salutes us and crosses the parking lot to his truck. He climbs in, starts it up, and drives off into the night.

Wren's still watching his taillights fade down the alley, her arms crossed over her chest. "Isn't Hephaestus the one who's married to Aphrodite?"

"Pretty sure." And good with mechanical stuff, but I suspect we're going to ignore that.

"He's so weird." She shakes off her interaction with Shepherd, turning back to me. "I forgot about all the cheating. I don't want a Greek god, after all."

They really don't have the best relationship track record. "Just someone who looks like one."

"Obviously."

I lean against my wagon's hatchback, not quite ready to head to the house. Mom was thrilled to have a movie night with August after we closed up shop. They're probably still watching *Cars* and snuggling on the couch right now.

Wren takes a spot next to me, her arm against mine.

"I'm sorry I jumped the gun yesterday," she says. "I

shouldn't have brought up putting your cakes on the menu with Mom until you were ready."

"It's okay. I pretty much knew that's how she'd react." I'm trying to forget the part where she seems to think my cakes could sink our business.

"We shouldn't give up, though. Mom isn't quick to make a decision, but I have to believe we can convince her. We got her to add your cupcakes to the case."

After a year of discussion. Getting her to add full cakes could take another decade.

"She's being careful and cautious." Even if it hurts a little when it comes to my cakes, I get caution. That's been my mantra my whole life. The one time I experimented with *not* playing it safe blew up in my face. I love the end result to the moon and back, but the journey was rough.

Wren nudges me with her shoulder. "There's such a thing as being too careful. You can wait so long that you lose your opportunity."

I say nothing. We're not talking about specialty cakes anymore.

"You don't want to miss out when you've got something good right there waiting for you." She's watching me like she's trying to bore a hole into the side of my head.

"Stop staring. You've made your point."

"If I had, you'd be in your neighbor's arms right now."

"That makes no sense." Even if it sends an odd thrill right up my back.

"Just promise me you won't shut down the possibility, okay?"

"You're awfully invested in my theoretical love life."

She laughs. "Yeah, because all I've got is sparring with Callahan."

Her gaze flashes down the alley where he drove off a few minutes ago, and she swallows.

"My point is," she says, dragging her attention back to me, "if you happen to find yourself in Ian's arms, don't waste the opportunity."

"I promise."

But only because that's even less likely than Wren realizing that when Shepherd said she should date Hephaestus, he wasn't really talking about the Greek God. He was talking about *him*.

EIGHTEEN
IAN

IT'S BEEN ages since I saw a night sky this clear and bright. I used to have them all the time on mountaintops, grand rewards for my efforts to reach new peaks. Now, I can't remember the last time I looked up at the stars. But I've been sitting on my back porch staring up at the sky for longer than I care to admit. If I was a wishing kind of man, I'd have a few in my back pocket from the meteorites that have zipped across the sky.

It's gorgeous. And oddly lonely. But maybe that's just me.

At my side, Dutch whines. I run my hand over his head. He really does have the softest fur.

Should probably do something about that breath, though.

"I know. I feel the same."

The lights are out next door. Have been all evening. Tess doesn't usually get home this late. I'm not keeping track to be a creep, but it's impossible not to notice her habits when she lives ten feet away from me.

I have no right to wonder where she is. She's not mine to deserve that kind of info. That hasn't stopped the questions from spinning through my head. Maybe we should exchange numbers. Just in case she ever needs anything.

No. She's got family. She would call them in an emergency. But...maybe it'd be good to have another option. Just in case.

I'm not *worried*. Worrying isn't my style. Anyway, it's not late enough to panic that something bad has happened to them. It's only a little after nine. The most realistic scenario is that she's with her sister or mom. Maybe out with friends.

Possibly on a date.

I catalogue the constellations I know by name, telling myself it's fine. If she is on a date, good for her, right? She deserves it. Well done, and happy for her.

Yeah, right. I've got the urge to throttle anyone who would even think to ask her out, like a knuckle-dragging Neanderthal declaring *mine*.

I stand and stretch my neck from side to side. "Let's go inside, Dutch. No sense pining by their door any more tonight."

We go inside, and I wander the small apartment, absently rubbing the center of my chest. I've been doing this all evening —moving from puttering around in the kitchen to trying to read a book to watching the stars. But I can't get comfortable anywhere I go. Everything's off.

Dutch must agree. He lies down in front of the back door, his face pressed to the crack like he's still sniffing for them.

"It's pathetic to miss them this much already."

I'm talking to us both.

I go into the living room just in time to watch headlights come up our lane and pull into the space out front. The weight that's been sitting on my chest all night melts away. *They're home*. Dutch gets up and does circles by the front door, tail wagging, hoping to play with his boy.

"Come on." I sit on the couch and pat the cushion beside me. He looks at the door another minute, but reluctantly joins me, laying his head across my thigh. I scratch behind his ears until his eyes close. "I'm disappointed, too."

We won't have any socializing tonight. Tess will surely put August straight to bed. Then she'll go to bed, too.

I do not need to think about her getting ready for bed somewhere on the other side of this wall. I definitely don't need to scroll through pajama options, trying to imagine whether she'd wear a nightshirt or one of those cute short sets.

I rake my free hand down my face. Keeping track of her schedule *and* entertaining a skimpy mental fashion show. I really am a creep.

Grabbing the book I tried and failed to focus on all evening, I settle in to read now that I'm relaxed enough to enjoy it. The front windows are open, and somewhere in the distance, frogs croak back and forth to each other.

After a while, Dutch must decide if he can't play with August, he's done for the evening. He slinks off the couch, probably heading for my room. He's got a plush bed of his own out here, but I'm likely to find him sprawled out on mine with his head on my pillow.

Right when I'm debating if I should call it a night too, a scream punches the air, followed by a crash. I'm on my feet in an instant, my heart hammering as I rush through my front door and onto the porch. Tess's light is on, her door closed, but the sounds definitely came from that direction. I'm about to hammer on her door when I hear scrambling on the far side of the house.

Blood thunders in my ears as I storm that way, on alert for intruders or pushy dates or I can't think what else. I round the corner of the house and run straight into something soft.

Tess screams again, but then throws herself into my arms. "Ian!"

I hold her close, her body trembling beneath my touch. Whoever hurt her is going to pay. Looking past her, I try to assess our surroundings, but we're on the edge of the puddle of light from the porch, and the neighbor's house is dark. The rest of the side yard is too thick with shadows to make much of anything out.

I cup her face in one hand, the other tight around her. "Are you okay?"

She nods, but even in the dim light I can see how pale she is, how wide her eyes have grown.

"What happened?"

"I think it's a bear." She barely whispers the words.

I'm still trying to figure out if I heard her right when a muffled sound comes from behind her, like something's going through the big plastic garbage cans she keeps back there.

I release her, putting myself between her and the other end of the alley. "Go inside."

She clutches the back of my shirt with both hands. "Not without you!"

I love that she thinks I might actually try to confront this bear for her. I fully intend to go inside with her, but if I'm going to report a bear sighting to wildlife management, I need to know what we're dealing with.

I slip my phone from my back pocket—not an easy thing to do with her clinging to my back. Quickly thumbing across the icons, I turn the flashlight on.

Her recycle bin is lying on its side, paper strewn around it. Past that, the garbage can sits against the wooden fence, a trash bag abandoned on the ground next to it. We're effectively boxed in by the house and the two lengths of fence, creating a tight alley a bear could accidentally corner itself in. But there's no sign of one.

"Was it right here?" I ask quietly. Best scenario is it climbed the fence on its way to the green space beyond the neighborhood and is already lumbering up the hillside.

"It's in the can."

"*In* the can?" I take a step closer, but the trash bag Tess left behind moves.

She stifles a shriek, plastering herself to my back. I peer at the bag. A mother wouldn't abandon her cubs in a spot like this, so what—

The garbage can lid lifts a few inches, revealing a furry black face, rounded ears, and beady eyes. Definitely a wild animal, but not a bear. The raccoon hisses at us, white teeth gleaming as its paws scramble with the lid. Tess gasps right in my ear.

The trash bag on the ground splits open as a second raccoon rears up, paws out in a defensive stance. This one lets out a shrill scream, and one of Tess's hands comes around to clutch at my stomach, her other holding tight to my shoulder.

"It's okay," I say, trying to soothe all three of them at once.

I lower my phone so the light isn't shining in the raccoons' faces, and attempt to back away. Not an easy thing to do with Tess glued to me like a koala, but I'm not putting a stop to that before I have to.

"We're all going to leave each other alone," I say gently.

When Tess and I reach the light from the porch, there's a loud scramble at the dark end of the alley. Pretty sure our intruders left in search of a meal with fewer interruptions.

I exhale the last few minutes of stress from my body. Not what I expected, but a good outcome all in all.

Tess rests her forehead against my upper back, her hands still wrapped in my shirt. "Those were really small bears."

She starts giggling, and soon, we're both shaking from laughter. I turn around, lightly placing my hands on her hips while hers come to rest on my shoulders. My heart's still racing, but it's got a new source of adrenaline now.

"You were brave to take on two dangerous predators like that," I tell her solemnly.

She rolls her eyes. "It's so dang shadowy back there. What else was I supposed to think?"

"Could have been anything."

She purses her lips at me but can't maintain the frown. "This is your fault, you know. You're the one who told me about bears and bobcats and snakes. You got in my head."

I flex my fingers tighter on her hips. "Good to know I'm in your head."

Her mouth curves up into a smile. "You were prepared to fight whatever was out here."

"Seemed like the neighborly thing to do." That, and the thought of anyone hurting her made me see red.

Now...I just see her. In my arms. Where I've been picturing her since we met.

The moment drags out too long, begging me to act on these impulses swirling through my head. But the second my gaze drops to her lips, she slides her hands from my shoulders to my forearms, taking a step back as though just now realizing how close we've been standing. I don't want to let her go, but I'm not brute enough to hold tight if she's pulling away. When I finally release her, my hands feel strangely empty, like I've lost something essential I'm meant to be holding.

"I'm sorry I freaked out over nothing." She glances to the dark end of the alley, the scene of her freak-out.

"Raccoons aren't nothing." She got close enough they could have scratched or bitten her. They could have been rabid. But pointing that out would probably have the opposite effect from the one I want.

She levels me a flat look. "I thought they were a bear."

"And I'm glad you were wrong."

She laughs, but then winces. Folding one arm up, she reveals a bloody scrape just below her elbow. "Oof. I forgot about that."

I step closer to gently take her arm in my hand. "They didn't do this, did they?"

Do not say anything about potentially rabid raccoons. Do not even think it.

"No. I, uh...kind of fell over the recycle bin when I saw the first one." She cringes adorably.

"That explains the crash I heard. Are you hurt anywhere else?" It's all gravel and decorative rock out here.

She pauses a second to assess. "I mean...my butt hurts where I landed on the bin."

I chuckle, refusing to consider any of the ways I could help her out with that. "I'll focus on the elbow. Do you have a first aid kit?"

"Of course, but you don't have to do that."

As I watch, blood pools and drips toward the point of her elbow. In this light, I can't tell how badly she's scraped up, but the smear of dirt is obvious. I want to be sure it gets clean and that nothing under there needs stitches. "I'll feel better when I know you're patched up."

She watches the blood, too, and her face pales again. "Maybe that's a good idea." She tilts her head toward the duplex. "Follow me, Dr. Vaughn."

At this point, I'd follow her anywhere.

NINETEEN
TESS

OF ALL THE ways to get your mountain-climbing next-door neighbor to notice you, crying, "Bear!" when you, in fact, only have raccoons isn't a great option. Tumbling over your own recycle bin and gashing your arm trying to escape those same raccoons is possibly a worse one.

But I let Ian into my apartment with one hand cupping my bloody elbow. On top of everything else, I'd hate to have to try to get stains out of Amy's stylish rugs.

I take him into the kitchen and open the plastic storage unit where I stash all of August's medical supplies. In the bottom, I've got a big red first aid kit, just in case. I start to unlatch it, but he gently takes it from me.

"I've got it." He opens the kit and assesses the contents before pulling out a few items and setting them aside. "Let's wash this first."

He takes my arm with the lightest touch, guiding me closer to the kitchen sink so the spray wand can reach my elbow. He turns on the water and tests it, making sure it's a comfortable temperature before turning it on my arm.

I wince at the contact, but I know the scrape needs to be cleaned. Now that we're inside, I can see how dirty it is.

"Okay?" he asks softly.

He's only asking clinically, wanting to make sure he's not causing me extra pain, but he's *so close*. And he smells *so good*. Like aloe and cucumber. I'm definitely smelling his deodorant right now, but I don't even care. His "okay?" feels like he's checking in on a whole different level.

Two lines crease between his eyebrows, and I realize I've taken too long to answer. Sweet that he's this worried about me over a scrape. I didn't hit my head out there. It's his nearness that's got me so dazed.

But I'd better start acting normal or he's going to figure it out.

"It stings a little," I finally say.

He nods and goes back to his task. He gently washes away the blood and dirt, only turning the water off when he's sure it's entirely clean. Bringing my elbow back up, he examines the wound, presumably checking for any remaining grit. Then he doubles up a couple of paper towels and presses them against the scrape.

"Let's put some pressure on it for a few minutes. It's bleeding more than I'd like." He helps me hold my arm up, folded so my elbow's out, while he keeps the paper towels on it in a firm grip. Once it's secure, he glances around. "Am I being too loud? I don't want to wake August."

This last part he whispers, and I can't help my smile. "You're okay. He's slept through worse."

Ian nods, his gaze tracing over my face. I indulge in the same, admiring the freckles scattered over his forehead, cheeks, and nose. He's got so many, it looks like a light tan at a distance. This close, they differentiate into too many freckles to count. I wouldn't mind trying, though. It would take a long, long time.

Deep lines frame his mouth, disappearing beneath his beard. Once, I would have said they were smile lines, but now, they emphasize his frown.

Maybe frown is the wrong word. He's watching me so intently my stomach swoops, that's all I know.

"You were out late tonight." It's not a question, but he's still asking.

"My sister and I went to dinner with a couple of friends."

He nods, and his gaze drops back to where he's holding my arm. His mouth flattens beneath his beard like he's had a bite of lemon pie without any sugar in it. It takes me a minute to realize my explanation might have given him the wrong impression about my night out.

"It was a girls' night," I clarify. "One of our friends just got back from a week-long hike. She's *not* a hiker, so we wanted to hear all about her adventure."

I leave out the part about Lila coming back with a new man in tow.

"Oh. Sounds like fun."

"The adventure or the dinner?" Despite his history as a guide and an adventurer, I haven't seen any evidence he still does things like that. I'm not sure the walking trail behind the duplex counts when you've been on top of actual mountains.

"Both. It's good that you've got friends like that."

"I don't have many close friends, but they're two of the best I've got." Hope has been best friends with Wren since they were kids. I've grown closer to her since Mom started subletting part of our bakery space to her a couple of years ago. She's creative and funny, but more practical than Wren.

I never really knew Lila before, but since she moved back to Sunshine last year, I've found a kindred spirit in her. I love her sunny attitude mixed with an eager enthusiasm for everything bright & beautiful. Both those women have excellent taste, too.

And then there's Wren. "My sister's probably my best friend. Along with my biggest cheerleader, loudest critic, and pushiest busybody."

He laughs softly. "Sounds like me and my brothers. Sometimes I love them, sometimes I can't stand them."

"Is it hard being away from them out here?" I was only separated from Wren for six months, but it was probably the loneliest I've ever been.

"Not at all."

I chuckle at that. "You keep in touch, at least?"

"More than I would like." The glint in his eyes lets me know he's only mostly joking.

"Okay. What about friends?"

His gaze returns to my arm. "I used to have a lot. It was easy to meet new people. Now...not so much."

It's no more than I'd already guessed, but hearing him say it is like a little thorn in my heart. He used to be so vibrant and outgoing. It's hard to see how he's walled everyone out of his life. Is it all because of his injury? Or something else?

"You haven't connected with anybody in Sunshine?"

"One." He tilts his head to the side. "One and a half."

I probably grin too wide over him simply admitting he sees August and me as his friends, but the knowledge makes my heart swell like a rising soufflé. And not because of any deal I'm getting on this duplex. I don't just want Ian to let me befriend him—I want to see him shine again.

"Maybe you could make more friends, too."

He watches me like he's sifting through my words, looking for hidden meaning. "Maybe."

He lifts the now-bloody paper towel from my arm and examines my injury. "Looks better. I'll bandage it up."

It's fascinating to watch him tend to my arm. This methodical side of him is all new to me. He applies an antiseptic cream with a cotton swab gently so it doesn't aggravate the wound. Then he lays a wide bandage over it, smoothing the edges down to make it secure.

It's comforting, letting him take care of me this way. I have so many responsibilities when it comes to August's diabetes, it's almost soothing to let someone else be in charge, if only of a simple scrape.

"You're good at this." My breathy voice reveals way more than I mean it to, but the sentiment's true.

"It was part of my job." He lowers my arm and gathers up all the trash. I point him in the direction of the garbage can, and he throws everything out, then closes up the first aid kit with a snap. When he returns to me, he slips right back into my space. "How does your arm feel now?"

"Better. Thank you."

"You might want to take some ibuprofen for the pain."

I smile over this new side of him. *Paging Dr. Vaughn.* "Did people get a lot of injuries on the climbs you took them on?"

He rests one hand on the kitchen counter behind me, leaning just a touch but not quite caging me in. "Sounds like you don't think I was a very good guide."

I poke him gently in the side. A bad call, really, when I already know just how firm his body is. "You know what I mean."

"If I was lucky, I only had to deal with a scrape or two. Once in a while, I'd have someone develop altitude sickness or dehydration. Mostly, I took good care of my clients."

I love the glimmer of pride in his voice. Even if I haven't read all the articles about him Wren mentioned, it's obvious he loved his job and was good at it.

"Well, I would trust you."

His gaze rakes over my face again, lingering on my mouth. "Yeah?"

"I just wouldn't trust myself."

His eyes lock on mine, brimming with silent questions. I mean it in every way he thinks. I'm definitely not a mountaineer, but with him standing *this close* and smelling *this good* that's not at the top of my reasons for self-doubt.

I want to close this absurdly small distance between us and kiss him. I want to throw my arms around his neck and lose myself in the moment. But I haven't done any of those things in so long—and the last time I experienced that with someone, I wished I hadn't. I can't just give in to the impulse.

My awkward laugh is like a wedge pushing me out of his orbit, and I take a step to the side. "I don't think I'd last very long on a climb like that. My friend, Lila, only went on a week-long hike around here, and it sounded like more than I would be able to manage."

"I think you're more than capable, Tess."

His earnest vote of confidence lifts me up like a buoy, even though my behavior just now proves him wrong. I am terrified of every potential outcome from this night—scared to move closer to him and scared to lose ground. When I don't know which step to take, it's easiest to stay exactly where I am. In this case, that means scurrying out of his reach.

"I will remember that if I ever decide to climb a mountain." I move away from him so I can tuck the first aid kit back into the plastic drawer. And take whole lungfuls of air again.

"If you ever climb a mountain, you'll do it with me."

I stop my fidgeting and meet his eyes. He looks a little like he did when I met him on the trail that day—intense and deadly serious. "You don't trust anyone else?"

"Not with you."

Can words sink into your skin and light you up from the inside? That's the most romantic thing anyone has ever said to me, and I'm not even sure he means it that way. Maybe he's just confident he's the best guide around. But as keenly as he's watching me, I don't think that's it.

"I will keep that in mind." Quite literally. "Thank you again for taking care of my arm."

Apparently accepting my cue that I need a little space, his gaze settles into something less intense and more strictly friendly. Neighborly.

This is what I wanted?

"Thanks for letting me."

We cross the small apartment to the front door. It's only a few steps, but it feels like crossing an ocean—tumultuous and uncertain. He lets himself out and steps onto the front porch, but turns around to face me again.

"Do me a favor?" he says. "Don't take your trash out at night anymore."

He dips his head to look at me from beneath his heavy red eyebrows, his mouth quirked up into a smirk.

"I promise." I hold my hand out to shake on it. Even though I'm afraid to try for anything more with Ian, I don't want him to leave without touching me one more time.

Mixed messages, maybe, but Ian doesn't seem like he's confused. He takes my hand in his, warm and firm and absolutely enveloping. He doesn't shake it like this is a business deal. He just holds it. Like he wanted one more touch, too. Then, he sweeps his fingertips along the inside of my wrist.

Not neighborly.

I draw in a soft breath, and his gaze warms. I might shudder, too, but I'm too focused on his touch to pay attention to anything else.

"I'll hold you to it," he says.

TWENTY

TESS

I SHOULDN'T FEEL like a criminal on the lam when I'm working in my own business. Okay, technically it's not mine— Mom brought Wren and me in as partners after we each turned twenty-five. I'm a co-owner. Still. My heart's racing while I blend new frosting flavors in the back, like I expect to be raided and handcuffed any minute.

Unlikely, since Mom left to pick August up from daycare an hour ago. She promised him an afternoon at his favorite park, so she won't come here again today unless absolutely necessary. She's dedicated to Blackbird's Bakery, but she's even more dedicated to being the best grandma.

I carefully pipe thick buttercream over filled cupcakes, agonizing just a touch over the flavor ratios with this batch. Peanut butter and jelly sounded like the perfect summer cupcake, but I'm not certain putting peanut butter in the cake *and* icing was the right call. The jelly should offset the nutty taste, but I don't want the peanut butter to overwhelm. At least I have a willing taste tester.

Smiling to myself, I frost the rest of the cupcakes on the baking tray. I've been swooning around all day, earning a dozen knowing looks from Wren. I told her a little of what happened last night when I explained about the big bandage on my arm, but it was more than enough for her to get carried away with her own ideas. Probably ridiculous scenarios where Ian's shirt comes unbuttoned as he runs through a field toward me.

What actually happened last night was better. I mean...I wouldn't hate the running toward me scenario, but bandaging my injuries is a romance book trope, too. I think. I don't read much of that genre, but I'll just assume that it is.

And rescuing me. That's a romance book thing for sure. He got right between me and danger. The fact that the danger was only raccoons going through my trash isn't important.

"Tess."

I startle and look up. Wren's poking her head into the back room, a sly smile on her face while she watches me work.

"Daydreaming about someone?" she wants to know. "I had to say your name a couple of times."

I straighten my back and set the piping bag aside. "I'm focused on my cupcakes."

Her smile spreads and curls across her mouth so slowly, it's like she's means for it to worm straight under my skin. Having a sister is a constant love-hate relationship.

"Whatever you say. Someone's out front to see you."

She hitches her eyebrows up before disappearing back through the swinging door. My stomach dips. Nobody ever comes to the bakery to see me. Except once.

I smooth my hands over my hair and straighten out my apron for good measure. I consider checking my face in the back bathroom, but nothing could be worse than the state Ian found me in last night.

Pushing through the door, I step out into the bakery, quickly scanning the space. Wren's helping a mother and her children at the front counter, with a man waiting in line behind them, and standing off to the side is Charlie Callahan.

No Ian.

Wren looks from me to Charlie, dipping her head in indication.

Oh.

I brush off my silly disappointment and cross to where Charlie's waiting. She's Shepherd's younger sister, but you'd never know it by looking at them. He got their dad's black hair and tall, lean frame, where she got their mom's red hair and petite, curvy figure. Meanwhile, Wren and I are carbon copies of our mom, personalities excluded. Genetics are weird.

As soon as I get close enough, the anxious look on Charlie's face breaks into relief. She actually clasps her hands together as if she wants to give me a standing ovation just for being here.

"Tess. Hi. How are you? Everything good?"

"Yes." I drag the word out, trying to do some calculations about what's going on. Charlie runs Moonlight Lodge with her parents. They sometimes request pies for special events, but they usually talk to Mom about those.

"I know I'm being weird. I'll get right to the point." She pushes her brown plastic glasses farther up her nose. "I have a couple staying at the lodge who have decided to elope while they're here."

She pauses to make jazz hands for the happy couple.

"They're throwing together a scaled-down event, but it's still our first real foray into weddings. I'm a little frazzled trying to help them pull in everything they need, can you tell?"

I just smile, but yes, I noticed. Charlie's usually less frantic than this. "What do you need from me?"

She stares at me a beat. "The wedding cake, obviously!"

"I..." My first request for a wedding cake, and that's all that croaks out of my mouth.

"My parents showed them pictures of the cake you made for their anniversary in the spring. The couple would love for you to make their cake, too. They probably want something different, and smaller since they don't really have many guests, but I told them I would check to see if you're available. I know it's crazy last-minute, but...do you have any space to make a wedding cake?"

"Uh..." Everything she said's still filtering through my sluggish brain like it has to go through a translator app a few times first. "When?"

"They'll have their license in three days, and we're planning for a ceremony then. If you can't do it, I completely understand, but I'd really love to keep everything sourced right here if I can."

She flashes a tentative smile. I'm flattered beyond reason—I can't even think straight—but I've also never made a wedding cake before. Birthday cakes, yes, anniversary cakes and holiday cakes, sure. All beautiful, all results I'm proud of. I even have a folder on my computer stuffed with photos of my work. But a wedding cake is a big deal. *The* big deal when it comes to cakes. I can't mess around and get it wrong.

"Are you sure you wouldn't rather call a bakery in Bend?" The question comes out at the same time I think it.

Over my shoulder, Wren makes a strangled sound of protest.

"I will if I have to, but I'm sure their specialty bakeries are already booked solid. I mean, it's June—everybody's getting married, right?"

That's true. Any bakery that offers wedding cakes probably has a waitlist months out by now. Her couple won't be able to find anything custom with only three days' notice. I don't want them to have to resort to a grocery store sheet cake when I could create something just for them. And I *could* make time...

Charlie watches me with a hopeful expression, waiting on

my answer. I'm frozen, mentally scrambling over possibilities. Flavor combinations and decorative styles, tiers and frosting and aesthetics. It's just another specialty cake, right? I can do this.

"I'll make the cake for them," I finally say.

She grins again. "I'll give them your contact info. You are the best. I know it's going to be amazing!"

Charlie finishes singing my praises and leaves to secure a few more vendors for the last-minute wedding. I return to Wren's side behind the counter, calculating how my next few days will have to adjust so I can bake and decorate the cake in time. I've already got a cake on my calendar next week for Hope's engagement party, but I can absolutely swing this.

Wren has a hand up, waiting on a high-five. "Bring it in."

I roll my eyes but slap her hand.

"I'm proud of you. This could be a game-changer for your cake business."

"Maybe. It might just be another one-off." I hope it's not. I've wanted to make wedding cakes for years. It's just never felt like a feasible possibility. It still doesn't, honestly, but I'm doing this for the sake of the couple having the best day possible.

From Wren's dubious look, I guess those hopes aren't much of a secret. "Or it could be the start of something big."

Visions of wedding cakes dance through my head until I can almost smell them. I'm not usually one to get caught up in daydreams and fantasies, but I guess this is the day for it.

"Let's not get ahead of ourselves. This couple might not like what I make."

"Shut up. It's going to be beautiful and delicious. I don't even know why you doubt it. You're the Cake Whisperer or something."

Hopefully, the couple will call soon so we can discuss flavors and any cake inspiration they might have. Who knows? They might want a style of cake I can't even do, and this opportunity will fall apart before it begins. I don't want to totally crush my cake-making dreams, but I need to be at least a little realistic.

"The only real question," Wren says more ominously, "is are you going to tell Mom about it?"

Yep. There's the dream-crushing I was afraid of.

TWENTY-ONE
IAN

TESS WATCHES me with one fist up to her mouth, her thumbnail caught between her teeth. Her gaze dances from me to the box of cupcakes she set on the back patio table a minute ago like she's waiting for the desserts to explode. Seems extreme. Worst thing I can imagine is her raccoon friends might scamper through and steal the treats before I get a chance to eat any.

"They look perfect. The frosting makes a nice—" I swirl a finger in the air. I don't know the terminology, but it's wavy like a soft-serve ice cream cone. It's honestly a lot of frosting, but judging by the ones I had last week, that might be my favorite part.

Her lips tilt into a smile around the tip of her thumb, and she drops her hand. "Thank you. But I need you to taste them."

"Pushy. I like it."

I pull one from the box. There's no pretty way to eat a cupcake this big. I'm guaranteed to get frosting in my beard. But Tess asked me to try her new flavor combination, so you better believe I'm going to follow through.

My first bite is half frosting, half cupcake, all delicious. The second bite captures some of the red jelly filling, bringing the J in the flavor's PB&J theme. The last two bites are just me in a shark frenzy, my eyes rolled back in my head.

"It's really good," I tell her when I've swallowed the last of it down. I decimated the fat cupcake in four bites. I think she can draw her own conclusions.

Her eyebrows lift. Maybe that wasn't the most helpful review. I cast about, digging deep for any hidden food critic skills.

"The cake's rich without being overpowering. The buttercream has the right amount of flavor, and the peanut butter flakes add interesting mouthfeel. The strawberry jelly has a brightness that gives the whole thing a nice kick."

Her eyebrows hitch even higher. Possibly because I said the word *mouthfeel* for the first time in my life.

"I would eat another, is what I'm trying to say."

She grins, and her shoulders ease into a more relaxed posture. "Go for it. How about a glass of milk to go with it?"

"Please."

August leaps onto the porch and heads Tess off before she reaches her door. "Can I try, too?"

"Sure, buddy. Take a seat with Ian."

In a minute, Tess comes back out with two glasses of milk and three forks. We sit at their patio table and share one of the sample cupcakes, August swinging his feet in the seat between us. The sun's just starting to ease into twilight, the harsh light of day fading into something softer for our cozy little taste-testing.

"Does Dutch like cupcakes?" August wants to know.

"He'll inhale them if he gets close enough." He's already standing between August and me, his nose an inch away from the tabletop. He's well behaved most of the time, but he's not too proud to lick up the crumbs that fall onto the patio.

"Can I give him a bite?"

Can't hurt anything. I nod, and August grabs a forkful of

cake between his little fingers. He passes it to Dutch, who takes it from him with an excessive use of tongue.

August squeals with delight. "He likes it!"

"I thought he might."

August eats another forkful, watching me as he stretches his tongue to reach all the frosting left around his mouth. "Can I see your bunny?"

I pause, my fork hovering over the remains of the cupcake. "My what?"

"Mama and Aunt Wren said you have a boy bunny. I want to see it. I like bunnies."

Tess and I share a look over his head, but she just makes a "no idea" face.

He looks so eager, I hate to disappoint him. "Dutch is the only pet I've got, kiddo."

His hopeful expression falls. "But they said you have a man bun."

Tess throws one hand in front of her face, coughing and spluttering around her last bite of cupcake. It's not enough to hide how her cheeks wash with pink, though.

"Oh, did they?" I lean closer to August. "What else did they say about my man bun?"

"Aunt Wren said she didn't think Mama liked them very much, but Mama said she *really* likes yours."

"Okay," Tess chokes out. "Why don't you go play in the yard a little longer. It'll be bedtime soon."

"But the bunny—"

"It's not a bunny." Her gaze lifts but doesn't quite reach my eyes. "We were talking about Ian's hair. He wears it in a *bun*."

"Oh." August scrutinizes me for a few seconds, taking in my hair I've tucked up. "I like that, too, I guess. But I'd like a bunny more."

He hops off his chair and finds a kickball in the yard, Dutch up for whatever. Tess's gaze is locked on them, her lips pulled tight between her teeth. She's trying hard not to look at me, which makes the whole scene that much more adorable.

She *wants* to look at me. Because she likes my man bun.

An absolutely stupid thing to preen over, but I'll take everything I can get with this woman.

"You've really got a thing for my hair."

She makes a sound of mock exasperation. "Don't gloat. It's not a good look."

I lower my voice and tip my head toward her. "That's not what I just heard."

She laughs but finally meets my gaze. I break out my most rakish grin—because yes, I will do whatever it takes to keep her thinking of me as a sexy pirate.

If I'm a pirate, her sharp intake of breath and soft "Oh" in response are all the treasure I need.

"That's the Ian I remember."

I go still even as my heart throbs at her words. For years, I've resented it whenever people brought up who I was in the past. It shone a light on a comparison I could never win. But this isn't a better/worse scenario. She's pointing out a glimpse of the man I used to be. Maybe he's not completely lost in here, after all.

"About that. You said we'd never spoken, but you talk like you knew me well." I've racked my brain these last two weeks trying to remember her, but nothing much comes to me from back then. I spent my days leading white water rafting tours about an hour north of here. Despite what Tess seems to think, I spent most of my nights crashed on Amy's couch.

She shifts in her chair as if she might like to escape, but she doesn't break eye contact. "You stood out."

I scratch my beard as if I'm pondering that. "Even without the man bun?"

That earns an eye roll. "I won't pretend you weren't cute," she starts.

I grin wider. It's been fifteen years, but come on. I'm only human.

"But it was your personality. The way you carried yourself. Like you weren't afraid of anything." Her gaze drifts to August in the yard. "I was afraid of everything."

"Shy kid?" I ask. She hasn't seemed like a shy person from what I've seen, except occasionally when it comes to me.

"Not exactly, just...timid. I looked for the safe path. I never would have thought about climbing a mountain or white water rafting or even talking to a cute boy."

"He would have been thrilled to have you talk to him." He sure is today.

She cringes. "I doubt it. I was only seventeen. I don't think I would have been on your radar."

"My loss." She's right, though. I might have been a shameless flirt, but I wasn't so thoughtless as to seek out someone underage.

"You know," she says, "all these years later, I'm just as terrified about making wrong choices as I was back then."

"What choices are you afraid of getting wrong?" Maybe I'm pushing, but this doesn't sound like a hypothetical.

Her gaze stays on me, and I could swear she's debating just how to answer.

"Cakes, for one," she finally says.

"Cakes?" Not the choices I thought we were talking about.

"We mostly do pies in the bakery, as you probably saw. But a few years ago, I started experimenting with cakes on the side." She shakes her head, a wry smile shining out. "That makes it sound so illicit, but it kind of is to my mom. The thing is, I love making fancy cakes. I love pairing the exact right flavors together. I love coming up with simple but elegant decorations.

And I love knowing I helped make someone's special day that much more memorable."

Her heavy sigh tugs at something behind my ribs.

"I got my first wedding cake request today. I talked with the couple this afternoon—they're so excited, it's impossible for me not to be excited, too. My mother, though. She's *not* excited. I want to add my specialty cakes to our website and menu, but Mom doesn't think the business can support it. And I have to trust she knows best."

"Does she?"

Tess splays a hand as though obviously she must. "She says it's too much of a risk."

"Sometimes a little risk is a good thing."

She huffs out a breath. "Why am I not surprised you'd say that?"

"My brothers and I risked a lot when we pooled our money together to start our guiding business. We grew faster than maybe we should have. But it worked out because we weren't afraid to try." I can just imagine Pierce's indignant reaction if he'd overheard that trite explanation. "I'm oversimplifying, and we had setbacks along the way, but we wouldn't have our successes if we'd played it safe."

I am keenly aware I haven't lived by that motto in years.

"Do you miss it?"

It wasn't all standing on the tops of mountains. So much work goes into a climb, the preparation and planning, both mental and physical, knowing weather could turn us away before we make it to the top. But mostly, I remember the exhilaration of reaching new heights, the views still stamped in my memory, the sense, however fleeting, that I could do anything.

"Every day."

Hurts to admit when I've spent so much time running from

that truth. I miss it, but I can't recapture it. Not like it used to be.

"It wasn't just about conquering mountains and the rush of adrenaline," I go on. "I always knew exactly where to go, where I was headed, and how I would get there. I didn't question any of it. Now...I've lost my way. Like a compass without a needle."

I don't like admitting as much to her. I'm stuck, in a way I've never experienced before. For the first time in more years than I can count, I don't know what I should do next. I'm not even sure what's possible.

"You can find your way again," she says softly.

I want to trust her. I just don't know how anymore. "Easier said than done."

Tess watches August secure a cape around Dutch. It matches the one he's wearing, and when they take off, the capes billow in their wake like superheroes. I want to take a picture and preserve this memory to make sure I never forget it.

"My father left us when I was twelve," she tells me. "Mom, Wren, and I banded together. Maybe too tightly. Wren and I didn't go away to college. We went to culinary school right here and worked with Mom in the bakery. I like to think it's what we both wanted, but I was still that timid girl, afraid of making the wrong choice.

"When I was twenty-five, I decided I didn't want to be that girl anymore. I wanted out of Sunshine, out of the house I still lived in with my mother and sister. I thought I could reinvent myself. So I got a job at an inn in Lake Tahoe and set off on an adventure. A small one, maybe, but it would be mine."

"Leaving everything you know takes a lot of courage." Clearly, she came back, but trying takes guts.

She shakes her head at that. "I wasn't brave. I was naive. I came home six months later, pregnant and alone."

"The father...?" I have to ask even though I can tell already I won't like the answer.

"Uninterested in ever being called that."

I want to track the guy down and punch him in the face on her behalf. And August's. And one just for me.

"It must be tough to do it all alone." The small glimpses I get show she's a dedicated parent who puts her child ahead of herself. Some kids don't give half so much attention even when there's two parents on the team.

"I have Mom and Wren. But I'll admit, being an unwed mother in a small town isn't for the faint of heart."

"Do people make it hard on you?"

"Some do. The first thing I had to let go of was worrying over what everyone thought about me. I'm not perfect at it, but that's the goal." A genuine smile touches her mouth. "And I got August in the end. No matter what anyone says about me, I could never regret that."

Her positive attitude in the face of public scrutiny puts my pity party in a harsh new light. She's not mired in feeling sorry that people are judging her in the first place, and she's sure not losing sleep over her choices or their results. Not like I have been.

"I haven't worn shorts in public since my accident. Eighty degrees out today, and I'm in sweatpants." I tug at the fleece over my prosthesis's socket. I went to the grocery store this afternoon, covered up as usual.

"Can't be comfortable."

"Nope." The sweat on my leg itches like mad as we speak.

"Are people weird about your prosthetic leg?"

"Sometimes. Mostly, they ask too many questions. Give me too many condolences for all the things they assume I can't do anymore."

Tess scoffs. "As though *you* are remotely incapable."

Kind of loving the way she said that. Like the thought of me not being able to do something is inconceivable to her.

"Maybe I need to take a lesson from you and not worry about what anyone else thinks."

Pretty sure the person I'm actually afraid of judging me for all my failings is me.

"For the record, I like how you look in shorts." She holds my gaze. "All of you."

My chest turns molten, the warmth of her praise seeping through my limbs down to my fingers and toes. There's nothing timid about Tess in this moment.

Even if, in the very next one, she scoops August up and takes him inside with a flurry of rushed goodnights.

TWENTY-TWO

TESS

I HAVEN'T BEEN SO afraid of dropping something since the day I brought August home from the hospital in his baby carrier. I'm eighty-five percent certain I'm going to somehow lose my grip and send the carefully crafted confection in my arms flying all over Moonlight Lodge's pristine lobby.

Several people taking up the comfy chairs and sofas in here are on their phones, so something like that would definitely wind up on social media.

Charlie Callahan spots me before I make it halfway across the rustic space and hurries around the front desk to greet me.

"You're here! Obviously you're here. This is it?" She nods at the cardboard box in my arms I constructed to fit the wedding cake. "Clearly it is. Ignore me. Let me show you into the reception room."

She's just a touch excited.

I follow her through the lodge to a beautiful room with plain log walls and simple white chairs and tables. The huge windows beneath the A-frame ceiling make extra decor unnecessary. The lodge sits secluded in the forest just outside Sunshine, and the windows reveal lush green pines and the river skirting by close enough to skip a rock in it. I can't imagine what else this room is used for, but an intimate wedding sounds just about perfect.

Charlie shows me the table where I can set up the cake. I take apart the box and stabilizing supports and place the wedding cake on a wooden stand in the center of the table. Inspecting every centimeter of the cake, I make sure nothing's amiss after transit. I'm meticulous with my deliveries, and I always triple check.

My phone is already loaded with pictures of this cake, but I take a few more of it in this gorgeous room, too. The couple chose a two-tier lavender cake filled with lemon curd and cream. I decorated it in buttercream tinted the bride's favorite shade of teal—she actually texted me the Pantone color swatch—with white mountains and green pine trees iced on with a palette knife.

Incidentally, I had Hope teach me how to paint mountains when I started experimenting with this decoration style last fall. I'm not much of an artist, but I can make a pretty good mountain out of buttercream now.

The cake is simple but elegant, perfect for this space. And hopefully, perfect for the couple.

"It's gorgeous." Charlie sighs over it. "I knew it would be, but seeing it...oh, it's lovely."

With praise like this, I might never have to go therapy again.

"Do you ever think about doing cakes full time?" she asks.

Her straightforward question pulls at something in my chest. *Every day.*

"Maybe someday."

The happy couple arrives a few minutes later to give their approval. People are usually excited to receive my cakes, but I've never had a man tear up over one. His bride-to-be cries, too, and they hover over their wedding cake like neither of them can contain their joy, hugging and kissing. It's one of the sweetest things I've ever seen.

I almost let myself miss out on this?

After they transfer me the other half of the cost I'd quoted, they leave to finish getting ready for their impromptu ceremony. Charlie leads me back through the lobby, grinning her face off.

"I'm working on convincing Mom and Dad to let me convert the barn into a wedding venue," she tells me as we walk past cozy leather sofas and a drinks cart offering hot cocoa. "It's our rec room space right now, so it will take a lot of work to spruce it up enough for weddings instead of just foosball bouts and table tennis. I'd love to have it ready by the new year, but they're not sure about the investment."

She scrunches her nose as though this attitude is ridiculous. I understand her sentiment a little too well. "So hopefully this first wedding is a major success and will convince them to expand. If not, you'll never hear me speak of it again."

"I can't imagine this place not getting booked up for weddings all year round."

We step outside into the warm June sunshine. I don't often come out here, but I can't get over how beautiful it is, both the scenery and the cabins. Charlie's transformed the lodge from a homey bed and breakfast into an upscale resort in just a few years.

"That's the dream. I've researched weddings in this area until my eyes went dry, and I think I've got a realistic business plan. It's just the last little hump I need to get past."

"It's hard to know what's going to be worth it in the end." I'm not sure why I'm echoing her parents' hesitation when I'm trying to convince my own business partner to expand our offerings. "You've had a lot of success so far. You don't worry about... hitting a wall?"

That's been Mom's concern. We'll reach some invisible barrier that triggers disaster, and the bakery will go up in flames.

Charlie makes a face. "The only wall is my dad's hard head. They don't always share my visions for this place. But I love building it out and turning it into a bigger name than my grandparents ever imagined it could be when they started it."

She looks around as if she's seeing past the parking lot and into the future where their family's business is even more successful. Knowing her, she'll bring her parents around. Pretty sure the couple getting married this afternoon is already writing up their five-star reviews.

"It must be hard not having Shepherd involved." I can't imagine carrying on our bakery if Wren were to leave. More accurately, I can't imagine Mom would react favorably to either of us abandoning ship.

Again. The last time I left the business, all her doom and gloom predictions turned out to be right.

Charlie scoffs. "Are you kidding me? Shep would just naysay everything. He's good where he is."

"Your parents don't mind that he went his own direction?"

"They're the ones who told him to quit. They knew he wasn't happy working here. And when we started all the upgrades—oof. Can you imagine Shepherd being involved in anything with the word 'luxury' attached?" She laughs as if she can see his sour face. "So no, they don't mind. And he's deliriously happy where he is."

"Deliriously?" He seems content with his bike shop, but I'm not sure I've ever seen him look especially happy. Maybe when he gets points in against Wren, but that's about it.

Charlie hitches a shoulder. "Well...as far as Shepherd can look happy. You know how he is."

Shepherd and I were in the same grade in high school, but I wouldn't say we know much about each other. I've gotten to know him a little better since he opened his business next door to ours a few years ago, but our friendship doesn't extend much beyond me running interference for him with my sister.

"Yeah. He and Wren have this fun 'trying to murder each other with eye contact' thing they do every time he comes in."

Her eyes narrow on me. "He comes into the bakery a lot?"

"Every week."

"Huh. Now I'm kind of mad he gets one of your pies every week and doesn't share."

I've got my own suspicions about that. We have our regulars, but nobody quite as dedicated to us as Shepherd is. Seems wrong to talk about it with his sister when I can't talk about it with mine, though.

"I've got to go make sure everything's ready for the big event." She flashes an all-tooth fake smile. "If we do expand to weddings, I'm hiring a coordinator. I am not cut out for this. But thank you so much for that beautiful cake. You really came through for us."

"You're welcome. It was my pleasure."

"If things go well with my plans, this isn't the last you'll hear from me." She points at me as she backs away. "That sounded like a threat, but I mean it in a good way!"

I laugh at her brand of enthusiasm. "Let me know how it goes."

I cross the parking lot, my ribcage full of fireflies. Mom might not be sure about me making wedding cakes on a more regular basis, but my heart is full. The cake turned out perfect, and the couple's reaction was better than I could have dreamed. Even my steps feel lighter, like my pride is cushioning me in a protective bubble where nothing can go wrong.

I'm almost to my car when my phone rings. August's daycare name appears on the screen, and that bubble bursts.

TWENTY-THREE

IAN

I STEP out onto the back porch to find Tess already there. She's at the edge of the patio, arms crossed tight around herself, staring into the trees like she doesn't see them. Something's off.

Might be a weird thing for me to notice about my neighbor, but I see it anyway.

"Hey." *Excellent opener, Ian.*

She turns and flashes a big, fake smile. Yeah. Something's definitely off. "Hi."

I move closer. Dutch joins August where he's playing with some trucks in an empty section of flower bed. He flops into the grass, begging for a belly rub. Without missing a beat, August scratches him with one hand and drives trucks through dirt with the other.

"Is everything okay?" They're home early, another thing I shouldn't notice but do.

"Yeah. It's just..." Tess drops her façade, her shoulders slumping, her fake smile crumpling.

"What happened?" I'm ready to get between her and whoever stole the sunshine from her skies. "Who do I need to throttle?"

That earns a faint smile. "Me, probably."

"Not happening." I close the last few steps between us until I'm close enough our shoulders brush. "Do you want to talk about it?"

I'm not sure I've ever asked anyone that before, but here I am. Ready to listen.

"August's daycare called this afternoon. The workers all caught some stomach bug, and they have to shut down for the rest of the week."

"Is August okay?" Kid looks fine from here, but the fact that he's sitting down to play instead of running wild could be a bad sign. Frankly, I'm not sure even projectile vomiting would keep him from petting Dutch.

"He's great, it's not that. It's just..." Her gaze lifts to the trees as though they have the answers she needs. Or maybe she's trying to fight off tears. "I have to ask my mom and sister for help while the daycare's closed."

I'm trying to understand the problem but coming up short. "I thought they'd want to help you."

"They do. That's just it. They'll adjust our schedules at the bakery, and we'll work out a system to take care of him while the daycare's closed. They'll swoop in and rescue me, *again*. It will be fine."

The look on her face doesn't feel fine. Feels more like I want to pull her into my arms and hold her close. Keep her safe until all her problems fade away.

"I wanted so badly to step out on my own and prove I can handle life, and here I am less than a month later, ready to crawl back to Mom and admit I can't do it. It just sucks to have to tell her I was wrong so soon, you know?"

I hate seeing her so distraught. I want to ease her burdens and help her smile again. Maybe I want to prove myself, too.

"I could watch August."

The words are out of my mouth before they've had a chance to fully form in my brain.

She breathes a laugh. "If only."

"I could." Her easy dismissal makes me more certain I want to do this. That I *can* do this. "I'm right here. My days are free. He could be in his own house so you know it's childproofed."

No need to mention I don't have a clue what childproofing entails.

She swivels her head to stare at me. "I sort of thought you didn't like kids."

I scoff. "I just don't know any. Doesn't mean I don't like them."

Her laughter comes out more genuine this time. "I can't ask you to watch August for the rest of the week."

"You didn't ask. I'm offering."

She opens her mouth but pauses. Considering. I've got a chance.

"You can ask Amy anything you want about me. Do a background check. Call my brothers." I would absolutely not enjoy knowing she's on a phone call with Pierce or Steven. But apparently, I would do whatever it takes to ease her mind about leaving August with me for a few hours each day so she can save face with her mom.

I know a lot about losing your pride. I don't want that for her. Not if I can help it.

Tess continues to stare at me. "Why, though?"

Because you're not alone. Because you don't have to prove yourself to me. Because you're worth the effort.

"I haven't challenged myself in two years. This would be a pretty big challenge."

Her mouth pulls into a frown. "You're not making your case with that."

"Maybe I just want to help you if I can. And I like the kid. He reminds me of me."

At least she laughs again. "He does not. He's very well behaved."

"Who said I wasn't well behaved?"

Her dark blue eyes glint at me. "Nothing you say could convince me you weren't a troublemaker when you were a kid."

And an adult goes unsaid, but I swear she mentally tacks it on.

"I could get my mother on the phone to vouch for me." Am I offering up *more* family members for Tess to talk to? Mom wouldn't vouch for me anyway—I fit the wild child accusation Tess lobbed at me to a tee. But I bet she'd love talking with Tess.

Getting ahead of myself here.

"I probably don't need to talk to your mom yet."

Not sure why that "yet" is such a hopeful little word. It's like a glimpse of a mountain peak that's been mired in cloud cover.

"I'm not worried about his behavior, but it's not like watching any other kid. You'd have to be able to manage his diabetes and be aware of any changes in his blood sugar levels. It's too much to ask of you."

"His blood sugar monitor has an app on a phone, right?" I wouldn't hesitate even if I had to do regular finger pricks to check his blood sugar and dip ketone strips in his urine.

"Yeah, we have one just for—wait. How do you know about the app?"

"I looked them up." My research isn't really the point. "I'm a certified EMT, and I have multiple first aid certifications. You're not going to find safer hands than mine."

She blinks hard at me. "Wow. Cocky Ian really is back."

I level her with a stern look. "It's not cockiness. It's fact."

"That's the whole definition of cockiness."

"The point is, his diabetes isn't a problem."

She stares at me so long, I'm convinced she's coming up with fresh ammo to reject my offer. But she takes a slow step back, her arm dragging against mine.

"I'm going to call Amy real quick. I should probably get at least one reference before I leave my child with you." Her true smile peeks out for the first time this afternoon. "Can you watch August for a minute?"

I frown harder at her, tilting my head indicating she can go inside.

"Right. Right. I'll just—" She slips inside the house.

I listen as August narrates what he's doing for Dutch, filling his trucks with tiny scoops of dirt. Kind of hilarious what all goes on in his head.

Wonder what Dutch would narrate back. Pretty sure it's circus theme music in there twenty-four-seven.

Five minutes go by. I'm not worried...but I do start to wonder just what Tess and Amy are talking about. She just needs a little reassurance I can make a good babysitter. Right?

Although...it might have been a mistake to offer up personal references. Technically, I've never babysat anyone. The closest I came was watching Steven and Iris's four dogs one weekend when they went off on an anniversary celebration. And even that wouldn't provide a pristine Yelp review—the Chihuahua, Bill, picked up the habit of walking on the dining table during meals.

I said that's what they get for having a dog the size of a skirt steak, but they still blamed me.

My heart is drumming a frantic beat when Tess finally walks back outside. She looks stunned, like maybe she got more information about me than she'd bargained for. Definitely a mistake suggesting she talk to my family.

"What did she tell you?" It comes out more accusatory than

I mean it to, but Tess's expression has me on edge. Like my heart's a Rubik's Cube with one side twisted out of alignment.

It takes her a second, but when she smiles, my heart clicks back into place.

"She confirmed everything about your EMT status. Said you're very trustworthy."

"Then why do you look so startled?" I can come up with plenty of other things Amy might have shared that I wouldn't be so thrilled about. Mostly about my lack of experience with commitment.

To be fair, nobody I dated in the past wanted to commit to me long-term, either. Which, now that I think about it, isn't a point in my favor.

"Oh, I just..." She pushes her hair over both ears at the same time, her gaze moving between me and her son. "I want to make sure August is comfortable with this."

"You can ask him. If he doesn't want to hang out with me, that'll be the end of it." Pretty sure he'll be thrilled to spend more time with Dutch. He'll probably rope him into another game of kickball. He let the dog win their last round. A point that further confirms August isn't much like I was as a kid. I hated to lose. But I also had two older brothers to rub it in my face when I did.

"August," she calls. "Come here for a second, buddy."

He nods and scrambles over—he's way more obedient than I was at his age, too.

Or am currently.

Tess gets down on one knee. "Honey, your daycare has to close for a few days. Miss Tammy and Miss Lori got sick."

"Like when Max threw up yesterday?"

She makes a face. "Probably exactly like that. But all the teachers got sick, so there's nobody to watch the kids."

"We can watch movies."

The kid's a problem solver, I'll give him that.

"It wouldn't be safe to leave all of you alone to watch movies."

"We know where the snacks are."

She grins at him. "I'm not going to take you to daycare without an adult. But what do you think about having Ian watch you for a few days? Just until all your teachers feel better?"

He looks up at me, his mouth open. "I could stay with you and Dutch all day?"

"Only if you want to," I tell him.

He leaps off the patio and runs through the yard screaming his head off. Dutch gets in on the action, barking until I call his name and put a stop to it.

"I think that's a yes," Tess says, standing up. "Congratulations. You're a babysitter."

"I prefer the term 'manny.'"

TWENTY-FOUR
TESS

ONE THING they don't talk about enough in parenting books is the importance of a strong poker face. Teaching emotional awareness is essential, but sometimes I just can't let August see my real reactions. Like how I'm supposed to treat every alert on his continuous glucose monitor as benign, without freaking out or seeming upset, no matter how urgent. Or how I shouldn't laugh when he wishes people luck, but he says it "Good yuck."

Or right now, when I'm about to hand my child off to someone new for the first time.

Someone I'm deeply attracted to and caring more about by the day. Who maybe, possibly, cares about me, too.

When I called Amy to get her vote of confidence yesterday, she offered it easily. Like she'd told me before we moved in, Ian's a good guy. Trustworthy and capable, if fairly inexperienced with kids. But she tacked on an extra part this time that I can't stop thinking about.

"Ian hasn't wanted to do much of anything in a long time," she'd said. "If he's offering to help you out by watching August for a few days, that means something."

"What?" I'd asked, even though I was halfway to the answer already.

She laughed softly as though she could read my mind. "It means you're important to him. You both are."

So I'm definitely trying extra hard to seem perfectly normal and not at all smitten when Ian knocks on my door just after five-thirty a.m.

But then I open the door. Something about him looking sleep-rumpled and bleary-eyed, standing on my doorstep holding two steaming mugs of coffee, makes me want to cuddle up with him. As though taking time for a morning snuggle is a thing we could actually indulge in.

My poker face had better be doing the absolute most right now.

His mouth tilts into the smallest smile. "I wasn't sure if you'd want a coffee. It's black."

"I would love one, thank you." I take the mug he offers me, cataloguing the way our fingers brush during the hand-off and the current of electricity that seems to arc between us. That's a better rush than the caffeine. "Come on in."

"Hi, Ian!" August waves from the dining table where he's finishing his egg and cheese breakfast quesadilla. Looking past us, his expression falls. "Where's Dutch?"

Ian chuckles softly. "He's sleeping in. We can take him outside later."

"Okay." August kicks his feet, content with this plan. We talked last night about how he needs to be on his best behavior for Ian. Fingers crossed he doesn't start repeating that bad word his aunt Wren accidentally said in front of him last week and give Ian the impression I'm raising a foul-mouthed little sailor.

Actually...I should probably cross my fingers he doesn't learn new words from Ian, either.

I open a cupboard in the kitchen to pull out a ceramic honey pot and add a generous drizzle to the coffee Ian brought for me.

"I should have predicted that," he says.

I glance at him as I take a sip. Mmm. Perfect. "What?"

"That you like it sweet." He sounds amused and maybe a little fond.

A weird thing for me to pin on a man for noting my coffee preferences. Definitely the effects of having him in my space before the sun has even crested the mountain peaks. While he's wearing sweatpants and an old T-shirt that looks oh-so soft and touchable.

I take another sip of my coffee before I give in to the urge. "You should see my order at Perk Me Up. White chocolate, milk chocolate, whipped cream, and a splash of vanilla."

"Does it have any coffee in it?"

"I've never asked."

His mouth tilts again into that not-quite-smile I'm growing addicted to. For a minute, we just watch each other over our mugs, drinking our coffees.

August pushes his chair away from the table, reminding me what I'm meant to be doing before I get too swoony over my guest. Although, I guess for the next few days, Ian's not strictly a guest. He's an unpaid caregiver. I offered him money for his time yesterday, but that brought his scowl back, so I dropped it. I'll find some way to make it up to him eventually.

For now, I go into business mode and get out August's medical kit. I show Ian the apps that monitor his blood sugar and insulin dosing. The juices and snacks in the fridge. How to track the food August eats, and menu suggestions for lunch. What to do if he needs to verify blood sugar levels with a finger prick. The emergency medication in case he goes hypoglycemic.

I look at everything I've laid out for him, the apps and monitors and emergency kit and *lengthy* note.

"This is a lot. Isn't it?" Maybe too much.

Yesterday, when Ian said that August's diabetes isn't a problem, my heart puffed up with unfettered hope. I didn't realize how much I'd needed someone to say those words. I want to trust him that it's really no big deal, but aside from the women at daycare, I haven't left August with anyone outside of Mom and Wren. They would understand if I called right now and told them the daycare had to close temporarily. I don't have to force this on Ian.

"Tess." He tilts his head closer until I meet his eyes. "I've got this."

His deep voice settles the wave of anxiety in my stomach. He holds my gaze, his entire demeanor speaking to his confidence. He's not afraid for me to hand over the reins. Not because he doesn't understand the risks, but because he knows he can take care of whatever comes up.

And I thought seeing him shirtless got me going. Competent and in charge? Oof.

"You're right. You've got this." I really need to leave before I put on a sultry voice and ask him to tell me more about his medical certifications. I didn't know that would do it for me, but on Ian, it works.

He nods, stepping backward. "We're going to have a great day. Aren't we, August?"

August hops around in the living room, apparently doing an interpretive dance to show his excitement about spending the day with Ian. It's mostly butt wiggles.

"So great!" he confirms.

I join him and kneel on the rug. "I have to go to work, buddy. Have a good time with Ian and Dutch, okay?"

"Okay." He gives me a huge hug, then squeezes my face in his hands. "I'm going to show him my Legos!"

Just like that, he's gone. Probably to find the latest spaceship he made or the mini figure he assembled that looks like him. It's got blond hair, a dinosaur on his shirt, and we painted white dots on the back of each arm for his monitor and pump.

"At least he doesn't drag out the goodbyes," I say as I stand again. "Legos are obviously fine, and he's got loads of other toys in his room. Art supplies are in the linen closet by the bathroom. He can watch PBS Kids if he wants. We have movies in the cabinet."

Ian steps closer, his hands in the pockets of his sweatpants. "I figured we'd watch either *Toy Story* or *Predator*."

I flatten him with an unimpressed look. "Ha ha."

"They're pretty much the same movie."

"I can't imagine which version of *Toy Story* you watched."

"They're both about friends banding together against a common enemy."

I consider that grossly oversimplified summary. "Isn't every movie *Predator* when you define it like that?"

"I'm hearing yes to the Arnold Schwarzenegger movie marathon."

I point a stern finger at him, but he lays a hand over his heart. "Don't worry. I'll stick with Disney."

"Okay. I have to go to work." I move for the door but turn around again. "I forgot. We should exchange numbers. I can see his apps on my phone, too, but you know. Just in case something else comes up."

No need to start thinking of all the non-diabetes trouble August could get into. Ahem. *Rattlesnakes.*

We trade numbers, and I glance around, searching for anything else I've forgotten. I'm supposed to be at the bakery in ten minutes to start on the day's pies and cupcakes. I can get there in time, but only if I leave immediately.

"Are you sure you're ready for this?" And I don't mean

medically. Kids can be a lot, especially for someone who's not expecting it.

He gives me a lazy nod. "I'm ready for anything."

Here's that cockiness again. It's surprisingly cute. "*Anything?*"

"If he asks me where babies come from, I'll probably choke. Everything else, we're good."

"So you're saying you don't know where babies come from." Not sure where this flirtatiousness was hiding. Safe to say, the confidence he was radiating earlier brought it out. "Surprising."

Ian takes a slow step closer until our faces are inches apart. The confidence has returned, and I am positively basking in it.

"Tess," he says in his deep, low voice. His gaze tracks from my eyes down to my mouth. "Go to work."

It's a warning as much as a command. Because if I don't walk out that door soon, I won't want to leave at all.

————

Hope's sigh is loud enough to carry through the bakery and her gift shop next door. "That's the most beautiful wedding cake I've ever seen."

Probably an exaggeration, but I'll take the compliment.

She asked to see what I made for the couple at Moonlight Lodge, and this is my first chance to step away from our counter to show her the pictures on my phone. She swipes through the shots I took of the cake set up at the lodge, her gaze dreamy.

"I couldn't have done it if you hadn't given me that painting lesson." Hope sells all sorts of handmade things in her store, but she's an artist in her own right, too. She gave me a painting of August's favorite lovey for my birthday last winter. Who knew a faded old ostrich could make me cry that much?

She hands me my phone back. "This is all you."

I quickly swipe over to check August's apps before I put my phone back in my pocket. His numbers are all in range and trending similar. I've texted to check in, and Ian said everything's fine.

More than fine.

"Will you make my wedding cake? That style is perfect for us."

"Oh..." I might as well be standing under a spotlight. Mom's at the front counter, and I know she can hear us talking.

"We would pay you, obviously," Hope rushes to reassure me. "I'm not asking for free cake. Whatever your rate is, I know it's worth it. We haven't set a date yet, but you're going to be the first person I call when we do."

"The audacity," Wren says from across the bakery.

See? No privacy in here.

"Don't tell Wren," Hope says in a loud stage whisper.

"I guess I'm in the market for a new best friend," Wren says. "Maybe I can join Ada and Isabel's book club."

"I'd go with you to that," Hope returns. "I need to know what they're reading."

"It's all smut," Wren declares. Mom tsks at her, but she's unrepentant. "You know it's true."

Mom apparently has no argument.

Hope keeps watching me, waiting for her answer. Will I make her wedding cake? To quote August: *duh*. I'll be thrilled to be part of her big day with Griffin in any way I can.

"Obviously, I will make your wedding cake for you," I tell her.

She grins, all happy sparkles, no doubt imagining herself getting married to her favorite handyman. They're achingly happy, and I love it for them.

A bell rings on her side of the pass-through, and she backs away into her shop. "We'll set aside time later to talk cakes!"

I return to the front counter, the giddiness of another wedding cake order tempered by Mom's apprehensive look. This is what makes it tough. She's not mean. She doesn't tell me I don't know what I'm doing, or that she hates my cakes, or that I'm a failure. She's *worried* about me—about all of us—and that's so much harder to argue with.

"I was always going to make Hope's wedding cake if she asked." A preemptive explanation seems like the best move here. I'm going to make the cake for her engagement party, too, but Mom will figure that out when she sees it.

"I don't have any problem with that," Mom says.

The *but* is implied. I hate implied buts.

Wren and I share a look. Waiting.

"It's so much extra work for you to take on," she finally continues. "I worry about you sacrificing time with August. That's all."

Her "that's all" is a mountain of guilt. Wren hung out with August so I could get everything done for the Moonlight Lodge couple's wedding cake. He loved spending extra time with his aunt, but he wasn't with me. Should he have been?

I want to fight back. Point out that I have to step up as August's mother *and* father. And I pay for everything. His up-to-date monitor and pump? They're not cheap. That extra money goes a long way to cover what insurance doesn't for his insulin and medical supplies.

And maybe I want to admit I need something for myself, too.

But Mom doesn't need to hear it—she lived it.

"You were a single mom, too."

"Yes." She straightens the napkin dispenser on the counter. It's her tell she doesn't want to have this conversation, and I hate the sense of déjà vu it gives me. I am she. She is me. "And I relied on your grandparents with you girls. They're gone now, so it's just us. We have to make the best decisions we can for our family."

Ugh. The scent of guilt in this room is overpowering. She's doling it out, and I'm soaking it up like a sponge. I love our family and our business. I don't ever want to jeopardize any part of it. And I hate that she thinks I might.

"I won't do anything that would negatively impact August or our family."

Mom squeezes my shoulder, her smile like someone offering condolences to the bereaved. "I know you won't, sweetheart."

We don't say it, but we're agreeing I won't pursue my wedding cake business. We'll maintain the status quo. I'll be happy with my occasional special orders, and that's it.

Disappointment curls and expands inside me like it's trying to fill in all my cracks. It's no less than I expected. Doesn't mean it doesn't hurt.

Her phone pings, and she startles out of her sorrowful encouragement. "That's Hans with the fruit delivery. I'll be in the back if you need me."

Wren and I stare at each other a long moment after she's gone. Trying to find the right words.

"This is some bull—"

I shush her as if August is close enough to overhear.

She glares. "You know it is. You can't pursue your own dreams? What about me? Can I chase mine, or is that forbidden, too?"

"What are your dreams?" Other than wanting to finally move out of the family home, Wren doesn't ever talk like she's missing out on something.

"I don't know, but I'd like the freedom to have them if they ever make an appearance." She slumps against the back counter, arms crossed over her chest. "You're a good mom to August. It's not fair to use him against you like this."

"She's trying to help me be practical."

Wren snorts. "You don't need help with that. Being practical is your whole deal. You need a shove into the *im*practical."

I would love to argue, but I am self-aware enough to know I'd be a raging liar if I did.

She sighs, making a show of cracking her knuckles and stretching her neck side to side. "I guess that's what I'm here for. I think you should open your own cake shop."

My gaze goes straight to the swinging door that leads to the back, as if Mom's as bad as Wren and is listening in. "I never even suggested that."

"You should. Have you researched it?"

I scan the bakery, hoping against hope someone will walk in to interrupt this conversation. "No."

Lies. I've looked at prices on storefronts, industrial ovens and refrigerators, website designers, the works. I've even spent more hours than I had to spare playing with logo ideas for Tess's Cakes.

Not the best name but good enough for a completely imaginary shop.

"Then you should. Get serious about it. Write up a business plan for a loan. Tour buildings with Hope's mom. Don't give up."

"I can't do this right now, Wren." I can't talk about starting my own business when Mom's in the next room. I can't seriously entertain the idea anyway. The status quo is where I thrive. Not in taking risks and trying new things. "Please."

"Fine. Tell me about the Ian situation."

I'm ready to launch into my default "there is no Ian situation" when a customer walks through the bakery door. *Finally*. I exhale audibly, relieved I neither have to lie nor admit any part of the awkward truth.

Like...*the Ian situation is he's currently my fill-in babysitter, hanging out with August as we speak, and one back yard has never been the source of so much bonding before, and I'm afraid that every sweet thing he does just corkscrews him deeper into my heart, but I don't actually know what to do with him once he's in there.*

Best to keep that to myself and just talk about fictional cake stores.

TWENTY-FIVE
IAN

I THOUGHT sprinting around in the back yard with Dutch half the day would wear the kid out, but that turned out to be a pipe dream. It's like activity only ramps him up with more energy than he had before. He's a tiny perpetual motion machine.

Enjoy it while it lasts, kid. One day, you'll be thirty-six and exhausted after a few hours of babysitting. I'm not complaining, though. We're having fun. It's not the kind of socializing Amy was trying to get me to do, but it counts for something.

He comes onto the patio to pick over the afternoon snack options every now and then. I set out grapes—cut in half, which never seemed necessary until today—pretzels, and cheese sticks. I'm keeping tabs on his apps, and all his numbers look good.

It's a bummer the kid has a medical condition like this, but diabetes care has come a long way in the last decade or so. He's not doing finger pricks all day or injecting himself with insulin for every meal. He's just a regular kid.

I do not think about how Tess treats me like a "regular guy," prosthetic leg and all. But I'd be lying if I said I didn't like how it's a non-issue for her. Or if I said I haven't thought about her breathy "I like the way you look in shorts" comment approximately seventy-five times a day.

I set down August's phone and pick up mine, swiping over to my text messages with her.

> Tess: On a break and checking in
>
> Tess: Is A giving you any trouble?

> Ian: He beat me at Candy Land
>
> Ian: Sang a whole song about it
>
> Ian: Seems a little much, but otherwise we're good

> Tess: He likes to win
>
> Tess: I think you share that

> Ian: I always win
>
> Ian: When I want something badly enough

The three dots appeared and disappeared twice before her response finally came through.

> Tess: It's the pirate in you

> Ian: Arr

Yes. I've been reduced to "*arr-ing*" at the woman. Twice now. Like a scurvy-riddled lunatic.

August flops into the chair across from me. "Do you like honey?"

My thoughts go straight to Tess trickling golden honey into her coffee this morning. I've always thought it too sweet, but I would very much like to taste honey off her lips.

Only a pirate would think about something like that right in front of her child. Still. I'm not sure I've ever wanted anything more.

"I don't mind it," I tell him.

He scratches the side of his face, leaving a trail of dirt. "I like honey, but I don't like bees. And Mama says we have to have bees to get honey."

"This is true. They put a lot of work in to make that honey." Although, if he knew exactly how bees make honey, he might not like it as much. Steven told me about *bee vomit* when I was nine, and I didn't eat the stuff again until well into adulthood.

"What else makes stuff?" August kicks his feet back and forth, his wide blue eyes stuck on me.

"Hmm. Cows make milk."

He lights up like I'm helping him solve world hunger. "Yeah, cows!"

"Chickens lay eggs." This game is surprisingly hard.

"I like eggs."

I snap my fingers. "We shear sheep to get wool."

He seems less impressed with that one. "What else?"

I'm running out of ideas that aren't just animal parts. Talking about ivory and leather doesn't really seem kid-friendly. "I can't think of any more."

"What about monkeys?"

I have to think for a second. "What do we get from monkeys?"

"Wrenches!" He bursts into laughter, revealing his gap-toothed grin.

I sure like to hear him laugh. "That's a pretty good joke."

"Max told me that one in Kindergarten."

"You already finished Kindergarten? Wow."

He nods, his little chest puffed up. "I'm going into first grade this year. After I turn six on July six. Isn't that funny? Six on the sixth."

It is funny, for more reasons than he knows. "July sixth is my birthday, too."

His eyes go as wide as saucers. "No lie?"

"No lie. But I'll turn a few years older than you will."

He laughs again. "A *lot* more years."

Harsh, kid.

"We can share a birthday party!"

Something soft and warm seems to fill my chest at his generous offer. "What are you doing for your party?"

"We're going to the park and we're going to have games and water balloons and dinosaurs everywhere and Mama's going to make my cake. Strawberry, because that's my favorite."

"Sounds like fun. Maybe I can just visit your party." I haven't done much of anything for my birthday in too long, but his excitement almost makes me want to join him and see what it's all about.

His little face turns serious. "We can't share presents, though."

I pretend to pout. "What if I like dinosaurs?"

He seems to consider. "Maybe I could share one present with you."

"It's okay, pal. I'm just teasing. Your presents are all yours."

"You can come to Fourth Fest with us, too! There's a parade where they throw candy at little kids, and at night, fireworks! You can come be with Mama and me."

"Maybe we should see what your Mama thinks of your plans first."

I probably shouldn't be making plans for birthdays and holidays with them without her input. Even if I'm ready to RSVP to his invite right now.

My phone rings on the patio table. Pierce. I'd avoid it, given where I am and all, but I suspect this is an important call.

"I have to take this, okay?"

"Okay." August slides off his chair and heads to the flower bed where he's stashed his trucks.

I step to the opposite end of the patio. "Pierce?"

"I caught you. Good." He sounds wrung out, which confirms my suspicions. "I'm a dad! Bonnie delivered our baby girl this morning."

"Congratulations. I'm happy for you." I truly am. I've never heard him sound quite this overjoyed. Other than on his wedding day, when he was also a little dazed and in awe of his luck. "What's her name?"

"Ophelia James. Seven pounds, seventeen inches long."

"I have no idea what those stats mean. Big baby? Small?"

"So tiny. With perfect little fingers and toes. She's got an impressive amount of hair on her head, too."

"Red?" We all inherited red hair from our dad. Mine's the darkest, Steven the lightest, and Pierce more of a pale red-brown. Bonnie's had her fingers crossed for a ginger baby since they met.

"No luck this time."

I won't point out he's already leaving the door open for another baby when they just had their first hours ago. It's actually kind of cute. In a sickeningly sweet way.

But sweet's been growing on me lately.

August runs up to me and taps my arm. "Ian? Can I watch a show?"

"Sure, buddy. I'll be in in a minute."

He dashes toward their apartment, saying goodbye to Dutch at the door. I wasn't sure Tess would appreciate him in her house all day, so we've played with him out here. Probably best to only spread dog hair after he's been invited in.

"Who was that?" Pierce wants to know. "And don't say the TV again. I'm not stupid. That's a little kid you're talking to."

I'm still not sure I want to share any part of this with my brothers. Then again, he did just tell me some of the best news of his life. Seems only fair. "That's Tess's son, August."

"Who is Tess?"

"My neighbor." The angel next door I can't get out of my head. But I'm not sure I'm even trying anymore.

"I haven't slept in twenty-seven hours, but I feel like I'm missing something."

I quickly explain about Tess's daycare shutdown and my offer to step in for a few days.

He seems to process this slower than normal. "So...you're babysitting. For your neighbor."

I don't like the way he says it so laced with judgment. I'm not sure just what he's judging, but it's probably me.

"I'm her manny," I tell him.

He barks a laugh. "I must have called the wrong number. This is Ian Vaughn, right? Notorious climber, guide to celebrities, and absolute attention hog is a...manny?"

"It's not that funny." I don't like the defensiveness in my tone, but I hate the incredulousness in his. "She needed help, so I'm helping. Is that such a shock?"

"Actually—"

"Forget I asked." I don't need a reminder of how unfamiliar this is for me. Not helping Tess out—I like to think I was always there for my friends who needed me in the past. But I never said Tess was just my friend. And I'm not sure I want her to be *just* anything.

"Is this something serious?" he asks, his mirth subdued with the weighty question.

I hesitate. I haven't had anything serious in...maybe ever. Nothing quite like this. Which is absurd to say, given that Tess and I *are* only friends. We're not dating. We haven't even kissed, much less considered anything more.

Well. I've *considered* more quite often. But that's not the point.

I sit with his question. And I offer Pierce the most honest answer I can.

"I don't know. But I'd like it to be."

TWENTY-SIX

TESS

LITTLE KID LAUGHTER has got to be the best sound in the world. Innocent and infectious, they laugh with their whole bodies, throwing everything into their enjoyment at top volume. August's laughter draws me through my apartment to the back door. I crack it open and bask in my little boy's giggles.

He's seated across from Ian at our patio table, coloring books and crayons spread out between them. Dutch is sunning himself nearby, flopped over on his side.

"Where do cows go on Friday nights?" Ian asks.

August's already grinning. I get the feeling they've been doing this for a while. "Where?"

"To the moo-vies."

August erupts in fresh laughter, his cheeks pink. "Another!"

Ian seems to think. "What kind of dinosaurs sleep a lot?"

"Dream-o-saurs!" August guesses.

"That's a good one," Ian says. "I was thinking of dino-snores!"

Once again, August laughs like this is the best thing in the world, his belly laugh echoing through the yard.

Ian catches me spying on them from the doorway. His

expression brightens, his mouth curves upward, and I think my heart performs a complete cartwheel.

Oh hello, sunshine Ian.

"Tess. Welcome home."

He doesn't mean it in some fantasy, "Welcome back to our shared home" situation. He's stating the obvious, that's all. But the greeting does something funny to me anyway, twining with his smile and August's giggles to create a warm hug I want to burrow into.

"Mama!" August waves. "Ian's telling jokes. I told you he was funny. Now tell one for Mama, Ian."

I join them on the patio and drop into an empty chair at the table.

Ian looks me over like he's sizing me up, trying to figure out the best joke for me. "How about I help you tell her one?"

August agrees, so Ian leans closer to whisper in his ear. It must be a good one because August starts giggling before he can even repeat it.

"I hope you know CPR." More giggles. "Because you take my breath away!"

August drops his head to the metal tabletop as if that joke is the height of comedy.

"A little EMT humor?" I ask Ian.

His gaze never leaves me. "Something like that. How was your day?"

"My sense of smell is fried from all the key lime pies we're making this week, but it's good." I smell the same tart scent everywhere I go now. An occupational hazard in my line of work.

"I like lime pie," August tells me.

I lean closer to run my hand over his pale, soft hair. "You like everything sweet. How was your day here?"

"Great!" he says. "We played games and washed Dutch, and we walked on the trail!"

"You were busy." I shift my attention to Ian, who hasn't stopped watching me since he spotted me in the doorway. "How are you holding up? Tired?"

His eyes sparkle at me. "Sounds like you expect me to wave the white flag and surrender already."

I'm honestly relieved that wasn't the first thing out of his mouth. *Welcome home. I quit.* I guess I should have had a little more faith in his dedication to the challenge.

I will *not* think about him possibly being dedicated to anything else.

"I read somewhere that babysitting kids is twice as hard as climbing mountains," I tell him.

He narrows his eyes on me, looking as stern as he did the day I first pulled up to this place. It's messed up that his glower makes my stomach tumble, right? But there it goes, dipping and swooping like a kite caught in a draft.

"Your source is wrong," he says. "It's three times as hard."

He breaks his teasing scowl, but not our eye contact.

"No unexpected questions, I hope?" I'm not prepared to tell August about the birds and the bees tonight. I need some kind of kid-friendly book to help me out, at least.

"Only about my freckles."

"He said a fairy painted them on him at night when he was a little boy," August pipes up. "The Freckle Fairy."

"She ran out of freckle juice when she was done with me." Ian runs a hand over one freckle-covered arm. From the memory of him shirtless that's seared on my mind, he's covered in them. "Had to start painting spots on ladybugs instead."

"You're silly." Judging by his grin, August is a big fan of the sillies. He whips his head around to me. "Mama, can Ian have dinner with us?"

"Ian's probably tired and needs a break," I answer before he can turn his request into a whole thing. I don't want to impose on Ian more than we already have today.

But he glances away, a hint of his genuine scowl returning. I thought I was giving him an easy out, but it doesn't look like the prospect of being alone appeals to him the same way it once did.

"Unless you want to stay for dinner," I add. "I'm thinking tacos, nothing special. But you're welcome to join us. If you want."

He looks from August, who's already cheering, to me. "I like tacos."

To be honest, I cheer a little, too.

We go inside to the soundtrack of August's shouts of triumph. He opts to stay on the patio to work on his coloring, so I leave the back door open. Dutch shifts positions to follow his sunbeam but doesn't come inside.

Ian waits for me in the kitchen. "What do you want me to do?"

"You don't have to help with dinner. You can just sit and relax if you're tired, and I'll—"

He stalks closer to me. "Angel, if you keep accusing me of being tired, I'll throw you over my shoulder and set you outside with August while *I* make dinner."

If I'm a tiny bit frozen and struggling to come up with a response, it's because this man just called me *angel* while offering to make dinner for us. Also, he thinks going full pirate and tossing me over his shoulder is a deterrent? It just went onto my top ten romantic fantasies list. Which I created five seconds ago specifically to put that on it.

"I'm tempted," I finally admit.

"Believe me," he says, voice low. "I am, too."

Reluctantly, I break our stare down. We'll never have dinner if we stand around eyeing each other all night. The monitor and insulin pump make August's mealtimes easier, but I still like to keep to a routine as much as I can.

"How about you brown the meat?" I grab the ground beef from the fridge, find a pan in the cupboard, and hand Ian a spatula from the container on the counter. "I'll prep the veggies."

We work side by side in the kitchen until the air grows heavy with the scent of cooking meat and warm spices. I've prepped small bowls filled with lettuce, cheese, and avocado, and laid a platter of sliced fruit on the table. Now and then, his arm brushes mine, but neither of us shifts to give ourselves more space.

"Any progress with your mom and your cake business?"

I keep my eyes trained on the tomatoes I'm chopping. "I'll keep doing special orders on the side."

"So nothing's changing?"

It's just a statement of fact, not a judgment call, but it still stings like a rebuke. *Nothing's changing* could be the title of my autobiography. Just ride out the same old, same old until the end of time.

Am I really willing to accept that?

And how far am I willing to go if I'm not?

"I already owe Mom and Wren so much, I can't turn around and ask for more. I don't want to be greedy."

Mom has carried on like we never had the conversation about expanding Blackbird's menu to offer my cakes. Wren, of course, brings it up in subtle side-eyes and not-so-subtle remarks at every opportunity. I'm stuck in the middle trying to keep the peace. Mostly with myself.

"Angel, wanting something for yourself doesn't make you greedy. It makes you human. Pretending that you don't want it won't satisfy. Your unhappiness will eat you up."

"I'm not unhappy making pies and cupcakes." I remind

myself of that every day. I'm lucky to have a good job and a comfortable income. I have a strong support system, and excellent care for August. Not every single parent can say the same.

"Would you be happier making custom cakes?"

That's the question, isn't it? "I think so."

"Then isn't a little risk worth it?"

"Says someone who has climbed literal mountains."

"What would it take to start up your own place?" he asks.

"My own bakery?" I have thought about it, even if I don't like to share as much with Wren. But knowing doesn't make anything easier. "I'd need premises in a decent location, and those aren't cheap, even here. Best case scenario, it's already set up with industrial appliances, worst case, I have to buy all that. It could be anywhere from twenty-five to fifty thousand dollars."

That number alone sends a chill through me. Leaving Mom and Wren to go out on my own, putting August's future on the line, all for my own hopes and dreams? That's ice water in my veins.

"So either I get Mom on board one day, or I stop dreaming about a custom cake shop." My laugh sounds awfully fake.

"What if you had an investor?"

"I don't know anyone that irresponsible with their money." I have some savings, but not nearly the amount it would take to get an entire bakery off the ground. And I could never throw it all into a business anyway. Rainy day funds are for emergencies, not fantasies.

"You're not a bad investment, angel," he says softly.

As intensely as he's watching me, I don't think he's only talking about my business. It's hard to believe someone could see me like that when I literally had a man run away from commitment with me. But Ian's not running. He's being patient, letting me inch closer to him.

Honestly, that makes me nervous, too.

"I don't know if I'm ready," I finally say. I don't think I'm only talking about my business, either.

"You'll know what to do when you are."

Right. Take a little risk. Not my strong suit on any front.

"I got some good news today," he says after a minute. "I'm an uncle."

I lay down my knife on the cutting board. "For the first time?"

He nods, turns off the burner under the seasoned meat, and pulls his phone from his pocket. Swiping it open, he turns it toward me, revealing a small pink bundle, eyes shut tight, the fingers of one little hand splayed across their face.

"Ophelia James. My oldest brother, Pierce, is out of his head with happiness." Glancing at the picture, his expression softens before he tucks his phone away again.

"That's a lot of hair. August was a little cueball."

He chuckles. "They're trying to contain their disappointment she didn't inherit our red hair."

Oh, no. I can't start imagining sweet little redheaded babies. I'll want to do a whole lot more than *inch* toward him if I get that idea stuck in my brain.

"She's beautiful," I tell him.

"I should probably send a gift, right? I don't know what's appropriate for a newborn."

"You've never had a friend have a baby before?"

"I'm not sure any of my friends are ready for that." He catches my incredulous stare. "What?"

"You're almost forty."

His mouth thins. "I'm thirty-six, angel."

Loving this new nickname.

"And your brother is...?"

He seems to concede the point. "Forty-five. But he's not an irresponsible playboy or anything like that. He was preoccupied with our business before Bonnie came along and changed his priorities."

A braver woman would dive in and ask what Ian's priorities are. But I'm skilled at keeping my feet on dry land. "If you need help with baby presents, I have some suggestions of places to shop in town."

"I welcome any and all suggestions."

"*The Painted Daisy* would be my first stop. It's the gift shop right next door to the bakery. My friend, Hope, sells all sorts of handmade things there. She usually has a good selection of baby stuff."

"Baby stuff like...?"

I can tell his mind is spinning with everything from diapers to pacifiers. It's kind of cute that he has no clue. He wants to learn, at least.

I rest my hand on his warm, delightfully firm shoulder. "How about I help you pick some things out one day this week?"

He breathes a sigh of relief. "This is why you're an angel."

If he keeps calling me that, I might not be for long.

TWENTY-SEVEN
IAN

"IS AVOCADO A FRUIT OR A VEGETABLE?" August asks.

If I hadn't just spent the day with him, I might be alarmed at how quickly his train of thought swerves in new directions. He just asked Tess how sour cream is made, and after a surprisingly detailed explanation, he's switched gears to the avocado slices he left on his plate.

"It's a fruit," she says. "Its pit is on the inside like an apple or a peach."

He holds a round slice of banana in his fingers. "What's a banana? It doesn't have seeds."

"It's a fruit, too. See all those the tiny black spots? Those are the seeds."

He seems to think about this. "Pumpkins have seeds on the inside."

She nods earnestly. "They're fruits, too."

August laughs. "No they're not!"

To be honest, I share his doubts.

"It's true," she says. "So are the tomatoes in your taco."

"Cucumbers have seeds on the inside."

I can't tell if August is trying to win the argument or just coming up with more vegetables that might be fruits.

She dips her head at him, eyebrows raised. "They're fruits, too."

"I'm so confused right now," I mutter.

"Vegetables are leaves, roots, and stems," she explains, possibly to both of us. "Like lettuce, potatoes, and asparagus."

August makes a yuck face. "I like fruit best."

"I know you do. If you're done with dinner, put your plate on the counter, please."

He hops up and takes care of his plate as asked, then dashes into his room. Some noisy toy starts up, the soundtrack to my day here. I might need a Tylenol. Or five.

Tess's gaze hits mine as if I said that out loud. "Are you sure you want to endure this for two more days?"

I level her with a hard look. That's barely a step up from asking me if I'm tired. "It's not a problem."

Pretty sure she thinks I'll see August as something she's saddled with instead of the sweet, exuberant kid he is. Is that how the other men she's dated have viewed him?

That question sits like asphalt in my gut. I don't want to think about her with other men. Especially anyone stupid enough to let her go.

I stand to take both of our empty plates to the counter. Her mouth drops open, and I know she's about to protest—it's too much, she can handle it, I need a rest. I give her another stern look and start putting the dirty dishes in the dishwasher. She doesn't have to do everything by herself.

I'd lecture her on that, but I'm pretty sure that would make me a hypocrite.

So we clean up together, setting her kitchen to rights. I scrape the grease out of the frying pan I used and get it sudsy.

We put the leftovers in the fridge and clean the counters. It's domestic and simple, but natural, too.

When we're finished, we lean against the kitchen counter side by side. She dries her hands on a dish towel and passes it to me.

"Thank you for this. For staying for dinner, for helping clean up. Thank you for everything."

The thought comes crystal clear—I don't want her to thank me for any of those things. I want them to be a normal part of our days, not something she thinks she owes me for. I'm not sure where the thought comes from since I've never had that with anyone before. But she makes me want to try.

"You don't have to thank me. It's my pleasure, Tess."

She rests her hands on either side of her hips on the counter behind her. "It's nice to have it be more than just August and me. We're used to communal living, since we were with my mom and sister for so long."

She winces, as if wishing she hadn't revealed that.

"What's that face for?" I ask.

"It's kind of pathetic, isn't it? Living with my family at my age."

I tilt my head closer. "You're not that old."

A wicked smile touches her mouth. "True. Compared to some people."

Tease me about my age all you want, angel.

"Living with family is nothing to be ashamed of. Some people do it to save money, some people's parents need their help. Sometimes it's just the cultural norm. It doesn't mean you're somehow failing."

"Thanks." That soft word is barely a whisper. Once again, she's thanking me for something I want to do naturally.

"And you're here now," I say to lighten this pressing, aching sensation under my ribs. "You've got your own place, even if the neighbors are less than desirable."

"Aw. My neighbor's not so bad. Even if he could stand to smile a little more."

I mirror her pose, resting my hands on the counter behind us, letting my pinky and ring finger drape over hers. I have never been a man to think much about something as simple as touching fingers, but with Tess, that contact is a bright spotlight drawing all my attention.

"I think he has new reasons to smile," I tell her.

She holds my gaze, letting the moment drag out. The urge to lean in becomes a tangible thing, like a hand on my back pressing me closer. The need to kiss her and let my fantasies melt into a perfect reality overwhelms. But with Tess, it's more important for me to get things *right* than to get them *now*. I can be patient.

I think I can, anyway. I've never really tried before.

"Look at this!" August runs into the kitchen, paper in hand.

Tess shifts away just enough to break our small connection. In the grand scheme of things, a touch is nothing. Insignificant. But that one? I'll carry it around with me for days.

He shows us a crayon drawing of a jack-o-lantern with green and yellow things coming out of the top. "It's a pumpkin-cucumber-banana fruit!"

"I love it, buddy," Tess says. "It's getting late, though. Are you ready for stories?"

He slumps a bit, as if he doesn't appreciate this news. "Can Ian read me my stories tonight?"

They both turn to look at me. It should be obvious to Tess I've never been asked to read anyone their bedtime stories before. Is the little glow of pride that he'd even ask me just as obvious?

"I don't know," Tess hedges. "Ian might be getting tired—"

"That's it. August, grab your books." I shift Tess around so she's facing me, then bend over and notch her waist at my shoulder. I straighten, lifting her in the air, and I'm not sure who shrieks louder, her or August. I march her into the living room, one hand on her thigh, the other at her hip on my shoulder, searing the feel of her into my synapses.

Her hands on my back are just the icing on the cake.

When I deposit her on the couch, she lands with a soft *oomph*. Her cheeks are rosy, but her mouth's still open, indignant.

"I gave you fair warning." I drop onto the cushion next to her.

"I will remember the magic word," she finally says.

She doesn't specify that she won't use it again. Good.

"You carried Mama." August's standing in the middle of the living room, staring at me. "You must be really strong."

Tess makes a soft sound, crossing her arms over her stomach. As if there's a single part of her I wouldn't worship if she let me.

"Your mama's very light," I tell him. "Where are your books?"

"Oh!" He darts into his bedroom and returns again seconds later, a stack in hand.

To my surprise, he crawls into my lap instead of Tess's. He settles on my right thigh, leaning against my chest like he's been here a dozen times before.

I've stood on top of mountain peaks. I've had week-long camping trips with A-list celebrities. I've pushed my body to its limits in pursuit of records and accolades. But this small child sitting in my lap feels like a personal best.

Tess watches us with an expression I can't name. Whatever it is, it's as significant as August's sweet trust.

"This one's funny," August says, grabbing one from the

stack he'd given Tess. He rests his head on my shoulder. "Will you read it?"

I read them all. I even do silly voices to make them both laugh. With every book, the warmth blooming in my heart grows until I'm steeped in it. This moment doesn't belong to me, I'm only too aware. But I'm going to hold onto it for as long as I can.

TWENTY-EIGHT
TESS

THE SECOND DAY Ian fills in as August's babysitter, I arrive home to them working in the kitchen, both wearing aprons. Sugar canisters and baking ingredients are spread out across the countertops, along with cookie sheets, measuring cups, and extra mixing spoons. Flour coats everything in a fine dust like ash after a volcanic eruption.

The Type A in me wants to start cleaning immediately. My softer side wants to just memorize this moment.

"What's going on here?"

They turn around to face me. August has a streak of flour across his forehead and one cheek like he tried to follow a contouring video but got it all wrong. Ian's equally covered in flour, the streaks in his beard making him look almost as wild as he did the day we first met. But he's got a glimmer of mischief in his eyes he sure didn't have then.

He points a finger at August. "Blame the kid."

"Mama! We wanted to make cookies for you, so Ian found a recipe and we followed it exactly!" August's bouncing on his heels, a cookie scoop raised in the air. "We're bakers just like you!"

He runs to the table and plucks a cookie from a cooling rack. "Try it, Mama."

I'm still stuck on Ian wearing my pink frilly apron with his red hair tied up in a bun. The two sights clash so much, I can't tell if I want to laugh or take a picture and set it as my phone's wallpaper. But August's watching me sweetly, waiting for approval. Obviously, I'm going to eat the cookie. I take a bite and am pleasantly surprised to find they achieved classic chocolate-chip-cookie perfection.

"Isn't it good?" he says.

"So yummy!" I high-five him and come away with a sticky hand. "You guys did a great job."

"We shared a cookie to test our work," Ian tells me. It's a small thing, but the hint he hasn't been letting August gorge himself on sweets is reassuring.

"I'm impressed." I know how easy it is to forget steps and ingredients when you've got a small helper.

"My plan was to finish and clean up before you got home." Ian must catch the way I'm cataloguing the mess, trying to contain my freak out. "But we had a small setback."

"Our first batch of cookies is in the garbage can." August gleefully points at the stainless steel container in the corner.

I step farther into the kitchen, one eyebrow raised. "The garbage can, huh?"

Ian shares a look with August. "I thought we were going to keep that between us."

"Oops." August giggles over his eager confession.

"What happened to the first try?" A dozen scenarios dance through my head. I've had a lot of experience with failed bakes.

"The butter was too soft—"

"It melted!" August cuts in.

"The cookies spread everywhere." Ian ticks his head to the side. "And we added too much salt. They're raccoon food now."

"Our bandit friends had better get their dinners somewhere else." I put the lid on the flour canister intending to get a head start on the clean up while they finish baking the last of the dough, but Ian puts his hand over mine.

"This is our mess. We've got this."

"Your helper will probably give up on cleaning after five minutes," I whisper. August has turned his attention back to scooping out balls of dough and dropping them willy-nilly on the baking sheet.

"I can handle it." Ian's warm hand on mine tightens, his voice dropping into his *I mean business* register. "Go sit down and relax. I thought I'd make dinner, too, if you don't mind hamburgers."

"Dinner *and* dessert? I can help—"

"Not this time." He shifts his hand around mine until his thumb brushes the inside of my wrist. If this is his signature move, I'm all for it. "Let us take care of you."

His words curl around me like the coziest sweater, even as his thumb at my wrist sends a shiver down my spine. I don't know how to sit back and let someone else take over. Other than Mom and Wren, nobody's ever offered.

But Ian makes me want to let go. Just a little.

"Okay," I finally concede. "I will sit down. But first—"

It feels like a crime to pull my hand from his, but I have a goal. I lift both my hands to his face and gently rake my fingers through his short whiskers. A few gray hairs glimmer among the red. "You have flour in your beard."

We've barely touched since I wound up in his arms a few nights ago after the raccoon incident. It might be a flimsy one, but I'll take any excuse I can get.

I dust off his beard long after it's clean. This close, the fire in his eyes is melting all my defenses. I want to bask in it like a sun-warmed cat.

"There," I say when I can no longer reasonably justify touching him. "The flour's gone."

Without breaking eye contact, he reaches behind me, runs his fingers through the small flour pile on the counter, and drags his hand over his beard. His eyebrows quirk.

That little move sends heat coiling through my belly. One part command, one part plea, he's telling me what he wants. I'm not bold enough for that.

But I can follow directions.

I run my fingers through his beard again, shaking out the fresh spots of flour. Scraping my nails lightly over his jaw. Tracing the smile lines framing his mouth. I want to explore the freckles coating his face like an explorer mapping uncharted waters, but for now, I can be content with surveying his whiskers and jaw.

"Is this enough dough?" August asks behind him.

Right. Because I am not, in fact, alone here with no objective in life beyond fondling Ian's beard.

"I'll check, buddy," Ian says. His hands come to my hips, and he walks me back a step. "Rest."

After touching him all over his face? Not likely. But I do as told and sit on the couch in the living room. Breathing slowly, I will my rocketing pulse to calm back down. Close proximity to Ian Vaughn makes it impossible.

The way the apartment is laid out, I can't see them from here, but August's questions and Ian's gentle answers as they finish up the cookies carry to me. I stretch out on the couch and rest my head on a throw pillow, smiling over their conversation.

"Have you ever been arrested?" August wants to know.

Note to self: work on his "asking appropriate questions" skills.

"Never. Have you?"

August giggles. "No. But I met the sheriff the other day. He was nice to me and Nana."

A few weeks ago, I wouldn't have thought anything of it. Sunshine is a small town, and you're bound to run into the mayor or a town council member on any random day out. But now, I suspect the sheriff was more than just *nice* to Mom.

And really, good for her. From everything I've seen, Daniel O'Grady seems like a decent guy. Handsome, too, even if I prefer redheaded mountain climbers...

"Angel?"

I open my eyes to find Ian hovering over me, one hand lightly touching my shoulder.

"I guess I fell asleep." I stretch like a cat across the couch and sit up again. "I didn't snore, did I?"

"Tiny bit."

"Ugh." I drag my palms over my face. "You're not supposed to know about that yet."

His eyebrows hitch up to his hairline.

Clearly, coming home from work was a bad idea all around. With any luck, I'm still asleep, and this is just a nightmare. I lightly pinch my forearm. Nothing.

"I meant to say at all. Ever. You will never know about that." Definitely making things better, Tess.

He holds a hand out to me. Reluctantly, I slip mine into his, and he helps pull me to standing. We are way too close like this, practically pressed together, but he doesn't back away.

"I can live with *yet*," he says. "Come on. Dinner's ready."

My thrill over the promising possibility of yet is tempered by the reminder I'm behind schedule. "I have to give August an insulin bolus for his meal first."

"Already did it. Double checked his numbers and plugged in the values."

"Oh. Thank you." August's blood glucose numbers are the

never-ending background noise in my head. Sometimes, they're accompanied by alarms, both figurative and literal. Too high, too low, pump out of insulin, one of the cannulas has come loose—no day is ever completely free of a minor complication.

The best days, they're *only* minor.

He tilts his head to the side. "August did it all, anyway. I just supervised."

We go into the kitchen, which has undergone a miraculous transformation. The supplies from their baking extravaganza have been put away, the surfaces shiny and pristine. The only evidence of their afternoon fun is the plastic container full of cookies on the counter.

"Wow. It looks better in here than it did when I left this morning."

He side-eyes me. "That's because I got a solid five minutes of work out of my helper."

"Told you."

He leads me through the open back door to the patio table, already laid out with our dinner. There's a fat, juicy hamburger topped with a slice of cheese on each plate, condiments, and a bowl of watermelon chunks in the center of the table.

August sits in his chair, his plate already served up. "I watched Dutch! He didn't sneak a bite."

The dog's right next to the table, eyes locked on the food like a fluffy shark waiting to strike.

"You did good, kid." Ian ruffles August's hair as he passes him.

This can't be the same man who glared at us when we first pulled up to the duplex a few weeks ago. Yet here he sits, ready to eat a meal he made for us after spending all day with August. He's not fully smiling, but the slant to his mouth tells me he's inching closer.

Inching closer. I don't mind the theme.

August tells me about his day while we eat. My kid loves a good recap. He goes into detail about the games they played, the Lego buildings they made, the stories Ian read to him.

I'm sorry I missed that part...and also should probably never see it again. Watching August snuggle up in Ian's lap last night was like a too-tight bear hug—cozy and warm, but it left me hurting in unexpected places, too. Everything I want mixed with everything I'm afraid of.

And the silly voices? I had no idea a man reading tongue-twister rhymes in an affected British accent would be so attractive.

"Ian, what's your favorite kind of cake?" August asks, switching gears.

Ian seems to need a second to catch up. "Lemon, I guess."

August turns his big blue eyes my way. "Mama, can you make us a strawberry-lemon cake for our birthday next week? We're going to share a party."

Now I'm the one left behind. "You're sharing a what now?"

"We have the same birthday! July sixth. Ian said he wanted to share my presents, but I think maybe we should just share a cake." August shoots him a look like he wants to be sure Ian's okay with that. "Strawberry-lemon would be good. Can you make that?"

"Your birthday is really the sixth?" I ask Ian.

"It is."

Fate? Kismet? Or sheer dumb luck?

"So fun for you, turning forty."

His eyes sparkle at me in the evening sun. "Flirt."

"My best friend, Jake, will be there, and friends from my Kindergarten class," August tells him. "We can invite your friends, too!"

"Oh." Ian's sudden frown is a stark contrast to August's enthusiasm. "That's sweet, kid, but we don't need to do that."

He's already admitted he hasn't really tried to get to know anyone in Sunshine beyond his aunts and August and me. Honestly, from everything Amy told me about him before we moved in, he hasn't spent much time with them, either. But even turning thirty-seven, nobody wants to sit at home by themselves.

Ian won't be alone for his birthday. Not on my watch.

"What if we have August's party with his friends in the park, and then we have a barbecue here in the evening?" I offer. "We can invite Ian's aunts and my mom and Wren. Maybe a few other friends. We'll celebrate you both together."

August is all for it, as I knew he would be. But Ian's vote is the deciding factor. He's watching me like he's looking for a trap. Smart. I'm definitely planning one. My encouraging smile is maybe too obvious. If he's against even this much, I'll drop it. But if he's on board...

"Sounds fun," he finally says.

Perfect. I'll make some phone calls tonight. Hopefully, we'll introduce Ian to a few more people around town. Maybe rebuild his community a little. Remind him he's worth being celebrated.

And if I'm really lucky, I'll get to see this pirate in a party hat.

TWENTY-NINE
IAN

MY SPIDEY SENSES ARE TINGLING.

I showed up at Tess's apartment at five-thirty this morning for the third day in a row. She was somewhat frazzled to get out the door on time, August was eager to see me and start building Legos, and I saw Tess off to work with a ball of longing lodged in my chest.

All normal so far.

But as the morning drifts into lunchtime, August's energy is sinking. He barely tried to run in the yard with Dutch, and the solitary tennis ball he threw for him didn't make it ten feet into the grass. He's been content to read books inside, and although we've done that some each day, it's never been this much.

No knock against bookish kids, but this isn't normal for him.

For the twentieth time, I pick up his phone app with the glucose monitor reading on it and the device that syncs to his insulin pump. The one shows his numbers are in healthy range, the other doesn't reflect any issues with his insulin delivery. It's unlikely both could go haywire at the same time and reflect normal readings when he has a serious issue.

Unlikely...but those spidey senses keep ringing in my head.

Ten minutes. If he doesn't perk up, or his monitors don't show some kind of change, I'm going to do a finger prick and verify his numbers myself.

I lean against the doorframe to his room. He's sitting on a little cushion on the floor, books spread out around him, his Lego creations abandoned a few feet away. Normally, he'd be reading out loud to himself, at least, but today he's just looking at the pages.

My heart does this funny thing as if it's spreading out like our failed batch of cookies last night. That fits. My heart's probably overly salty, too. I've honestly never paid much attention to kids. Haven't had a reason. But this one...I know him. Something's wrong, and I need to find out what.

"How are you feeling, August?"

He lifts a shoulder. "I'm fine."

"Do you have a headache?"

He doesn't look up from his book filled with animals driving silly cars. "No."

"Hungry?"

"No."

"Tired at all?"

"No."

Great. The kid learned a lesson from me and is answering in monosyllables. My verbal check in isn't getting me any closer to an answer.

I would love to blow this off and tell myself everything is fine, but I can't. It's like the rare times on mountain trips when someone in my group complained of dizziness or headaches that turned out to be severe dehydration or altitude sickness.

Maybe August's low-key day is part of a normal pattern. Maybe. My gut tells me I need to make certain.

"I think we should do a finger prick with the other blood sugar meter in a few minutes. Will that be okay with you?"

Even though I'm convinced something's off, I still want to get his consent if I can. He's more on top of his diabetes than I expected him to be at his age. Each day, we've checked his numbers at meals together, and I help him input what he's going to eat so the monitor can calculate the carbs. I won't be surprised if he can do his own finger pricks and insulin shots without me even in the room to guide him.

If he doesn't consent, well...our cozy friendship is going to get mighty uncomfortable when I have to whip out my "dad voice" on him. Assuming I have one.

"I'm not sick." He still doesn't look up, though.

"I just want to make sure."

I go into the kitchen and look over his insulin kit again. He's got a few emergency medications in here I hope we won't have to use. I prep the lancet for the finger prick and get everything ready to check his blood.

I haven't called Tess yet. Right now, I don't have anything concrete to tell her. It's just a hunch. As soon as I know more, I'll update her.

August walks into the kitchen and glances at the insulin kit. "Finger prick time?"

He's a brave little trooper, but it's clear he'd rather not.

"I think we should."

He moves closer to me, crawling into my lap. He rests his head on my chest, one hand curling into my T-shirt. He's warm to the touch, but not burning up. I cradle him in my arms, wanting to do whatever I can to comfort him.

"I don't feel so good," he finally admits.

"I know. We'll do this, and then if—"

He tenses. Makes a guttural sound. And vomits all over my front.

Oh.

I run my hand over his hair. "I guess that explains a few things. Any more coming right now?"

He shakes his head, but after the last ten seconds, I don't trust his judgment there. Not much I can do about it if he needs to go again.

"Okay, buddy, let's get us both cleaned up, then we'll do the finger prick."

I strip both of our shirts off to deal with later and lead him into the bathroom. Grabbing the insulin kit on the way, I sit him in front of the toilet just in case we haven't seen the last of the yucks.

"I threw up on you," he says in a pathetic voice. "I didn't mean it."

I sit on the floor next to him, opening an alcohol wipe. "I know you didn't. Sometimes it happens."

Checking in with him first, I do the finger prick and apply the test strip. The glucometer readout is within five points of his monitor app. Just a stomach bug then, and not hyperglycemia.

But even a stomach bug can have devastating impacts on his blood sugar. We're not out of the woods yet.

"I don't want to have to go to the hospital again." August takes my hand as if someone's right outside, ready to drag him away in an ambulance. "I don't like it there."

I don't like the thought of him there, either. Clearly, he experienced some worrying visits before they got his monitor and insulin pump. But just because they're managing his diabetes better, doesn't mean he's forgotten what it's like to be in the hospital.

I haven't forgotten, either.

We're both shirtless, and there's a good chance more throw-up is on the way, but I wrap him in my arms and pull him into my lap. He's clammy but not feverish, scared but not shaking.

"I'm going to take care of you, okay? And when your Mama gets here, she'll take care of you, too."

He nods against me. "If I do have to go to the hospital, will you come with me?"

A month ago, I wasn't even sure I liked kids. I didn't know any and wouldn't have had a clue what to do with one if given the opportunity. Now, I think I would burn down this whole town to make sure this child knows he's safe.

I press an impulsive kiss to his temple. "I'll be right there with you, buddy."

THIRTY

TESS

DRIVING while on speakerphone isn't technically illegal. The way I'm barreling through town probably is, though. Thankfully, August wasn't with me when Ian called a few minutes ago to let me know about the vomiting. My poker face didn't even try.

"Did you give him the anti-nausea medication yet?" Forever grateful for the stash of emergency meds August's endocrinologist suggested I keep on hand.

"I did." It's weird that Ian's "in charge" voice can comfort me even when it's disembodied in the car, right? "Numbers are still good. Luckily, this happened before lunch, so he doesn't have extra insulin on board."

He could have crashed straight into hypoglycemia if he couldn't hold down food he already took extra insulin to accommodate for. He still could if it takes him too long to eat or drink anything. A shiver of worry floats up through my chest, but I force it back down. I have to keep a clear head and not get caught up in potential scary scenarios. Work the problem, not my fears.

"Ketones?" I ask.

"Negligible."

"Headache?"

"None."

"Fever?"

"Mild. Ninety-nine-nine."

Not bad, all things considered. But even with the anti-nausea medication, we're only at the beginning of this illness.

"I'm here," I hang up as I park in the gravel drive next to Ian's SUV.

Definitely a record commute time, and not one I hope to repeat anytime soon.

I'm through the door and across the apartment in an instant. Seeing Ian standing in the doorway to August's room, relief washes over me like a cleansing wave. We exchange small smiles, and I know I should thank him for everything he's done, but I can't shake out of Mama Bear mode. August first.

Voices come from his room, and I step inside, puzzled to see the small television from my room sitting on his dresser. It's playing his favorite educational cartoon show about underwater explorers. Who are also animals. And some vegetables. Right now, they're singing a song about lobsters.

It all makes sense when you're five.

"Hi, Mama." August's propped up against pillows so he can watch the show. He's got towels spread out around him and the small plastic trash bin from the bathroom at his side.

Dutch is also at the ready, sprawled next to him like he needs to maintain as much bodily contact as possible.

I curl up next to August and run a hand over his head. Warm, but not so feverish he's burning up. I'll take the small wins. "How are you feeling?"

He gives me a thumbs down.

"That sounds about right." I squeeze him closer. "How's your tummy?"

He shrugs. "Better."

"You have a friend in your bed."

Dutch chooses that moment to lay his head across August's knee as if daring me to kick him out.

"I wasn't sure what you'd think about that," Ian explains. "But he asked, so..."

"He makes me feel better, Mama." August turns to face me, both him and the dog giving me their cutest puppy eyes.

We've never spent this much time with a dog before. I don't know what's normal or acceptable, but...I don't mind this. Isn't this what dogs are for? Comfort and love and cuddles?

I pet Dutch's head until his eyes close. "I guess he can stay."

"Thank you, Mama."

"And the TV?"

More puppy dog eyes. "I asked Ian if I could watch while I rest."

Ian rubs one hand over the back of his neck, glancing from the TV to me. "I can't say no to a sick kid."

"It's fine." And actually, super adorable. I might have shown more restraint, but that would only mean August propped up on the couch watching the TV in the living room instead of in his bedroom.

"Isn't Ian so great, Mama?"

I lock eyes with Ian across the room where he's still leaning against the doorframe.

"So great," I confirm.

I mean it, one hundred percent. Ian is thoughtful and kind, and more patient than I ever thought a man could be. He's looking out for both August and me with a gentle sweetness I never expected to find. I'm absolutely scared of everything that could go wrong...but I don't want to keep pulling away from him.

I want to lean in.

"I threw up on him," August whispers.

Maybe I don't want to lean in right this minute.

I lift my eyebrows at Ian, but he just shrugs. The man has been a total rock, managing a medical emergency and enduring throw up, and he's brushing it off like it's just another day. It sure isn't to me.

"Do you need anything?" I ask August.

"No." He sinks deeper against the pillows. "I just want to watch for a while."

"That's a good idea." He's likely to fall asleep soon, and he needs the rest. I kiss his forehead, dismayed at the heat radiating from his skin. "I'll come back in a couple of hours for checks."

He nods, his sleepy eyes on his cartoon show. He's so used to finger pricks now, he might not even wake when I come back later.

I leave him to the creatures under the sea, keeping the door ajar in case he calls or Dutch wants out. Ian's waiting for me in the living room, a tentative smile on his face. I don't know why that smile does it, but all the adrenaline I've been holding at bay finally crashes over me.

I don't so much hug him as collapse against him in a jittery heap. He wraps his arms around my back, holding me steady in more ways than one.

"Thank you." I exhale the words against his chest, eyes closed, letting his warmth ground me.

He kisses the top of my head. "It's not a problem, angel."

His utter confidence—in himself, in me—lifts my heart like a bird in flight. It's new to flying and its wings are shaky, but it's still up there, doing its thing. I want to lose myself in this moment, maybe let it develop into something more. But I can't.

I pull back. "I hate to tell you this..."

"I smell like puke?" His mouth slanting into another smile

sends my wobbly heart-bird even higher. "I know. I snuck next door to get a fresh shirt, but I need to shower."

"You cleaned everything up already?" I try to peek past him as though I'll spot a tell-tale puddle somewhere.

"I'm offended that you think I would leave it for you to handle."

He can't be too offended. He's still got me snuggled up in his arms. "I'm grateful you didn't, if that helps."

"Depends on how grateful."

My traitor eyes focus on his mouth. Even though I was just thinking I wanted to finally take a risk and lean in...I can't. I'm standing here wrapped in his warm arms, and he gave me the perfect opportunity, but those last few inches between us feel like oceans.

"Very," is all I manage. Not flirty. Not bold. Barely even lukewarm.

He tightens his arms a fraction. "You'll be busy with August the rest of the day. What do you say to a movie marathon in between checks? Keep your mind from spiraling."

"I didn't say I was spiraling." I had a toe on the line, though.

He gently sweeps a lock of hair away from my forehead. "Maybe it's for both of us."

He's been worried, too? He hasn't shown it. I love his confidence, but I love this hint of softness even more.

"I can leave you to handle it if you want me to," he says when I stay silent too long.

"I don't want you to leave."

He nods like everything's been decided. "I'll order us something for dinner later. You just focus on August. And my movies."

"Is it going to be all Arnold Schwarzenegger?"

His smile quirks up. "You read my mind."

He leans closer to kiss my forehead, pausing whole seconds

in that sweet gesture. Then he releases me and steps toward the door. "I'll be back."

I point a finger gun at him. *"Predator."*

His thunderstruck expression tells me I might have got that wrong.

"Angel, no. That's..." He runs a hand over his forehead like he's trying to keep the exasperation in. "We're going to have a serious talk about this one day."

I wish I could save myself here, but I have minimal knowledge of his favorite actor. "I don't watch those kinds of movies."

"You don't have to watch it to know the quote. There's a whole cultural lexicon around *The Terminator*—" He lifts a hand in the air. "Never mind. We'll discuss later. I'll be back in fifteen."

He leaves me reeling from him using the phrase "cultural lexicon." Calm in medical situations, has a soft spot for my child, and well read. This pirate is the whole package.

I check in on August. He's already asleep, his pale hair stuck to his sweaty face, one hand on the dog's neck. Dutch's eyes shift my way, and his tail slaps against the bed a few times, but he doesn't move from his cuddle spot.

I grab the monitors off August's dresser, double-checking his numbers haven't sunk too low yet. I take everything with me into the living room and collapse onto the couch. Then, I have to check my own phone.

> Wren: How's A?

> Mom: Please give an update on August when you can.

> Mom: Take tomorrow off. Wren & I can cover for you.

> Mom: Let us know if you need help tonight.

Mom: We're here for you.

Guilt worms through my stomach. I didn't share the whole truth when I told them August was sick. I entirely left out the part about him being at home with Ian when it happened. Wren would get my reasoning, but Mom won't. I'll explain it someday, just not right now.

I text them updates on August's health and reassurances that I'll call if I need them. I know they're thinking about when he was first diagnosed and we had a few scary visits to the hospital. In that light, his stomach bug today isn't so bad. Hopefully, I won't even have to use any more emergency medications.

Hear that, Universe? Give us a softball this time.

Ian returns a few minutes later, movies in hand. He's slicked his wet hair into his ever present bun and changed into a fresh T-shirt and athletic shorts.

I like the clothing swap. Gray sweatpants might do it for some women, but I'm a shorts girl all the way. Not just because I like the hint of his exposed thigh. He's comfortable enough to wear them around me, and I don't take that lightly.

"You brought a lot of movies. Am I going to have to cover my eyes during the shoot-em-up parts?"

"I don't think so." Standing in front of the couch, he fans the movies out in his hands.

Twins. Kindergarten Cop. Junior. No action movies to be seen.

I point at the last one. "Um...is he pregnant in that one?"

"He's glowing." Ian smirks. "You're distracted already. My plan is working."

And honestly, it is. Ian and I get comfortable on the couch and watch silly comedies. We take breaks to check August's blood sugar and help him drink fluids. Ian orders us meals from a soup-and-salad place in town, and August manages some bites of dinner. Sick days are never routine, but this is the best one I could hope for.

It's almost midnight when we finish our movie marathon.

"I can't believe I cried over an Arnold Schwarzenegger movie. Stupid message about family loving you no matter what." Hit a little too close to home.

Ian chuckles. "He can do anything."

I yawn wide and check my phone alarm. I'll be doing blood sugar checks every few hours until August is totally well, which could be days. I probably shouldn't have stayed up this late, but Ian was right. Schwarzenegger kicked my anxiety's butt. Now, exhaustion is kicking mine.

"I should go so you can get some decent sleep." Ian stands and holds a hand out to me, helping me up. Our hands stay locked together as I walk him to the door.

"Thank you for tonight." Those few words feel awfully small in light of everything he's done for us.

"You don't have to keep thanking me, angel. I wanted to be here."

The soft lamp light makes his eyes sparkle like a rushing river. We stay like this, holding hands in front of the door, neither of us letting go. I'm waiting for him to do something—kiss me, hopefully—but I begin to realize that ball's in my court. He's letting me set the pace.

It's sweet. And way too much pressure.

His motto might be "What's life without a little risk?", but mine is "Caution." I don't know how to make the next move. I'm so far out of practice, it's laughable. We could wind up in this standoff until morning.

I'm tempted to tell him I haven't dated since before August was born. Admit I don't know what I'm doing. Throw the ball back in his court and let him decide our fates.

But is that really who I want to be? A woman who can't lean one foot closer to kiss the man she's crazy about?

In a flurry of nerves and adrenaline, I rush forward to press a kiss to his cheek. Not the bullseye, but it counts. Even if this sort of kiss gives him no chance to participate. His skin is warm, and I catch that soft cucumber scent I've been smelling all night. If I pressed my nose against his neck, it'd probably be even stronger.

That would be too much, right? Or would it...

But I lean back, my cheeks heating from even that brief kiss. It's a baby step, but it's in the right direction.

He holds my gaze, even though I'm tempted to tear mine away. It's like he can see straight through my eyes to every one of those thoughts.

"I should bring you dinner more often," he says with a smirk. He squeezes my hand once, a Morse code message I don't have the decoder for. "Goodnight, Tess."

He turns to leave, but I tug on his hand like a yo-yo, pulling him back to face me again.

"Do you want to come to the Fourth Fest with us on Saturday?" I ask. "As long as August's better, I mean. There's a parade and then a farmers market and live music. Wren and I will have a little cart selling hand pies, but it should be a fun time. You could join us for the fireworks in the evening, too. If you wanted."

It's not really asking him on a date if my whole family will be there. Which...now that I think about it, is worse than asking him on a date. *What are you doing, Tess? Oh, nothing, just casually asking Ian to spend time with the entire Krause clan.*

The slow smile spreading across his face is like a sparkler lighting—just a glimmer at first, but soon, it's too bright to look at directly.

"I'd love to."

My stomach tumbles down, down, down endless flights of stairs. I might never find my footing again if he keeps talking to me in this low voice.

"Text me how he's doing tomorrow," he says. "I'm here for you. Whatever you need."

I nod on autopilot. *Whatever you need.* These baby steps aren't enough. I thought they could tide me over, but I want more. It's time for a leap.

He starts to turn for the door, but I tug him back. And this time, I meet him in the middle.

My lips brush against his, so painfully uncertain, I'm convinced he can feel it in my touch. My hand on his shoulder might be trembling. But then his hands slide over my back, locking me to him. His mouth responds to mine, and oh, does he participate.

Our gentle kisses would pass for chaste if it weren't for the heat coiling through my belly. His lips press and pull, responding to mine without demanding more. There's a tenderness to his kisses that takes me by surprise. They're a kiss hello. A welcome home. A new beginning.

Sweet, like spun sugar.

I finally draw back enough to give us space, our arms still around each other.

"Thank you," I breathe out.

He turns his eyes to the ceiling, his mouth slanted to the side. When his gaze reconnects with mine, there's a fire of challenge in it.

"Don't thank me for kissing you yet." His low timbre is the closest thing to a legitimate growl I've ever heard. "Not until I've kissed you so thoroughly you can't open your eyes. Not until I've left you sighing for more. Not until the only word in your head is my name."

I draw in a shaky breath. It's a good thing his arms are still around me because I'm not sure I could stand on my own right now.

He nuzzles his nose against mine. "*Then*, you can thank me for kissing you."

I swallow, my swooning brain cells grasping for words. "Something to look forward to."

THIRTY-ONE

IAN

I HAVE NEVER SEEN SO many American flags in my life.

Maple Street teems with red, white, and blue. Sunshine's residents are decked out in everything from Captain America shirts to striped Uncle Sam top hats. I passed one storefront stuffed with so much patriotic merch my eyes watered.

Was that a hyper-American Gandalf doll in there?

It's over the top, but it's actually kind of fun. Durango had big celebrations, too, but I was usually booked for private guides over the holiday. I can't remember the last time I participated in a small-town Independence Day festival like this.

The day is clear, and the top of McKenzie peak is visible in the distance. That mountaintop calls me. Hard to believe I've been here four months and haven't explored the closest mountains. Honestly, I've barely explored my own neighborhood. Maybe it's time to change that.

But first, I have an urge for something sweet.

I weave through the farmers market aisles, not fully registering the handmade goods laid out at each booth. I'm on a mission to find one particular food cart helmed by one particular woman. Until then, nothing else can hold my attention.

Finally, I spot her. Tess and her sister are stationed at a red cart topped by a big glass display loaded with cupcakes and hand pies. She's talking with a customer and slipping treats into paper boxes, smiling the whole time. Her red-and-white striped shirt and dark blue shorts make her look like a flag. I have never wanted to salute anything more.

It's a warm day, but now all the heat around me seems to coalesce behind my ribs. My angel glows in the sunlight, a vision I can't stop staring at. I move closer without thinking. I'm a thirsty man crawling across the desert, drawn to the shimmering oasis before me.

August appears from behind the cart, wearing a shirt with the grumpy patriotic Muppet on it, waving glow sticks around. Glad to see he's feeling like himself again after the stomach bug. I stopped by yesterday to make sure he was on the upswing. Not because Tess can't handle his diabetes—just like August manages his pump on his own, she didn't really need me there, even in the worst of it.

Nope, I checked in for my own peace of mind. I needed to see his little smile and verify for myself she was holding up okay. I didn't stay long, just reiterated I was there for them if they needed me. Still am.

August catches sight of me and grins. "Ian!"

Tess looks around. When our gazes meet, she shines like she's made of sunbeams. Having that effect on her doesn't seem real. I want to see her shine like this every day.

"You made it." Her gaze drifts over me, her smile cranking up a few more degrees when she spots my shorts.

What can I say? It's a hot day.

Even hotter when she watches me like this.

Her sister waves a hand my direction. "Avast there, Ian!"

Tess's eyes go wide, and she purses her lips as though she's struggling not to scold her. Wren's smug smile makes me want to know what all she's heard about me. Clearly, pirates are a theme.

"Ahoy," I say, keeping my gaze on Tess.

Wren cackles and helps the next person in line, ignoring the withering side-eye Tess shoots her way.

August comes up right in front of me. "Ian, did you see the parade? And the horses? And the fire truck?"

"I missed it, buddy." I know my limits. Tess told me her mom would be with August at the parade while she and her sister prepared for the festival, cutting my incentive to attend in half.

He slips his hand in mine. "Next year, you have to come and sit with us."

I glance back to Tess. "Next year, I will."

"Do you want to—"

"Thank you for your service."

It takes me a second to realize an older man in line for pies is talking to me. When I meet his gaze, he salutes.

My good humor for the morning winks out. Why do they always make this assumption, like everyone who's lost a limb is Lieutenant Dan home from Vietnam? They offer me a moment of respect and recognition I don't deserve. "Thanks, I crashed my motorcycle" tends to kill their gratitude.

"I didn't serve," I say coolly. I was never that selfless.

"Oh." His gaze drops back to my leg as if he needs to make sure I've still got the prosthesis. "Then how'd you lose it?"

He manages to make it sound like negligence, as if I set my old leg down somewhere and forgot about it. As if it was entirely my fault. Which it absolutely was.

I have no desire to talk about one of the worst days of my life with him, but he's eagerly watching me, waiting for the whole bloody story.

And this is why I stopped wearing shorts in public.

Tess makes a sound of disgust. "Really, Mr. Miller? You're going to ask him that without even saying hello or asking his name?"

The man looks at her as if she's speaking nonsense. "It's a fair question."

"It's genuinely not. You're asking a stranger personal questions. It's rude."

I'm used to Tess's sweet, soft side, but this spitfire? I like her.

He looks around as if searching for back up, but the other people in line don't make eye contact with him. "Guy lost his leg, it's natural to ask why. Was it an accident, infection, what?"

Tess frowns harder at his eager fishing attempt.

He waggles a finger between the two of us, eyes widening as though he's caught onto something. "Diabetes, maybe?"

She takes me by the hand, glaring at the man as if she wants to set him on fire. "Maybe you should ask yourself why you're so focused on what he's missing. Personally, I think he's pretty fantastic just the way he is."

Oh, okay. It's *me* she's setting on fire. Just like her impulsive kiss the other night, this side of her is unexpected but suits her exactly right. I don't need her defending me any more than she needs me to tell her what to do about August's diabetes. But her standing up for me, being *here* for me, means everything.

"Wren, I'm taking a break." She pulls me away from the cart, and August trots along on my other side, still holding my hand.

"You got it!" Wren shouts from behind us.

The three of us walk through the market in a little chain. I'm not sure where Tess is taking us, but I suspect she just needed to get away. I've been there.

August lets me go and cuts in front of Tess.

"Mama, can I?" He points at a face painting booth.

"Sure, buddy." She waves him along to get in the short line.

Her attention stays focused on him, but I've seen this move before.

I lean closer to her. "Are we going to talk about how you ripped that guy a new one?"

She laughs but finally meets my gaze. "I know you're more than capable of defending yourself, but I have some experience with Mr. Miller. He would have asked a hundred invasive questions before tiring out."

"He's bothered you before?"

She gestures at August, happily waiting in line. "When we first got his monitor and insulin pump. The man's morbid curiosity knows no bounds."

I'd ask for specifics, but I doubt it would douse the protectiveness simmering inside me. "I might head back over to the cart and have a talk with him myself."

She pulls me closer, her free hand wrapping around my biceps, trying not to smile. "I think he's had enough for now."

"If it's any consolation, you're breathtaking when you're furious." My avenging angel, ready to cut somebody.

Her tiny smile has a hint of mischief to it. "Should I ready the CPR?"

I lean even closer, loving her flirtatious side. "Please."

She laughs but focuses on August. "Oh, no."

I turn to catch what's got her so dismayed, but it doesn't take much investigation. August's sitting in the face painting chair being made to look like a pirate. He's got a painted-on red bandana with a skull and crossbones in the middle, various scars on each cheek, and is currently getting a beard and mustache dabbed on.

"I might have talked about pirates too fondly." She side-eyes me. "He asked me yesterday if his hair is long enough for a 'man bunny.'"

"Not thrilled about the bunny, but I'm taking that as a

compliment."

"I thought you might."

August slides off the camp chair and rushes over to us. "Isn't it great, Mama?"

"You're the cutest little pirate."

I pay the face painter, ignoring Tess's attempts to scowl at me. It's a few dollars for some fun, what's the big deal?

A firetruck honks its horn as it pulls up the alley not far away from us. Kids stream forward to get a better look, and a few firefighters hop off the back, presumably to entertain their questions.

August's gasp is almost as loud as the firetruck's horn. "Mama! Can we go?"

"I know how much you want to, buddy, but I can't leave Aunt Wren to handle the customers alone." She turns to me. "I'm sorry we can't spend the afternoon together."

"I understand." She has a job to do, and I don't want to get in the way. "I can take August to see the fire truck."

August squeezes my hand again. "I'm ready!"

Of course he is.

Tess only pauses a second. "Okay. Sure."

August's happy squeals make my day. Yeah, they're mostly for the fire truck, but I'm coming to the rescue, too.

She pulls his monitor phone from her pocket and passes it to me. "You know what to do."

"That's what I like to hear."

She rolls her eyes, but her smile peeks out. "You might be getting more than you bargained for. August will probably want to stay with the fire truck until it drives away again."

"I can be patient." A total sham, since all my willpower is focused on not tugging this gorgeous woman into my arms right now and kissing her in front of everyone she knows.

Climbing mountains takes a lot of self discipline, but she's testing me like nothing else ever has.

"I appreciate that about you." Her soft little eyelash flutter kills me.

I die even more when she releases my hand and starts to back away.

"Thank you," she says softly.

I just nod her along, my resolve fraying when she uses that hushed voice. She gets about ten feet away from us and pauses to turn back. She holds my gaze, breaking out a secret smile just for me. That smile is a lit match to the tinder in my chest, making it burn white-hot.

August tugs on my hand. "Aren't we ready?"

I pull my attention from Tess walking away and look down at him. With his painted-on pirate persona, he looks like he might call me a scurvy landlubber if I don't hurry. I love it. I still opt to play dumb, though. "Was there something around here you wanted to see?"

"The fire truck!" He tugs with all his might.

I let him drag me along to where the firemen and firewoman are showing kids—and a couple of curious adults—around the big, red truck. We're within a few feet of it when I recognize one of the firefighters. Nathan Bridger, my enthusiastic job recruiter from the diner a few weeks ago.

"Can I go look at the truck?" August asks.

"Stay where I can see you."

Whoa. Having serious déjà vu to my childhood right now.

He runs off to join the kids listening to a discussion about the fire hose. Nathan comes forward, hand outstretched. I shake it, the reminder of my unfriendly behavior the other night sitting like gravel in my stomach. If he's concerned about that, his wide grin doesn't show it.

"Good to see you out here," he says. "Did you catch the parade?"

I'm guessing they were in that, too. "Missed it."

"There's always next year." He leans back, glancing me over. "You look different. Can't put my finger on it."

"Had a little makeover." Long overdue.

"That's not it." Good grief, this man's eyes shine like he's perpetually up to something. "You're smiling."

"Am I?" Pretty sure I'm not.

"Not now," he concedes. "But a minute ago, yeah. I'd have sworn you were happy."

"All right. I get it." I am happy. Sad that it's such a big change-up even this ball of chaotic energy can see the difference.

"I'm here for it, is all I'm saying." He nods August's way. "I know who his mom is. I ship it."

"What does that mean?" I don't manage to make the question sound casual. If it means something about how attractive Tess is, we're going to have a talk he won't enjoy.

He chuckles. "It means I can see you two together. Geez, you really are a dinosaur."

"Thank you. So glad I came over here."

If anything, he laughs harder. "You know, we just opened up two firefighter paramedic positions. It's a satisfying gig. Helping people. Being part of a team. Rising to unexpected challenges. And the schedule's good. Two days on, four off."

Sounds better than some of my guiding trips where I could be on for eight days at a time, sometimes under grueling conditions. And clearly, I'd have a fan in August if I decided to try my hand at firefighting.

Except...what am I doing? Nathan's got me thinking about *another* potential job?

"How many jobs do you have?" I ask.

"Just the two. I'm not part of the permanent team for Back-country EMT, only special events."

"I don't know if something like that's for me." I don't know what's for me anymore, and I sure can't figure it out in the middle of this festival.

"Ian, look at me!" August waves from the passenger seat of the fire truck, an oversized helmet on his head.

"Looking good, buddy," I call back. I whip out my phone to take a picture of him up there and text it to Tess.

"There it is again," Nathan says.

He's legitimately gloating. If he thinks this kind of crowing is a good pitch for me to become his coworker, he can think again. I wipe my face free of the smile August brought out. But he waves again, and he's so happy sitting up there, I can't help but smile back.

Nathan slaps me on the shoulder, a self-congratulatory grin stretched across his own face. "Good to see you again. Let me know if anything changes. My drinks invite still stands."

"Got it." His constant enthusiasm is insufferable. But...not all that different from how I acted at his age. Maybe even more recently than that. "I'll think about it."

Nathan walks away to command the attention of some kids at the back of the truck. "How tall is our ladder? I'm glad you asked."

I shake my head at his ridiculousness, but I can't deny his audience is loving it.

August listens to talks about the firetruck's knobs and dials, safety gear, and how fast it can go in an emergency. When he's touched every part of the truck he can reach and asked every last question in his head, he finally returns to me.

Good. I don't know if I would have had the heart to tear him away from the fun.

"Did you see me, Ian?" he says, taking my hand again.

"I saw it. You looked good up there." I turn us to head back through the market to the bakery cart.

"Can I be a firefighter when I grow up?"

"Sure."

"Could I drive the fire truck?"

"I bet you could if you're a good driver." Weird to imagine him as anything other than the innocent five-year-old he is now. Why does that make my heart ache so much? Did I become Pierce when I wasn't looking?

"Will they let me take it home?" he asks.

"I think fire trucks have to stay at the fire station."

Some of his enthusiasm fades, but then immediately perks back up. "I'll live at the fire station, too, so that's okay."

"Glad that's settled."

At the bakery cart, August runs up to Tess. "Can I get my snacks?"

"You know where they are." She waves at a small cooler tucked behind the cart. He roots around until he finds a cheese stick and a yogurt cup. He sits in a small camp chair they must have brought just for him, and digs in.

"I could watch him until you're done here, if that's easier for you," I tell her. Maybe take him to the park I saw when I was doing laps downtown, who knows.

Her bright smile kills me every time. "That's sweet, but my mom's got their afternoon planned out. Wren and I will take over in the store when the market ends in another hour."

"No problem." The small, sinking sensation in my chest says I'm disappointed, though.

She leans closer to me. "You're coming with us to watch the fireworks tonight, right? I have it on good authority it's going to be memorable."

With Tess, anything would be.

"I won't miss it."

And won't be able to think about anything else the rest of the day.

THIRTY-TWO

TESS

IAN and I exchange amused smiles as we make our way across the high school's parking lot in the growing darkness. We're loaded down with blankets, sweatshirts, and a cooler full of snacks—everything we need to enjoy the big fireworks show.

The same fireworks show August has talked about nonstop all evening. He's told us what his favorite fireworks from last year look like. How loud their bangs are. How he gets to stay up extra late. That maybe he'll make fireworks when he grows up.

You'd think he downed ten cups of coffee before we got in the car.

"Everybody sits on the football field to watch, isn't that funny?" he says. "But I lie down to watch. It's better that way. If you sit, your neck hurts. So I lie down."

"So I should lie down, too?" Ian asks as if he's having trouble getting it.

"Yup. And then they whoosh, zam, pow, right over our heads! There's going to be a zillion fireworks."

"A zillion?" Ian's mouth tips up at the side. "Are you going to count them?"

"It's too many to count. But my friend Lila told me there will be a zillion, and she knows. She's a fireworks expert."

I make a mental note to tell Lila to add that to her resume.

"Remember where we're headed?" I've reminded him a few times. We come to the field for New Year's fireworks, too, but that's a big break in between.

"The big forty-five on the field. Because Nana is forty-five!"

I snort. "She would love to hear that."

We move through the bottleneck at the entrance and stream onto the field. A few hundred people have already set up blankets and lawn chairs in anticipation of the big show. Somebody's playing "American Pie" on the guitar, kids toss a light-up Frisbee back and forth, and glow sticks shine like a sea of neon.

"I see them!" August sprints down the forty-five-yard line to where my mom and sister are sitting on blankets halfway across the field.

I catch the moment they notice Ian. Nerves fizz through me like a shaken seltzer bottle. I told them I'd invited our neighbor to join us and left it at that. But even in this dim light, I can see them reaching all the conclusions I was too afraid to say out loud.

I like him. I care for him. I'm completely smitten and need everyone here to be cool about it.

Ian already knows Wren, so I only have the one introduction to make. "Mom, this is Ian. Ian, my mom, Maureen."

"It's good to meet you." Mom stands to shake his hand. "August talks about you all the time."

"And Dutch!" August says from the blanket next to Wren.

"I'm a fan of August's, too," Ian tells her.

"I'm glad you could join us," Mom says with a smile.

It's not her relaxed smile, though. It's her bakery smile. I've always admired her customer service calm, but I don't like her directing it at Ian. As if he's not our guest and a friend, but a stranger waiting in line for pie.

If Ian feels her friendliness is forced, he doesn't show it. "Thanks for letting me crash your party."

"It's supposed to be a big production." She does it again— she flashes the smile she uses when she tells customers about our flavors of the week. I'm not sure if admitting Ian is more than just my neighbor would have made her more friendly or less.

"I keep hearing that."

I start laying our blankets next to theirs, and Ian moves closer to help me smooth them out. "Our friend Lila is revamping Sunshine's holiday events," I tell him. "We're excited to see what she does."

Wren sighs. "I wish I could have seen her when she put her slimy ex in his place."

Lila accidentally got sick all over her ex this morning, and Sunshine's grapevine has been working at light speed to share the tale. The poor thing must have the same stomach bug that August had. I doubt she'll be happy when she recovers and finds out her spewing on the sidewalk was a bigger topic of discussion than the festival she organized.

To be fair, people raved about the Fourth Fest. But our stylish, media-savvy local influencer losing her lunch on her snide ex was way juicier.

Poor choice of words.

"She's home sick with her Adonis, Hope's up in the canyon watching the fireworks with Griffin." Wren looks up at the stars. "Sure would be nice to have someone to cuddle up with, too. Wouldn't it, Mom?"

So subtle.

"Are you asking for a hug?" Mom opens her arms wide. "I'm ready, little gal."

Wren wrinkles her nose. "I was thinking of romantic snuggles."

I ignore her and sit on the blankets farthest from her theatrical sighs. I'm not any happier with her obnoxious nudges than I am with Mom's affected indifference. Maybe I just can't be pleased.

Ian moves closer to me and, yup—I *can* be pleased.

He crosses his prosthesis's foot in front of him and smoothly lowers to the ground next to me. It feels rude not to compliment his powerful thighs, but I manage to restrain myself. And, sadly, rip my gaze away from them.

"I'll hug August, then." Mom wraps him up in a quick embrace. "I don't get enough of these anymore."

"I hug you all the time, Nana," he says from under her arm.

She lets him go and *boops* him on the nose. "I will always take more."

A breeze drifts over us, and shivers ripple across my skin. Sifting through the sweatshirts we brought, I set August's aside for him, but I don't find my lavender one I'd intended to wear. Instead, I find two I don't recognize: a navy one and a gray one, both oversized.

"Didn't I give you my sweatshirt to bring?" I ask Ian, rubbing the fleece between my fingers. They're soft and perfectly worn in. "When we left the house?"

"I brought two of mine."

I hold them out to him as if he's going to slip them both over his head right now. Maybe I left mine in my car.

He chuckles and leans closer. "Indulge a man a fantasy and put on his clothes."

Oh. *Oh.* My stomach dips, but I pull the gray one on. The sweatshirt smells like him, cucumber and soap and a hint of something spicy. I'm surrounded by my new favorite smell in a cozy fleece cocoon.

"Thank you," he whispers low.

I've got so many lights glittering and twinkling around inside me, I don't even need the fireworks.

"It's probably a busy night for crime, huh? I bet Sunshine's sheriff and deputies don't get to enjoy the show." Wren has decided to create her own fireworks by bashing Mom over the head with hints tonight.

Is it bad to say, "better Mom than me?"

Mom shushes her. "You'll give Ian the wrong impression of Sunshine."

"Oh, he knows about our seedy underbelly. They've dealt with bandits and thieves over at their house."

Mom's attention whips over to us, but I hold up a hand. "We had raccoons, one time."

Probably more often than that, but I've followed Ian's request to avoid taking out the trash at night. What I don't know won't hurt me. Or startle me into hurting myself.

She relaxes, but her attention stays fixed our way. "How do you like Sunshine, Ian?"

"I haven't explored enough of it. But it's growing on me. Tiny bears and all."

Hopefully, it's too dark for Wren to see my goofy grin.

A streak of brilliant white shoots into the sky, to the delight of the crowd around us. Must be ten.

August squeals and flops onto his back next to Wren. Lifting his head, he points a finger at the rest of us. "You have to lie down."

"He's a commanding little pirate captain," Ian mutters as he lowers onto his back.

I stretch out, too. "He's not wrong. It's a pretty good way to watch the show."

They launch the fireworks from a meadow a few blocks away.

This close, they really do burst right overhead, a series of spinners, blooms, and fountains lighting up the night. It's peaceful, even with the occasional loud bangs and the "oohs and aahs" from the crowd.

August's little sounds are my favorites, though. He's a fan of every single firework, and lets us know how pretty they are with a round of applause after every shower of sparks.

I realize Ian is facing me instead of the sky. I turn my head toward him. Even in the darkness, his slanted smile shines through.

"You're missing it," I whisper.

"I'm not missing a thing, angel."

Fireworks illuminate his face, revealing his gaze steady on me. Between us, he finds my hand and threads our fingers together. Looking into his eyes is like walking through the door of a house and realizing I'm home.

Despite my intentions to keep my heart anchored in a safe harbor, I'm sailing through uncharted waters. I'm falling for Ian, and if I don't reroute soon, I'll coast right off the map.

Here be dragons.

But maybe also a pirate with a good heart who'll sail along with me.

August crawls over me to snuggle into the small space between me and Ian. We let go of each other, scooting over a touch to make room.

"Isn't it good, Ian?" he says, staring up into the night.

Ian's gaze never leaves mine. "The best."

If there's something better than seeing Ian carrying my sleepy son into the house, I don't know what it is. August's arms are wrapped around Ian's neck, and the man's got him hefted onto his hips like he's precious cargo. My heart can't handle these levels of adorableness this late in the day.

Inside, Ian takes August to his bed.

"Goodnight, Ian," he says with a big yawn.

"Goodnight, buddy."

Ian slips out while I help August change into his pajamas. I run my fingertips over the adhesive around his sensor and pump to make sure we're good for the night. They're both on his belly tonight, and his muscles flex from the ticklish sensation, but otherwise, he barely stirs. I kiss his forehead, whisper goodnight, and leave him to dream about fireworks.

In the kitchen, Ian's leaning against the counter, his arms crossed over his chest. I tuck August's insulin kit away in the supply cart for the next time we go out.

He nods at the cart. "You've got yourself a mini clinic here."

"He needs a lot of supplies. As you know."

"All that can't be cheap."

"Mom changed to an insurance plan with good coverage as soon as he was diagnosed. It's not free, but I manage."

"Forgive me for asking, but is your ex paying his share of August's medical expenses?"

I can't help the incredulous sound that bursts out of me.

Ian's gaze hardens. "Please tell me he's not a deadbeat, and he's doing right by you two."

"Ian, my ex didn't want me to have August at all. When he found out I was keeping the baby, he left Lake Tahoe the next day. Changed his phone number, blocked me on all social media. I have no idea where he is or how to contact him even if I wanted to." I stopped running internet searches on him a long time ago, but he did his best to stay off the grid.

An amicable break up and co-parenting situation would have been almost normal. Fleeing the state? That's brutal.

"I didn't put his name on the birth certificate, so legally, he's

MAKE MINE SWEET   255

not August's father. I would have to sue for paternity before I could ever get child support, and that feels like a lot of effort for someone who didn't want either of us in the first place."

With his mouth set into a frown and his eyes a little wild, Ian looks as dangerous as I've ever seen him. "I hate that he couldn't be bothered to step up and know his own child. I hate that he's not here for you."

I can only shrug. Even if my ex were right across town, I can't pretend he would magically be an involved dad. He simply never wanted to be one.

"I can take care of August without him."

"I know you can." Ian strides over to me until our chests are practically touching. His gaze is still stormy, but there's nothing dangerous about him now. "I take it back. I hate that you're doing everything on your own, but angel...I don't hate that he's not here. I think I'd go mad if he were."

He cups my face in his hands and covers my mouth with his. His tender kiss conveys reassurance, a reminder that I'm worth sticking around for. It's so soft I could cry, but I don't want that tonight.

Thankfully, neither does Ian. Gentle kisses give way to something untamed. I open up to him, and he groans. The rough, uninhibited sound makes my belly swoop as he absolutely plunders my mouth.

It's no theft—I'm his for the taking.

He slides one hand into my hair, the other moving to my upper back as if he needs me even closer. As if he will never get close enough. I fist my hands in his shirt at his sides, robbed of the faculties to do much more than hold on.

His kisses the other night were soft and sweet, but this? This is an unquenchable fire, spreading flames from my ribs out to my fingers and toes. I am wafer paper on a burn-away cake, completely consumed.

He breaks the kiss—to do what, I don't know—but I'm not having it.

"Ian," I whisper without opening my eyes. I don't even know what I'm asking for, but he grants my wish and returns his mouth to mine.

Only, this pirate has chosen torture. He slows the kiss to an agonizing crawl. Every touch of his hands and stroke of his tongue become a deliberate attempt to tease. To get me to whisper his name. To beg.

I'm ready to run up the white flag and surrender.

When he draws back a second time, I need a moment to gather my thoughts beyond the word "more." I open my eyes to find him gazing back at me, burning with the same heat running through me.

"Thank you," I whisper.

He lived up to his conditions for gratitude and then some.

He groans again and moves in for another devastating kiss. I will happily be conquered by him.

August's door creaks, and we draw apart in earnest. My eyes fly open to find my son blearily taking the short trip to the bathroom.

"Have to potty," he says, shutting himself in.

Ian and I watch each other in silence. I'm not sure I ever knew eye contact could be this sexy, but my skin blazes with as much fire as it did when we kissed.

The toilet flushes and the bathroom sink runs for a minute. August comes out, still rubbing his eyes. "Night, Mama."

He pads back into his room. His door is ajar, reminding me I can't go completely wild with Ian, no matter how much I want to. Maybe if we were quiet on the couch...

"I should probably go let Dutch out," Ian says.

Oh. I guess we're not on the same wavelength with the couch thing. I walk him to the door, duct-taping the mouths of all the voices in my head telling me I messed up. Got ahead of myself. Gave too much.

He opens the door and turns around. "See you tomorrow?"

Relief floods in. "Yes, please."

He leans close enough our mouths almost touch. *Almost.* His breath ghosts over my lips.

"I like the *please*," he purrs.

Purrs. A month ago, I might have described him as a grouchy lion with stabby claws. Now, he's a ginger kitten. Still dangerous, but the only thing in the firing line is my heart.

His kiss goodnight is full of promises of more kisses to come. When he pulls back, he smiles wider, tempting me to lean in to keep saying goodnight.

"August was right," he says. "A zillion fireworks."

THIRTY-THREE

TESS

HAVING August's birthday party two days after the Fourth Fest was a bit like going to Six Flags and then hitting up Disneyland —excitement overload. He had a blast at the park with his friends, getting caught up in party games and running wild on the play structures. They had strawberry cupcakes with dinosaur toppers, sliced fruit, and a veggie tray I'm bringing home in its entirety.

Mom and Wren alternated being in charge of the bakery so each of them could come down for an hour to celebrate with August. It's just more proof that we need to hire another employee, no matter how little Mom likes the concept.

Mom floated the idea of having his party yesterday when Blackbird's was closed, but that would have resulted in *three* party days in a row, and I refused on principle. Mama needs a minute to rest.

August and I are on our way across town still giddy from the party and loaded down with presents from his friends, and the day isn't over yet. Later tonight, we'll have the barbecue at the duplex with friends and family. This event will be more low-key since I only invited adults, but he's just as amped up about it as he was for the afternoon with his classmates.

"Everybody can see our new house and meet Dutch, and we can play my new game," he tells me.

"The one that throws whipped cream in people's faces?"

He giggles. "Yeah."

"Maybe play it with just Aunt Wren." I will be front row, center with my camera ready to see my sister take a fake pie to the face.

"When will everyone get here?" he asks as I pull up to the duplex. We just left a party and he can't wait to get the next one started. His social battery doesn't quit.

"Not for a couple of hours. We have some time to relax." Even though asking him to relax is like asking the sun to tone it down with its cheery rays. Not likely.

"This is the best day ever."

I make eye contact with him in the rear-view mirror. "I'm with you, buddy."

I have my own good news to celebrate.

We take his party loot and leftovers inside. Naturally, the first thing he wants to do is rush out the back door. Not even brand-new Lego sets and a marble run track can keep him from some playtime with Dutch. The dog is sunning himself in the yard but leaps up when August runs out with his new soccer ball, ready to start a game of one-on-one.

I haven't figured out his rules, but he always knows the score.

Ian's back door is wide open, so I head that way. I step over the threshold as I knock on the glass.

"I have exciting news—"

And that's it. That's all I get out before I'm stopped cold in my tracks. Staring is a real problem for me with this man. Just when I think I've got myself under control, he throws me another curveball. Usually, the shirtless kind.

He's standing in his kitchen in athletic shorts and nothing else. His hair is damp, and his chest glistens like Edward Cullen with a death wish. He's downing a big glass of water, his armpits braced on a pair of crutches. He's not wearing his prosthetic leg, and one side of his shorts hangs empty.

It's a weirdly intimate moment, and not just for how little he's wearing. This isn't a side of him he lets most people experience. And I am painfully aware I wasn't actually invited.

"Oh. I'm sorry. The door was open. I shouldn't have barged in."

His mouth tips on one side. "It's fine. Dutch and I just got back from a run on the trail, and I needed a shower. How was the party?"

Taking his cue that this isn't a problem, I step farther into his apartment. "Wild. Twelve kids doesn't sound like a lot, but when they're all screaming and running around, it's mayhem."

I have a slight headache from all the noisemakers, and I don't mean plastic toys.

"No, twelve kids sounds like a lot."

"I guess you're right. They had a good time, if lack of volume control is any indication."

His gaze warms. "I like to think so."

Okay, that's...oof. I can't focus when he's watching me like this. Or saying things like that. Or standing around shirtless and barefoot like it's no big deal. I drift closer to him, my body acting apart from my mind.

Ian sets his empty glass aside and leans against the counter. "I want to hear about your exciting news."

That, at least, snaps me out of my bare-chest fog. "Right. Charlie Callahan at Moonlight Lodge called me as we were packing up the party. She got the green light from her parents, and they're going to convert their barn into a wedding venue. When they're ready, she wants me to be their preferred wedding cake vendor."

I am a professional. I didn't squeal or jump up and down. I saved that for when I got off the phone with her.

"That's amazing news, angel." He holds a hand out, and I step into his embrace.

On the "Leads to Risky Activities" scale, shirtless hugging has got to be way up at the top. He's just so perfect and warm like this, even slightly damp from the shower. And looking good shirtless is one thing, but *smelling* good shirtless? Doesn't seem possible, but here he is, smelling so fresh and clean I actually sniff him.

I regret nothing.

I let him go, but don't move out of his space. He keeps one hand on my side, tethering me to him. Outside, August's happy shouts carry as he frolics with Dutch in the yard.

"What does this mean for your family's business?"

That turns my excitement down a notch. "I don't know. I'll have to talk to Mom and find out if we're going to do this together or if I step out on my own."

I'd much rather have my cakes be an arm of Blackbird's Bakery than start a new business by myself. But I'm willing to fight for it. Right this minute, though, I just want to enjoy the moment before reality sets in.

"I'm proud of you."

I can't help it—I let out the tiniest squeal. "I'm so excited. Charlie said it will be a few months before they get the venue ready for weddings, and it will probably take a while for them to build up clientele and a solid reputation."

Given how popular Moonlight Lodge has become, their calendar might fill a whole lot faster than she's thinking.

"I have time to figure out my menu and get my website in

order. Obviously, not every couple will choose to work with me—"

Ian scoffs, his fingers flexing on my side. "Impossible."

I love how much confidence he has in me. It's not the source of mine, but I like having the extra layer. "It will most likely build little by little. It's probably ridiculous to be this excited about a business that doesn't exist."

"Yet," he says. "Always remember the *yet*."

"Yet," I confirm. So many *yets* right now. "But I want this. One way or another."

He dips his head closer to mine. "I'm loving this fearless side of you."

Fearless. Not a word I've ever used to describe myself. But maybe I'm becoming my own definition of it. Looking out for my son. Getting my own place. Pursuing my custom cake dreams.

Being so at home in Ian's arms.

I love the fearless side of me, too.

THIRTY-FOUR
IAN

THE SUN RISING OVER DENALI. The Milky Way stretching out over Mount Shasta. Glaciers atop Mount Rainier. I've seen a lot of magnificent sights, but nothing compares to having Tess in my arms. Her bright smile soaks through my skin until I'm made of it, happiness by osmosis.

I look past her out the back door to where August is kicking a ball with Dutch in the yard. Pretty sure I heard him declare the dog the World Cup winner, the adorable kid.

"You should celebrate," I tell Tess. Making custom cakes is a huge deal for her.

She tilts her head to the side, pretending to think. "Maybe I should throw a party."

"Definitely."

"With barbecue and cake."

"Always a good combo."

She chuckles. "And presents."

"Only for August, right?" Even if we share a birthday, this get together is supposed to be about him. I don't need anything more than what I've got right here.

Her mouth ticks up. "And party hats."

I frown at her. "Seems unnecessary."

"Mandatory."

"I object."

She leans a fraction closer. "There might be incentive to wear a party hat."

My fingers tighten on her side. "I'm listening."

She slowly moves in to press a kiss to my mouth. Soft, sweet, brief—not nearly enough.

"That's a quarter of a party hat kiss."

Her laugh exhales over my jaw. "I guess we'd better go for the whole hat."

She kisses me again, lingering this time. I let her lead, savoring the moment she sets aside her initial timidity for boldness. Her hands come up to my sides but retreat after contacting my bare skin. I slip both of mine around to her back as well as I can while still maintaining my balance on the crutches.

When she walked in, it was like being caught naked. Maybe the wrong comparison, since I've never really minded being seen that way. But being caught without my prosthesis on is an all-new ballgame. For half a second, I wanted to escape to my bedroom and secure my leg back on.

But Tess's gaze warmed so quickly, I realized she wasn't bothered by anything she was seeing. Or not seeing. I don't need to keep anything from her because she accepts me exactly as I am.

Her hands return to my sides. Tentative, maybe, but steady. I love watching her learn to let go—in all ways, but especially with me. She deepens the kiss, and just like that, I'm lost. Nothing exists outside of Tess. Her mouth, her hands, her soft little sighs against my skin.

Until August squeals in the yard.

She draws back, robbing me of her touch. But the spark in her eyes as she gazes at me is a prize all its own.

"I told August we were supposed to relax before the next party." Her mouth tilts to the side. "I don't think either of us are doing a good job with that."

"I have no complaints."

Her laugh is a red thread wrapped around my heart. "That's a relief. Maybe we could—"

My doorbell rings, cutting her off.

"Amy and Jodi said they might come by early," I tell her. Then I turn toward the living room and shout, "Door's open."

The door creaks, and steps sound on the hardwood floor. "Hello?"

My stomach sinks. That's not either of my aunts.

I crutch to the center of the kitchen to confirm for myself. But yes, that's my brother Steven walking through my living room, with Iris right behind him.

His thousand-watt grin seems designed to irritate. "Surprise!"

"Surprise is right," I mutter.

His gaze drifts to my side, locking in on Tess. His steps falter comically. "Are we interrupting something?"

I frown at him. From the hint of pink in Tess's cheeks, it's clear he caught us in a private moment. Asking just amplifies the embarrassment.

For her, anyway. I'm not embarrassed for a second.

"Tess, this is my brother, Steven, and his wife, Iris."

"It is a *delight* to meet you," Steven says, shaking hands with Tess. He gives me a meaningful look, just in case I don't know all the assumptions forming in his head. His glee is overkill. It doesn't take Sherlock Holmes to deduce what's going on.

"It's good to meet you, too," Tess tells them with a warm smile.

"What are you doing here?" I've got considerably less enthusiasm than she does.

"Amy told us about your birthday party," Iris explains. "We decided to fly in for a few days to celebrate with you."

"That's...nice."

It is, on the face of it. But Tess and I had a cozy little bubble going, and they just burst right through it.

Tess wraps a hand around my biceps. Not sure if it's a signal to be more appreciative or just a reminder she's with me, but it works either way. They're trying to be supportive. It's not their fault their support irritates me.

Not entirely.

"I need to go wrangle my son and make sure everything's ready for this evening," Tess tells them.

I turn to her. "I told you I would handle the food tonight. You've already helmed one party today. Don't worry about this one."

"I know, but I told *you* I'm still in charge of dessert."

I smile down at her. "That you are, angel."

We linger too long, considering present company, but I never want to pass up an opportunity to look at the vision before me. She finally says goodbye to our interlopers and escapes out the back door.

I turn, watching her talk with August before they both go inside next door. Dutch sits in the grass, stoically looking toward the hillside as though he alone stands guard.

"*Angel*, huh?" Steven says. "That's a new one."

I cut my gaze to him. "Shut up."

"What he means is, we're happy for you." Iris glares, but Steven doesn't notice. He's too busy gloating.

He looks me over. "Amy didn't tell us the dress code for the party was this casual."

I make a rude gesture at him. "Make yourselves at home."

I go into my bedroom and quickly put on my prosthesis and pull a shirt over my head. When I come back out, they're on the couch. Iris is flipping through my book collection, and Steven still looks far too happy.

"You've been keeping secrets." He grins at me as if he's got a few favorites.

I take the chair across from them, saying nothing. They won't be secrets if I admit to them.

"Tess seems really sweet." Iris's attempt to temper the situation isn't working.

Mostly because I'm tempted to expound on how Tess is so much more than sweet. She is that, one hundred percent. But she's also fierce and capable and tough around the edges, with the softest center I think I might die to protect. But they've got plenty of incriminating information on me already. I don't need to offer up more.

"She's the single mom?" Steven wants to know. I nod. "That's a new thing for you, isn't it?"

He says it like being involved with Tess and August is the same sort of inconsequential choice as wearing socks with sandals or changing the station from rock to hip-hop.

I just stare at him. I'm not ready to ruin this unexpected reunion with raised voices. Yet.

He finally takes the hint and eases up on the smug smile. "Whatever it takes to get you in the land of the living."

"I can always go back to my crypt," I grumble.

"Leave Ian alone," Iris says to my brother. She turns back to me. "Sunshine is a cute little town. You'll have to show us around while we're here."

"That'd be a short tour." I haven't been to many places here. I could point them in the direction the bakery. That's about it.

But it's the best stop in town.

"You could ask Tess for some ideas tonight," I add. "She'll know all the good spots."

Iris's slow nod tells me I said too much. Seems to be the theme of the last ten minutes.

"Have you bagged any of these mountains yet?" Steven asks.

"Not yet. I've been reading up on a few trails I want to tackle, though."

He claps his hands and rubs them together. He's always been overly dramatic. "That's what I like to hear. Anything we can get up to tomorrow?"

"Probably." Nothing serious, since we don't have gear, but some mountain air might do me good. "There are some half-day hikes we could do."

"I'm in. Iris?"

"As long as it's a true half-day, and not one where you pull this 'just one more mile' garbage on me for five miles." She glares at him so hard, I'm surprised he doesn't whimper.

"I did that one time, babe."

She purses her lips, still staring at him like she's waiting for him to turn to stone. "We hiked back in the dark."

He lays his hand over hers. "And we'll carry those treasured memories with us for the rest of our lives."

She snorts at his syrupy tone. "I'll trust Ian to pick the hike."

"I'll come up with something that will have us home long before dark." Possibly because I don't want to miss seeing Tess and August tomorrow evening.

"Pierce will be relieved." Steven's wide grin unsettles me. It usually means trouble. "He's been freaking out about your little sabbatical. He was afraid you'd never come back."

"Yeah." I can't put much laughter behind it when I wasn't sure I'd ever go back, either.

I'm even less sure now.

THIRTY-FIVE

TESS

IT'S OFFICIAL. I'm a starer.

No matter what anyone else does during the party, my gaze keeps returning to Ian. Across the yard kicking the soccer ball with August. Grilling our dinners at the barbecue with Jodi. Talking politely with Mom. I watch him like we're having a staring contest he doesn't know about, and if I look away, I'll lose.

He's just so happy tonight. He seemed a little disgruntled by the surprise arrival of his brother and sister-in-law, but he relaxes more and more as the evening rolls on. I can't stop marveling over his casual friendliness with everyone. I'm a scientist observing her subject in an all-new environment, amazed by her findings.

The findings are: *I am in deep.*

"Uh oh," Hope says. "Ian just asked Griffin about the best local hiking spots. They're going to be there a while."

Griffin, Steven, Iris, and Ian are in the yard with sodas in their hands. Ian's nodding along while Griffin describes something. He looks over and catches me watching. When he flashes a small, slanted smile just for me, we might as well be the only ones out here.

"It's too bad Lila's sick," Wren says. "I bet her new guy would love to get in on this conversation."

I pull my attention back to my friends.

"How do we keep getting the outdoorsy ones?" Hope's gaze darts to her fiancé as if she can't help herself, either.

"I won't be part of your little group." Wren tips her nose up. "I'm holding out for an indoorsy type. A bookish guy. Someone who plays chess and drinks tea and never has grease under his fingernails."

Hope takes a sip of soda, glancing away. That list got suspiciously detailed.

"You don't play chess," I point out. It's my safest response here.

Wren makes a face at me. "It's part of the vibe I'm looking for, though."

August slips between me and Wren. "Mama, can we do cake and presents now?"

"Sure, buddy." He's been as patient as I can reasonably expect. Probably because he already had cake and presents once today. "Want to ask Ian to come to the patio?"

"Yeah!" He pumps his fist and sprints across the grass.

I go inside and pull the cake from the fridge. Wren follows me to grab plates, forks, and napkins but pauses when she sees the cake.

"That is the cutest freaking thing. Has August seen it?"

"I told him not to peek. We'll find out by his reaction whether he resisted the urge or not."

Outside, everyone gathers around our patio table, with Ian and August standing in the place of honor. I set the cake in front of them. It's a strawberry-lemon cake as requested, but I kept to the dinosaur theme. I frosted the single-tier, three-layer cake in light brown buttercream and piped big, green leaves all around the outside to give it a rainforest effect. On top, I added a T-rex footprint filled with chocolate ganache.

I do know some movie references.

August slaps his hands on both cheeks when he sees the cake, his mouth forming a perfect 'O.' Oh, yeah. He peeked.

"Where did you buy that?" Iris asks me.

"Tess made it." Ian sounds as proud as if he told her I'm a brain surgeon. "That's what she does."

I press two candles on either side of the T-rex footprint, smiling to myself.

"Seriously? This is so impressive."

Hope slides over to her, phone out. "Check out what she made for our engagement party. Chocolate cake with mascarpone cream and salted caramel."

Iris looks from the phone to me. "I want to eat this picture."

"Best cake I ever had," Griffin adds.

"Shall we sing for the birthday boys?" Mom says. I tell myself she's just trying to keep the party going.

"One more thing." I grab my secret stash and pass them around.

Ian exhales a playful groan when he sees the party hats. I secure one on top of August's head and turn to him. "They're part of the fun."

He frowns, but his gaze is on my mouth. "I'm going to need more bribes."

"I can do that," I whisper, securing the elastic beneath his beard and settling the hat on his head.

I light the candles, and Ian hefts August onto his hip while we sing the birthday song to them. August tilts his head to touch Ian's chin, smiling like a goofball and hamming it up for the phone cameras turned their way.

I take pictures too, but mostly, I just watch them. They're so adorable together, soaking up the attention of our small group of friends. Ian locks eyes with me and winks. Pretty sure Wren and Hope hear my sigh. I am a hopeless case.

They each blow out a candle, my two birthday boys.

I slice the cake, and Wren passes out plates. My happy little heart goes on floating as everyone praises the Meyer lemon cake with strawberry cream filling.

"Oh my gosh." Iris covers her mouth with one hand, her eyes wide. "Steven, I'm sorry. I'm leaving you to run away with this cake."

Steven swallows his bite. "I knew a baked good would get between us one day."

"Why aren't these on Blackbird's menu?" Jodi has no idea the weight behind her innocent question. "I haven't even finished my slice, and I want another one."

I stuff my face with cake, making eye contact with nobody. I'm planning to talk with Mom, but a joint birthday party really isn't the time for me to put my foot down.

"We're still working out her terms." Wren's saucy answer earns some laughs. "She demands a raise and a bigger workspace."

"She deserves it." Amy shoots a meaningful look Mom's way.

Hope makes a strangled sound. "You're not avoiding adding cakes to the menu because of me, right?"

Mom sets a hand on her arm. "We're glad to have The Painted Daisy right where it is."

Hope relaxes again and takes another bite of cake. "Thank goodness."

She convinced Mom to sublet part of our bakery space to her a couple of years ago. Before Mom took it over, our shop was a restaurant, and the extra floor space made sense. But we never quite figured out a good use for so much room as a bakery. We're not really an eat-in location, and so much empty space was honestly kind of dreary. Hope moving her gift shop in was the perfect solution.

Still. Sometimes it hurts that Mom believes in Hope's small business dreams more than mine.

"Presents now?" August asks.

I wipe the chocolate frosting mustache from his upper lip. He only had a sliver of cake, but half of it made it onto his face. "Presents now."

Mom helps me roll out the August-sized bicycle I've had stashed away in her garage for the last week. He puts his bike helmet with dinosaur overlay on immediately. He starts pedaling around the patio, thanks to the training wheels I had installed. Wobbling steadily from one side to the other, but he's moving.

"That's so perfect for him," Wren says.

"Shepherd helped me pick everything out."

She purses her lips, clearly torn on whether or not she still likes the bike.

August receives a few more gifts, including a giant T-rex from Ian. It roars and shrieks and even makes thudding sounds as if it's stalking prey. He uses it to harass the squishy stuffed animal Hope gave him.

"Now Ian's presents!" August's clutching the T-rex in one hand, the squishy in the other, still wearing his new bike helmet.

Ian tries to go all scowly on me, but it's too late. Presents are happening whether he likes it or not.

I pass August the two packages I set aside. "Can you give these to him?"

He takes them and trots to the other side of the patio. That's right. I'm stooping to having August deliver the gifts. Ian's already admitted he can't say no to him.

Ian takes them, watching me from beneath scolding

eyebrows. He unwraps one like he's trying to defuse a bomb. August *was* the bomb when it was his turn to unwrap presents, decimating paper in a blink.

"That one's from Mama," August tells him.

"Is it?" Ian moves even slower. He peels back the paper, revealing a small leather case. He pauses, staring at it in his hand.

My heart pounds, desperate to know what he thinks of it. I can't tell if he recognizes the stamped logo on the case. He swallows. Then carefully pulls out the vintage compass.

His gaze collides with mine, holding me in place as firmly as if his arms were around me. Emotions crash across his face. Gratitude. Surprise. Affection. *More.* His lips part, but no words come.

I lift a shoulder. He said he was lost. I want to help him find his way.

"What is it?" August wants to know.

Ian shows it to him. I picked up the classic brass compass at a secondhand store. They said it's a good brand, but older and scuffed. Still works exactly as intended, though.

"It's a compass." His voice sounds gravelly as he points at the dial. "This needle helps you figure out where you are, and where you want to go."

"Thank goodness," Steven says. "You were always getting clients lost on trips."

Laughter moves around as August grabs the other present. "This one's from me."

He wiggles the whole time Ian unwraps it.

"A joke book." Ian holds it up like a trophy. "Just what I needed, buddy. Thank you."

August is pleased as can be. His focus lasts about five seconds before he asks for a fire in the fire pit. Griffin offers to help, and he follows August into the yard to inspect what we've got. The rest of our little group disperses, cleaning up the dessert plates or taking empty seats around the two tables.

Ian slips his hat off and makes his way over until he's standing in front of me, staring so intently my toes curl.

"Let's help Griffin get that fire going." Hope pulls Wren away, glancing between the two of us.

Honestly, I barely notice them.

Ian pulls me into his arms, holding me tight as if he's trying to fuse all my cracked and broken pieces back together. Or maybe he's trying to fix his. He sighs against me, pressing a kiss to my neck. Joy fizzes through me like I'm made of tiny, perfect bubbles. I'm not even sure my feet touch the ground.

"Thank you," he says softly.

When he draws back, I'm ninety percent sure he's going to kiss me in front of our families, but he must think better of it. "Can we talk tonight?"

"Of course." As if I'm in the mood to deny him anything.

"Great." He squeezes my shoulders, but if he's tempted to lean in, he doesn't indulge.

I wouldn't mind a little indulgence.

August calls for him to join in the fire-starting adventure. Ian hooks a thumb over his shoulder. "I'd better go help."

He leaves to take up position around the fire pit with the others. We haven't used it yet, and frankly, I didn't realize we had all the supplies for a fire. But Griffin's arranging small pieces of wood in it and using the lighter I got out for the birthday candles. In a minute, they've got a good fire going. The sky is fading into twilight, blue deepening to purple, making the flames glow.

Iris and Steven approach me while I'm still gazing dreamy-eyed at Ian. I try to tone it down, but I can't do anything about how flushed I still am after our hug.

"That cake was so good," Iris tells me. She's got short, black hair and olive skin. Her gorgeous turquoise necklace makes her look effortlessly stylish like Lila. "I'm a wedding photographer, and I can't tell you how many times a cake looks beautiful but tastes like it's been frozen for a month."

"Thank you. I still make everything fresh." And don't intend to ever change.

"Do you make wedding cakes too?"

I can't help but look over at Ian. He's talking to Griffin, with August and Dutch making cute little bookends on either side.

"That's the plan."

Iris follows my gaze. "We're so happy Ian's made a friend out here. He wasn't very friendly when he left Colorado."

"No." I smile, remembering those first days. "He wasn't very friendly when we first met, either. But he's come out of his shell."

Iris laughs softly. "Pretty soon, you'll wish he would go back into his shell. Ian at full blast is a lot to handle."

"Oh, no," Steven puts in. "We need him at full power when he comes back."

All the light, effervescent bubbles inside me pop at once, slamming my feet down to earth. My lungs ache like I'm breathing in cement. I keep my smile on, clinging to the fragile, sham of a thing as if it can save me from drowning.

"Is he going back soon?" I hope I sound casual, and not as if my heart is fissuring like a crinkle-topped cookie.

"As soon as possible. We've been waiting on him to sort himself out for two years." Steven seems to realize just what he's said. "I get it. He went through a lot with the accident and recovery. It's understandable he needed to work through some things. But look at him now."

I do. He's smiling and happy and *himself*. I can't turn around and be sad when I got exactly what I wanted. I befriended him. Maybe helped him get his spark of life back.

I dug my own grave, lay down in it, and now the dirt's raining over on me.

My throat sticks as I swallow. "Look at him now."

Isn't this what he wanted when he came out here? To rest and recuperate. So he could go home to the business he built with his brothers. So he could go back to the life he worked so hard to create for himself. The life he misses *every day*. This was never a permanent move.

He catches my eye again, and his smile glows in the firelight. It hits me like a sucker punch. *I love him, and now, I'm going to lose him.*

I told myself not to sail into dangerous waters, but here I am. Shipwrecked.

THIRTY-SIX
IAN

I NEVER COULD HAVE PREDICTED I'd be wearing a party hat when I realized I'm in love. It was festive, at least. But in the moment, I couldn't even regret the ridiculous thing. When I opened that compass, all the pieces clicked together, and I *knew*. Tess is the one. She sees me in a way I haven't let anyone try in years. Maybe ever. She accepts me for the man I am today —and that just makes me want to be a better one tomorrow. She's the woman I want to spend the rest of my life with, now and forever.

My heart stutters in my chest as I finish loading her dishwasher. Forever isn't a word I'm familiar with. Most things in my life, no matter how good, have been temporary. A collection of excellent memories, fun while they last, but they don't stick around. And a few months ago, I would have thought the idea of *the one* as juvenile. Something out of fairy tales, not real life.

But now? I know that angel is meant to be mine.

"August is ready to say goodnight."

I look over my shoulder to find Tess smiling softly from his doorway. She's been getting him ready for bed while I finish the after-party clean up. Another small, domestic thing I want more of. I just want to be with her, in whatever capacity she'll let me.

I dry off my hands and head into August's darkened room. He's illuminated by his night light, tucked up in bed, his arm around the T-rex I gave him. Dutch is curled up next to him, already used to this new sleeping arrangement.

My phone's wallpaper is a picture of the two of them in their party hats.

I sit on the bed beside him. "Did you have a good birthday?"

"So good. Did you have a good birthday?" He giggles at the reminder we share the day.

"The best." The happiest. The most significant. All the superlatives.

"Will you take me on a hike one day?" he asks. He over-heard some of the conversation between Griffin, Steven, and me. "A big hike? Up a whole mountain?"

"Anything you want." And I mean it. Mountains, lakes, valleys—there's nowhere I wouldn't go for him. He owns my heart as much as his mom does.

"And help me ride my bike?"

"I think you're doing a pretty good job already. But absolutely."

He nods. "Okay. Night, Ian."

"Goodnight, buddy." I kiss his forehead and leave the room, calling Dutch to follow.

In the kitchen, Tess is waiting for me. My heart thumps a painful beat, desperate to get closer to her. "Do you want to watch a movie or something?"

The bone-deep need to tell her I love her is being edged out by nerves, of all things. I have no experience with these kinds of conversations. Declarations. Am I supposed to do something romantic, set the scene, just blurt it out and lay everything on the line?

I've never said those words to a woman before. The idea feels like a steeper climb than I would have thought. It's a bit like those dreams where I'm back in high school, taking an important test I didn't study for, and also, I forgot to put on pants. I've never felt so unqualified.

I'm fully clothed, at least, but drastically unprepared.

"Maybe we could go outside?" she says.

I nod and follow her onto the back patio. Stars shine overhead, our faces visible by the soft glow coming from her apartment. I thought we were heading to the deck chairs or maybe the coals in the fire pit, but Tess stands at the edge of the patio, her arms wrapped around herself.

"Hard to say, but I think August had a good time," I tell her.

Especially when we played the game where people randomly get splatted in the face by a dollop of whipped cream. Wren, Griffin, and I got messy, but August came out unscathed. I don't want to call the kid a cheater, but...

She exhales a soft laugh. "Pretty sure he'll never forget it."

She winces as if something hurts, like the night I tended her scraped elbow.

I move a step closer. "What's wrong?"

She shrugs, her expression hard to read in the weak light.

I rub a hand across her upper back. "Talk to me, angel."

All the discussion about her cake business might have been too much, right there in front of her mom. Hopefully, it didn't make her doubt herself or what she wants. She was a vision this afternoon, so certain she's ready to take this next step for herself. I don't want her to let that spark die out.

Tess sucks in a breath like she's preparing to dive into the ocean. "I don't think I can do this."

"Do what?" But I already know. I hear it in her voice. It's not her cake business she's doubting. It's me.

My ribcage aches as if someone's tightening a slip knot around me.

"I don't think it's a good idea for us to keep seeing each other...like this."

Funny how a whisper can echo louder than any shout. My ears pound with it.

I let my hand fall away from her back, all the words I wanted to say to her disintegrating like ice in a lava flow. The feelings behind them don't fade, though. They burn me up from the inside.

"Why not?" As if I want to know all the reasons she thinks I'm not a good bet. I could list them for her. Just give me a paper and pen.

"I need to make good decisions." She's stoic, like she's reading off a notecard, something she planned in advance to say when the time was right.

Or everything went wrong.

"And I would be a bad decision." It's not even a question. Of course I would. I'm thirty-seven and I've never had a lasting relationship. I'm out of work and not even looking for a job. I don't know the first thing about being a good dad to August.

Why does that one feel like the biggest failure of all?

She turns to face me. "How long are you staying in Sunshine?"

Her soft question might as well be an accusation. But of course Tess would soften the blow as much as she can. She's kind as she slices me to ribbons.

"I don't know." No job, no plans, no prospects. No wonder she thinks this would be a mistake. What do I have to offer her?

"I've got August to think about. He's already so attached to you, I don't know how he'll handle it when you leave."

The idea of hurting him makes my own heart ache, but he's

not the one I'm thinking of most right now. "And you? Is this just about protecting August's feelings?"

Her gentle smile is a knife finding its mark between my ribs. "I'm attached to you, too."

I take her shoulders, clinging to that scrap of hope. Maybe I can still save this, save us. "Angel—"

"But you're not staying." Her voice breaks as a tear tracks down her cheek. "You have a business and a life to get back to. And I'll be left to pick up the pieces when you leave. I need to do what's best for us."

"And that's not me."

Her sad smile is the deathblow that finally splits my cracking heart in two.

"I'm sorry, Ian."

I brush the tear on her cheek away with my thumb. "So am I."

I drop my hands from her, closing her tear into my fist. She seems to struggle over what else to say but must decide she's said enough. After a minute, she goes into the house with a soft "goodbye."

I sit in the deck chair closest to me, crumbling away. The smell of gasoline and motor oil come back to me, the air seemingly thick with it. I just spun out again, but this time, I don't have the heart to save myself.

I just bleed out.

THIRTY-SEVEN
TESS

HOT TIP: nobody can tell you're crying when you're swimming in a lake.

Wren put together a day trip to distract August and me. She didn't say it in so many words, but I can do the math. She's been tiptoeing around me ever since I told her I...well, that I chickened out with Ian.

It's not really a breakup if you were never together. And technically, we're still friends. I didn't sever ties, I only said I couldn't see him *that way* anymore. But since then, we haven't seen him at all. I guess we're both avoiding each other.

The duplex has never felt so stifling.

Wren invited Hope and Lila along with their men to come out to Caldera Lake with us. It's a gorgeous day, clear and hot, and the water reflects the mountains in the distance. We're splashing around in the sun, having the time of our lives.

Or looking like we are.

"But why couldn't Ian come, Mama?" August asks.

I can't count how many times he's asked about Ian in the last three days. I foolishly hoped he'd be focused on Dutch, but it's Ian he keeps asking for. Every time he asks, my heart crushes into a finer dust, knowing if I'd been smarter, I would have spared him this.

But I let him get attached, just like I did. The single-parenting advice columnists would be so disappointed in me.

"Ian's brother is still in town." It's the truth but also a lie. I know they're still here because their rental car keeps showing up next door. But since I never invited Ian in the first place, it's a shabby excuse. "So we just came with friends today."

"But he's our friend, too."

My little guy has no idea how he's twisting the vise around my chest.

"Hey, buddy!" Griffin swims over to commandeer the purple hippo float August is perched on. "Want to play I Spy?"

Hope rests her elbows on the edge of the float. "Griffin's good at I Spy. He needs someone who can really challenge him. Think you can?"

"Yeah!" August bounces on his knees on the big float, holding onto his life jacket.

They swim a little distance away from me, looping him into their game and taking his mind off of Ian.

I guess everyone knows about the real reason behind lake day.

Wren swims closer to me. I hate the concern on her face—she's supposed to be a sassy spitfire teasing me for being a stick in the mud, not a worried sister checking in on my broken heart.

"When are you going to talk to Mom?"

Oh. I lost my momentum for that conversation after I...did what I did with Ian. I don't know how to describe it. Smashed my own happiness in order to avoid worse heartbreak in the future? Doesn't feel like such a hot bargain right now.

"I have some time. Charlie won't be ready to start hosting weddings for a couple of months."

"If you keep putting it off, I'm afraid you'll back out entirely."

It's crossed my mind. However this shakes out, I'll be rocking the boat at the family business. And as I reminded myself this week, I'm not good at staying afloat. Dry land is best for me. I can be happy making pies and cupcakes. The status quo isn't so bad.

"Don't give up on this," she says gently. "Don't be like Mom and put off your own happiness for literal decades."

I dip my head under the water, washing away fresh tears.

"I'm trying to preserve my happiness, Wren."

She shakes her head, bobbing in the lake. "Not this way. Not by never risking a little heartache."

"It's not *a little*," I choke out.

I paddle a few strokes until she's behind me. Pulling away from Ian has left a visceral pain beneath my ribs. I knew I'd gotten in over my head, but I didn't realize I was this close to the bottom. Every day we don't talk on the back patio is a fresh ache, every night we don't share a few moments together a new cut. I hate every minute of it.

But doesn't that prove this is for the best? Better to get out now before I'm in any deeper. Better to spare August from caring even more for someone we can't keep.

All those *betters* don't bring me any comfort.

Wren swims back into my line of sight. "Hey. I'm here for you no matter what."

"I know."

She tries for a smile. "I push because I care."

"I know that, too."

Past her, August and Hope shout at Lila and Grant, who seem to be making out in the water a short distance away. They tone it down, but barely.

"They're so cute together." And not just because the man

truly is an Adonis sculpted by Michelangelo himself. They haven't known each other long, but it's obvious their affection goes beyond any casual acquaintance. They really seem to bring out the best in each other and want the other's happiness.

It's both adorable and selfishly painful to watch.

"He's going back to Texas soon, though," Wren says.

"I guess Lila can handle the heartbreak." Not sure how, after everything she's been through. She's a lot braver than I am.

"Or she knows whatever time they have together will be worth the risk."

Wren's pointed look cuts just as sharp as her words.

Risk. Caution. Here, both paths lead to heartache.

"I think you're giving up too soon," she tells me.

"You're terrible at distracting people." I duck my head under the water again.

She swims even closer. "I saw you two at the party. I've never seen you look at anyone that way."

Because I've never felt this much for anyone before. That's the whole point in trying to protect myself. Even if I'm pretty sure it's too late.

"Both you and August were so happy, Tess. And the three of you together? You looked like a fam—"

"Don't."

She winces at my clipped tone.

"Please," I say more gently. I know she's trying to help. But I can't take it right now. I can't hear how great things might have been *if only*. "It hurts too much to think that way. Just...don't."

Wren's gaze grows sad, but she swims over to join August, Hope, and Griffin.

And me? I let my tears run into the lake water.

THIRTY-EIGHT

IAN

GETTING into a fistfight with your brother at a family dinner is rude, right? I need the clarification because Steven's sorely tempting me.

"I can't figure out what's gotten into him," he's saying to the others.

Amy and Jodi invited the three of us to their house for dinner on the last night before Steven and Iris fly back to Colorado. I thought about hiding out in the duplex, but my former refuge has turned into a brutal reminder of everything I want but can't have. So I joined them, and I've regretted it since I walked in the door.

"He sure had a better attitude at his party." Steven looks me over. "His scowling is back up to nuclear levels, too."

"Stop talking about me like I'm not here," I bite out.

"You've barely spoken to us tonight. I wasn't sure it mattered."

I look away, my arms crossed over my chest like a petulant child. I shouldn't have come. I'm not in a mood to be around anybody, especially not people who find my bad attitude amusing.

"Ian." Amy tries to soothe me with gentleness. "What's wrong?"

"Nothing's wrong." Nothing I want to explain, anyway.

The woman I love made a preemptive strike. Ended things before she could get hurt. For her sake, I hope it worked. For mine, well...let's just say, my heart's an open wound, and I'm not even trying to stanch the blood.

"You were so happy at the party." Iris watches me like she's trying to figure out the best angle to capture my morose mood. "What went wrong?"

Only a fool would say Tess was my sunshine and now that she's gone, my days are full of oppressive rainclouds. But I am a fool, so...

"We all know heartbreak when we see it." Jodi opts for a scalpel straight across my flesh.

I want to rage. Tell them it's none of their business. Pretend my heart isn't bleeding in my chest. But that road has never taken me very far. And honestly, I've lost the fight for pretending.

I sigh, dragging a hand over my hair to tug on the knot at the back of my head. "Tess doesn't want to see me anymore."

They seem surprised by this news, as if they didn't suspect something like it from my attitude these last few days.

"What happened?" Amy wants to know.

I run my thumb over the condensation on my water glass until I catch a drop the same way I caught her tear. "She told me she can't risk her heart on someone who's not sticking around."

It's all I've been able to think about. She's afraid of seeing in me the ghost of the man who left her pregnant and alone. I want to rail at the comparison, but am I really so much better than that guy? I was ready to tell her I love with no clear plan for a future with her. Just living in the moment the same way I always have. She deserves more than that. They both do.

Across from me, Iris raises her hand. "That might be our fault."

I look between the two of them. "Which part?"

Iris lifts her eyebrows at Steven as if that will jog his memory.

"What?" he says. "I didn't say it to break them up. That's just a fact."

"What did you say to her?"

He spreads his hands wide. "The truth. That you're coming back to Durango and the business as soon as possible."

The women at the table groan over his obvious stupidity. Even I can see it, but as the one his stupidity devastated, that fits.

"What?" he says again. "This is just a short-term thing, right?"

Fleeing here started out that way, but nothing about it feels temporary anymore. Especially not how I feel about Tess.

"I know you like her," he says. "But you're not actually serious about a woman with a kid, are you?"

I bring my hand down hard on the table. "That 'woman and her kid' are everything to me. *Everything.*"

Silence rings in the room. I've said too much already, but I keep talking.

"Tess is all things sweet and soft and gentle. But if you cross the people she loves, she'll make you regret it. She is sunlight on my skin. A warm embrace when I'm cold. She is laughter on my worst day. She's a better woman than I deserve, and I want her anyway. Her *and* August, Steven. I want them both."

They stare at me for a full five seconds. Yeah, I got a little poetic there. Love and rejection will do that to a guy.

"Ian." Iris reaches across the table to where my hand still rests. "I know the plan was to come back to Colorado when you were ready...but you can always change the plan."

"What?" Steven sputters. "That's not what we're—"

"It's your life," Jodi says over him. "And I believe you *do* deserve the love you want. Maybe even more so because you think you don't."

"It's the shabby men who think they deserve it all who actually don't," Iris adds.

That shuts Steven's mouth.

"Nobody deserves her," I tell them. "Least of all me. And it's not just about Colorado. It's everything she's too good to say. I've never had a relationship like this, never had anything close. The old me wouldn't have wanted one."

Then, I would have been stupid enough to walk away from her. Now, I want her more than anything, and she's still slipping through my fingers.

"You keep saying you're not the same man you used to be." Amy's steely gaze pierces me. "Maybe that's true in more ways than one."

"Do you love her?" Iris asks gently.

"Yes." I would rather tell Tess before anyone at this table, but I can't sit here and deny it. "It scares the hell out of me for all the ways I could ruin this, but yes. I love her."

"Then don't let her get away."

"Are we just going to act like our business isn't even in the picture?" Steven asks.

Iris shoots him a withering look. "Yes."

"As long as I understand what's going on," he mutters.

"I'm pretty sure there's this thing about accepting a woman's 'no' the first time." I've thought about knocking on Tess's door fifty times a day since she rejected me. But I can't barge my way into her life if she doesn't want me there.

"I'm not talking about violating her trust," Iris says. "I'm talking about earning it."

"The last guy Tess fell for didn't stick around to catch her,"

Amy tells me. "Be her soft place to land so she knows it's safe to fall for you."

I would be that for her if I could. Right now, that feels like a big if.

"I don't know if I can be the man she needs. She deserves so much more than I've ever tried to give. I don't want to fail her."

Steven huffs. "Since when do you expect to fail? You're the guy who stands in front of a blizzard and says, 'Do your worst.' You're the guy who sees something nobody's ever done before and says, 'I will.' Are you Ian Vaughn or not?"

For a long time, I thought maybe I wasn't. If I didn't have my career or my reputation, I wasn't sure I could claim to be the same man. But I'm not willing to live in limbo anymore, unsure of who I am or what I want.

I want Tess and August. I want a life here with them. I want my family.

"I am Ian Vaughn," I tell him.

And I don't run from challenges.

———

I might not run from challenges, but I sure am walking slowly to meet the one on the other end of my front porch. Possibly because I don't want to burn my hands on a hot casserole dish. Or look like a creeper who's been watching out the front window, waiting for Tess's car to pull in the driveway. One or the other.

I ring her doorbell with my elbow, a platter propped in my hands. I get about ten seconds to prepare myself before she opens the door.

I was not prepared.

She's just so...soft. Light. Open. Blond tendrils stray from her bun, framing her face with strands of sunlight. Her blue eyes widen when she sees me.

"Ian." Her breathy greeting makes my stomach dip.

"Hi, angel," I finally say.

Her gaze drops to the items in my hands. "What's this?"

"I made dinner for you and August. Chicken enchiladas with steamed broccoli, and sliced mangoes and kiwi." It's probably too much, but I need to start somewhere.

She hesitates as if maybe she wishes I hadn't started anywhere. "That's really sweet of you."

"I like taking care of you."

Her mouth drops open, but I keep talking.

"Tess, I understand your fears, and I know why you have them. You need to do what's best for you and August. But, angel, I'm going to try my hardest to prove to you that *I* am the best for you both."

She's still staring at me, mouth slightly agape, when August runs to the door.

"Hi, Ian!" He hugs me around the middle without a second's pause. "I've missed you."

I never knew that little phrase could make me so happy. "I've missed you, too, buddy."

He stands on tiptoes to peer at the items on my tray. "What do you have?"

I lower the tray so he can see. "I brought enchiladas for you and your mom."

"What's that white goo on top? I don't know if I like white goo."

I pull a silly face. "That's queso. It's cheese."

"Oh. I might like it okay. Are you going to eat dinner with us?"

"I can't. I have some things to do tonight." I hate to disappoint him, but promising him I will another time would be over-stepping.

"With Dutch?"

"Not with Dutch." I've been trying to make things easier on August by not taking Dutch into the back yard these last few days, but I don't think it worked for either of them. My dog's pining hard.

Just like his owner.

"Why don't you set the table for us?" Tess tells him.

He frowns as if he might argue but eventually wanders into the kitchen. I'm not certain he'll actually set the table, but at least he had the intent.

Tess and I watch each other over my steaming casserole dish. Reminds me of another food-related impasse we had. I move it a few inches closer to her, and she blinks as if waking up. She takes it from me, and her fingers brush over mine.

Not nearly enough, but I will take anything at this point.

"You didn't have to go to all this trouble," she says softly.

"Yes, I do. I want to do more than this, Tess. So much more."

"Why?"

"Because I looked at that compass you gave me, and I found my true north." I lean in so I can whisper. "It's you."

Her jaw works but no sound comes out. I've left my angel speechless. That's okay. I have more plans to set in motion.

"Enjoy your dinner, Tess."

———

I forgot how exhausting going to a bar with a twenty-something could be. Nathan Bridger not only knows everyone in here, but he's a chatterbox. He's introduced me to at least a dozen people tonight, every one eager to welcome me to Sunshine.

I don't hate it. I'm still not as comfortable as I used to be in a situation like this, but I'll get there. Or maybe I won't. Maybe I'll stay here in the middle of the sociable scale. It's not the worst place to be.

A few people have asked about my leg, but most have asked me more mundane questions. And even the ones who did ask haven't made it weird. Not a Mr. Miller among them. I'll run into another one eventually, but I can't let people with no social filter make me hide away anymore.

"Guy came to the medic tent every day of that festival covered head to toe in hives," Nathan's telling me. Our conversation has devolved to "dumbest things we've seen." "We give him the same line of questions every time, trying to pin it down. He says he's allergic to tree nuts but he's careful to stay away. No trail mix, no coconut oil, nothing. But we go through everything he's eaten anyway. Come to find out, he's been eating Nutella all weekend." Nathan's laugh is almost as good as August's, hearty and just slightly too loud. "He'd never had it before and was gorging on the stuff."

"Most accidents I've seen in the wild are self-inflicted." Didn't pack enough supplies, drank water that wasn't filtered, thought it'd be cool to pet a wild animal—you name it. We're all our own worst enemies.

I sure have been.

"My older brother, Graham, is the poster child for that stuff. He's a hopeless case on camping trips. These days, he sticks to field trips with his high school science class."

"Is it just the two of you?"

"Nope. First, there's our oldest brother, Luke. He's taken over our dad's hardware store. Very responsible, that one. Then Reed, who is the opposite of Graham in every way, and would rather live alone in his cabin in the woods than be around a living soul. Then Graham, then our sister, Lucy. She's the wild card. *Then*, me."

"And I thought two brothers was a lot."

"Oh, it was chaos growing up. That's what I want when I have a family. Kids everywhere."

Not that long ago, I would have said that sounded horrible. Now, after spending time with one rambunctious child...it's not such a bad plan.

He points the rim of his beer bottle at me. "Did you tell your brothers you're staying yet?"

I stare at him. I haven't mentioned a word about that.

He flashes me a cheeky look. "Come on. I'm a very persuasive guy."

I can only chuckle. "It was all you, huh?"

"And the help of two cute blondes."

I point a finger in warning. Call me old-fashioned, but I don't like him talking about Tess that way. "Yeah, I told them. They're dealing with it."

Maybe I could have figured out a way to do the kinds of rigorous guides I used to do. Invested in specialty prosthetics and foot attachments, made modifications to my trips. But those aren't options now that I know what I'd be missing out on here.

Everything.

"I submitted an online application to Backcountry EMT." It wouldn't be so bad if the next phase of my life is more about helping other people than helping myself.

His grin is an obnoxious thing to behold. "I should have been a salesman. Look at me go."

"You're going to give yourself a gloating injury."

He holds his beer bottle out. "Did we just become best friends?"

It's a little much. But I've missed this, no matter how exhausting or obnoxious.

"Best friends," I confirm.

His attention fixes on something past my shoulder. "Hey. Want to meet Leo Dalesandro?"

"The football player?" Should probably tack on *former* football player to that, after his brutal injury last season and retirement announcement.

"He's over there with Shepherd Callahan."

"Do you know Leo?"

"Nah." Nathan grins. "But I know Shepherd, and that's close enough. Should we go say hello?"

My attempt to make a friendly gesture has turned into more introductions than I ever expected. But hey. Might as well keep on trying.

"Why not?"

THIRTY-NINE

TESS

I CANNOT TAKE ALL the side-eye today. Mom and Wren need to keep their eyeballs to themselves and knock it off with the weird looks. I'm fine.

I'm just...shaken. Anyone would be after a man tells her she's his *true north*.

I was so stunned last night, I just stood in my doorway, staring like a fish. Ian said goodnight and walked away, and it still took me a full minute to come to my senses.

August asking where the plates are helped break the spell. Kids are fun like that.

I can't stop hearing Ian telling me he found his true north, and it's made me wobbly. I'll be boxing up a pie and those words will tumble around in my brain, and my fingers get too shaky to close up the tabs. I keep mis-keying in customers' totals. My piping work this morning was far from the best. I'm distracted.

They've noticed.

"Wren," Mom says. "Why don't you close up early?"

We stare at her. Blackbird's Bakery is closed one day a week and major holidays, and that's it. We only closed early a couple of times when August had to go to the hospital years ago. I check my phone as if maybe she's having some kind of freaky premonition, but his numbers are just fine.

"What's going on?" I ask. Calm. Normal. The shaky hands mean nothing.

"Come sit down." She takes a seat at one of our rarely-used tables. "I want to talk to you girls."

Wren does as she's asked and locks the front door, spinning the sign in the window to *Closed*. Somebody could theoretically walk over from Hope's shop, but I guess we'll deal with that if it happens.

We sit across from her, exchanging glances as though we're trying to figure out which one of us is in trouble. I already know it's me. I went from walking around like a Barbie doll the last few days, with dead eyes and a plastic smile, to fumbling over my own hands. I haven't been lectured about my job performance since high school, but I probably deserve it today.

"I want to tell you both that I'm seeing someone." Mom's a little too stiff, like she doesn't know how to approach this personal revelation. In typical Mom fashion, she opted to tackle it straight on.

Wren and I exchange glances. Not where we saw that going.

Also: *finally*.

"Are you trying to tell us we're getting a stepdad?" Wren jokes.

"Maybe. Yes. If you want him to be that to you."

That shuts us both up. This is *serious* serious.

"Daniel and I have been friends for a long time." She spins the garnet ring our grandma gave her on her right hand. "I knew he wanted more with me, but...I was afraid." She smiles gently. "At my age, I was afraid."

It's hard to think of her as being afraid or fearful, and not because of her age. Fifty-five is the new forty, right? But she's stepped up to do so much for us, she's been more like a super-woman than somebody who would ever cower in fear.

"After your dad left us with nothing, I promised myself nobody would ever put me in that position again. I wouldn't rely on anyone again, financially or emotionally. I never wanted to be hurting and alone. So I focused on you girls and the bakery. My friendships. It worked for a while. Maybe too long."

As close as we are, she doesn't talk about this with us. It's odd to hear her talk about Dad at all, let alone how much it devastated her when he left.

"When Daniel came along, I clung to that mentality. I turned him down whenever he'd ask me out. It hurt, but I thought it was for the best. I thought I was being strong. Saving myself heartache. It took me too long to realize Daniel wasn't the one hurting me—I was."

She focuses her laser beam eyes on me. "I didn't mean to, but I think I passed those lessons onto you girls."

I tear my gaze away to stare out the front window. That's what I've been doing, isn't it? Protecting myself from hurt by pushing Ian away. But I haven't protected myself from anything. It still hurts, and I did it all to myself.

Maybe Wren was right. Maybe I was too quick to let him go.

"Where did all this self-reflection come from?" Wren asks with her usual tact.

"I've been talking with Kat McBride. And Amy and Jodi."

I meet her gaze again. *Do not ask. Do not ask.*

"They're the ones who helped me realize I was hurting us both by refusing Daniel." Her eyes soften, and she takes my hand. "And that maybe you're doing the same thing in your life."

We are carbon copies, after all.

"Maybe," I whisper. "I don't want August or me to get hurt."

"Does it hurt anyway?"

I nod because a *yes* would break me.

"I can't tell you what to do," Mom says. "I've been lucky that Daniel's been content to be my friend all this time. He's been patient, but he's been here for me whenever I needed him, too. In big and small ways."

I think of Ian stepping up to watch August. How he cared for both of us when August got sick. How patient and understanding he's been with me. The way he kisses me with his whole soul. My need for a guaranteed future made me write off everything he's already been proving to me every day.

"I found my true north. It's you."

I think maybe I've been an idiot. I still don't know if he's staying in Sunshine, but those aren't the words of someone planning on packing up and leaving.

"How did you fix things with him?" I ask totally casually and not at all fishing for ideas.

"The next time he asked me out 'as friends,' I kissed him." Mom's slow smile has a touch of cheek to it. "We figured it out from there."

"You are blowing my mind right now." Wren stares as if she just suggested we add mincemeat pies to the menu. "I had no idea this side of you existed."

Mom rolls her eyes, but honestly, I'm not that far behind Wren.

"Out of curiosity, how long has Sheriff O'Grady been trying to date you?" Wren always comes through with the important questions.

"You know it's Daniel O'Grady?"

Wren shrugs. "Tess is a snoop."

We laugh because she's fooled nobody.

Mom glances to the side. "It's been three years."

Wren slaps both hands on the Formica table. "What? You rejected that silver fox hot cop for literal years?"

Mom laughs, but a hint of blush hits her cheeks. "It wasn't easy. But that's not quite my point in telling you all this. I don't want you girls to live your lives in fear like I did for so long. I want you to be brave. Choose your own happiness."

They both keep their eyes on me, since I'm the one in need of this life lesson. What's that saying? A ship in the harbor is safe, but that's not what it was made for. I don't want to live my whole life—or even the next twenty years—stuck in the same safe harbor because I'm afraid of storms.

"I love you girls," Mom says. "I want all the best for both of you. I hope you know it."

"We do," I say with a nod.

Mom seems satisfied and starts to get up, but I take her hand to hold her in place. "We have more to talk about."

"Oh. Okay. I'm ready."

I'm not sure she is.

"I want to start a custom cake arm at Blackbird's."

Her mouth falls open, but she snaps it shut again. I'll take that as a good sign.

"I love making cakes. I get a nice bonus from the private orders I get, but I want to make more than just a few a month. Moonlight Lodge has asked me to be their wedding cake vendor, and I agreed."

Mom's watching me as if she's calculating costs and mapping work hours. "Wren and I won't be able to keep up with our menu if you're doing something else every day."

"That's easily solved," Wren says. "We hire on another baker. Or two or three."

Mom draws in a long breath. She looks to the front counter as though trying to imagine someone new standing there. "Doubling our employees? I don't like having to rely on anyone else."

"But then you could take more time off to be with your hot cop."

Wren knows how to find a silver lining.

"The amount of money I could make on my cakes is significant," I tell Mom. "I don't want to do this without you guys. But I will if it's my only option."

She blinks hard at that. "I never wanted to be unfair to you girls. I was just trying..."

"To protect us," I finish for her. "To keep us safe. But sometimes a little risk is worth it."

"Ooh, look at us, going against type," Wren says. "Mom kissed a silver fox, and you're all about taking risks. Maybe I should go be nice to Shepherd."

"You really should," Mom tells her. "I've heard how you talk to that man."

Wren crosses her arms over her chest. "I changed my mind."

Mom shakes her head at her, but she's smiling too much for the scolding to stick. "I love you girls. I want the best for us—and Blackbird's. Maybe we should give this a try."

"Really?" I know she's not a liar, but I need the confirmation.

"My friends have been encouraging me about this, too. Your cakes are popular around town—I get asked about them more than you can imagine. It's a smart business decision." Her eyes are suspiciously wet. "And I want to support you however I can."

We do the least Krause-women thing ever and group hug.

"I love you emotional dummies," Wren says.

Mom kisses her cheek. "Thank you, sweetest daughter, for that beautiful declaration. I love you both."

"I love you, too," I say, squeezing them tighter.

"Now what are you going to do?" Wren asks me when we finally let each other go.

"I think I'm going to sail my ship out to sea."

Mom's eyebrows lift, but Wren smirks.

"She's going to go find her pirate."

————

I don't have a plan. I should have a plan, right?

When August and I get home, he heads straight for the back door the way he's been doing for weeks. But unlike the last few days, he has happy news to report.

"Dutch is outside, Mama! Can I go play?"

My heart thunders, and nothing's happening yet. Ian isn't even in sight. But it rumbles in there anyway, and I'm back to being a wobbly bundle of energy.

Poker face, don't fail me now.

"Sure, you can."

I follow him into the back yard. He finds a tennis ball and starts up Dutch's favorite game. They're so cute together.

Ian's door snicks open, and I turn to see him cross the patio toward me. He's got another plate in his hands, this time filled with what might be baked goods. He holds them out in offering.

"They're honey scones. I made them for you and August. Seemed the neighborly thing to do."

His mouth ticks up a tiny fraction, and my heart rate doubles. Definitely not safe. I take the plate from him, and the soft scent of honey drifts up from the warm scones.

He slips his hands into his shorts pockets. "That's a lie, really. It wasn't to be neighborly. You bring so much sweetness into my life, I thought you deserved a little back."

All the possible grand gestures and meaningful speeches that flew through my mind on the drive home disappear. I just need to take a page out of Mom's book.

I set the plate on my patio table and take the two steps into Ian's space. I cup his face in my hands, his red beard scratchy beneath my touch. His eyes light with an almost painfully cautious hope before I go on tiptoes to crush my mouth to his.

My enthusiastic kiss is a little desperate, but I do not care. His arms circle my back, pressing me against him, just as frantic. I fit against him so perfectly, I just *know*. This is where I belong. But I need to tell him, too, and not just show him.

Showing him is pretty great, though.

I pull back enough to look into his eyes. "I don't want to be afraid anymore, Ian. For all that you are, and all that you've been to me and August—I couldn't help but love you."

More than I planned to say, but my heart has its own agenda.

"Oh, angel. I love you. I've never been this full of love for someone." He kisses me again, more softly, repeating those words in every touch. "And I will do whatever it takes, however long it takes to convince you I'm not going anywhere. I've been applying for jobs right here in Sunshine."

I drop back down onto my heels. "What about your business? Colorado?"

"I loved what I used to do, and I have a lot of great memories from those years." He tightens his grip on my waist, drawing me in again. "But I want more for my future. I want a future with you."

My baby bird heart takes off into the clouds. If a ship can be joyous, mine is. I am all the things.

"Are your brothers okay with that?"

"When I told them I'm staying in Sunshine because I love you, they understood. Gave me a hard time about it, but they understood."

I run my fingers along his hairline and down across his jaw. I can't stop touching his face. "Are you sure about all this?"

"I don't know how everything will shake out with work. But

angel, I am in this. With you and August. You're all I want, and I'm going to prove that to you every day."

I can't help it. I tear up. "You already do."

He kisses me so tenderly, a few more tears fall. I don't want this moment to end.

Which is exactly when August runs up onto the patio to get in on the action. He throws his arms around both of our waists in a double hug. "You guys kiss?"

"We do." I expect more questions. And I'll answer them... within reason.

"Can Ian stay for dinner?"

I laugh, standing here in the arms of the two guys I love more than anything. "He can stay for dinner."

He can stay forever.

EPILOGUE

TESS

ALL OF THESE mountain men were definitely a mistake. First Hope, then Lila, then me, and even, reluctantly, Wren fell to the charms of an outdoorsy man. But none of us are complaining.

Except maybe me, right this minute.

Ian's leading me on a short hike. Short is relative, I've found. Thankfully, he knows my limits and doesn't try to push me to walk too far or too fast. But the spring air is crisp today, and the sky is a stunning blue. I can appreciate the beauty, even if I'd rather be cuddled up with him on my couch watching *Conan the Barbarian*.

What can I say? Ian got me hooked on Arnold's movies.

"Are we pretty close?" I try to sound eager and not like I'm counting every step until I can sit down somewhere.

He takes my hand. "Very close."

He grins at me, and—okay. Yeah. The hike is worth it to see him glowing like this.

His love for the mountains is undeniable. He's climbed practically everything he can get a permit for around here in the last ten months. Some of that's been through his job as a wilderness EMT, and some he's explored with his new friends.

I've gone on a few of the shorter hikes with him, and it's always the same. He's brilliant out here. I love that he doesn't deny himself what he enjoys anymore.

I don't, either. Especially when it comes to him.

But if I start thinking about that I'll want to stop for entirely new, inappropriate reasons. I turn my thoughts to the work ahead on my calendar. Two wedding cakes this weekend, three the next, with a dozen or more custom cakes in between.

Charlie's modest hopes for Moonlight Lodge's wedding bookings were totally blown out of the water. Not every couple orders a cake from me, but the numbers who do increases every month. And now that my cakes are up on Blackbird's menu, it seems like everyone in town has a birthday or an anniversary to celebrate each week.

I love making every one. Most special of all was the wedding cake I made for Mom and Daniel a month ago. They opted for a courthouse wedding, and a casual reception at the lodge. Seeing her so happy in all ways just reminds me to grab my happiness when it comes around, too.

Which I will. Just as soon as I catch my breath.

We round a bend, and Ian squeezes my hand. I glance up to find a small lake spread out in front of us. Surrounded by pine trees, its gorgeous dark green waters seem like they were dropped here just for us.

"It's beautiful," I breathe. More of a wheeze, really, but it's still a pretty sight.

"Griffin told me about it a few months ago." Ian draws me closer. "I had to bring you to your lake."

"My lake?"

He gestures toward the water. A rough-hewn forest service sign declares it *Angel Lake*.

"Oh, Ian." I turn to face him, and my already overtaxed heart stutters harder.

He's on one knee, holding a tiny box revealing something shiny, smiling up at me as if I am the best thing he's ever seen.

"Angel, I love you more than I ever thought possible. When my world was bleakest, you gave me hope. Joy." His mouth quirks, and his eyes grow shiny. "A family. I want to go on loving you for the rest of our lives. Will you be my wife?"

I drop to my knees with him, ignoring my muddy pants. "Yes!"

He grins even wider as he plucks the ring from the box and slides it on my finger. The pale purple emerald-cut gem has green and white gemstones on either side making it look like a flower blossom. It's perfect.

"I love you so much," I tell him between kisses. "I couldn't be happier."

"I told August I was going to ask you to marry me." His pale blue eyes glisten in the sunlight. "He, uh—"

Ian swallows a couple of times, needing a second to gather his words. I run my hands over his shoulders, waiting. Seeing him choked up gets my tears falling, too.

"He asked if this means he can call me Papa." He grins despite the rush of emotions overtaking him. "So. I can't imagine a better day."

"Yet," I remind him. I crush him against me as close as I can. He holds the back of my head, his face in the crook of my neck.

"I love you with my whole heart and soul," I tell him.

"My angel," he whispers against my skin. "My wonderful Tess."

We're a tangle of limbs and overwhelmed smiles and pure joy. But after a few minutes, I have to pull back.

"When did you ask August? I can't believe he kept this a secret." Keeping his lips sealed isn't exactly his forte.

"Oh, he didn't. I asked him when we dropped him and Dutch off at Wren's an hour ago. He wanted to run out to the car to ask you for me."

That sounds more like it. "So Wren already knows."

"Everyone already knows," he confirms.

"I'm good with that." I wrap my arms around his shoulders. "Will you say it?"

His gaze heats. "We're in the mud."

"That makes it more perfect. Just say it once for me?"

Once now...more later.

"It's always for you." But he tips his face closer to mine and growls. "Arr."

"That's my pirate."

Want two more scenes of Tess and Ian? Sign up for my newsletter to get a cut scene of Ian shamelessly begging for kisses, and one of a special family day a few years in the future. Keep reading for a peek at Wren's book...

BONUS EPILOGUE

WREN

Is this what it's like when the presenter calls your name to come up on the stage and claim your Oscar? It's got to be a close second.

I walk up the pine tree-lined residential street carrying two boxed pies, my body fizzing with triumph. After months of gentle prodding and a tiny bit of bribery—the pies, obviously—I finally snagged an invite to one of the most mysterious clubs in Sunshine. Today is the day. At long last, I get to sit in on Ada and Isabel's smutty book club.

To be clear, I adored their romance pick for the month—a Highlander hero, this one wheedling his way into marriage via blackmailing his intended with her embarrassing letters to an imaginary beau. It automatically went on my favorites list. But I've pictured Ada and Isabel's secret meetings as something subversive for too long for me to just stop referring to them as risqué.

Even if I'm now included in the get-togethers.

I've got a dopey smile on my face when I ring the bell of the classic single-level ranch house. I haven't been this excited to be part of a group since middle school. Maybe it's silly, but it's *mine*. And I need something that's all mine right about now.

Ada swings the entry door open wide. Her chic gray bob accentuates her sharp eyes and bright smile. "Well, if it isn't the newest member of our little enclave. Welcome in, Wren."

She waves me inside, and I step over the threshold into the cozy home.

Enclave. I like that. I'm one of the lucky few included in their super-secret, ultra-exclusive—

"Callahan?"

A dozen or so older women mingling throughout the open-concept living room and kitchen turn at my outburst. But standing in the middle of them wearing a blue flannel shirt layered over a black tee like a grunge rocker among cardigan-clad grandmas is Shepherd Callahan.

How is this my life?

For a second, he's frozen mid-conversation, a polite smile stuck on his face. But then it morphs into a smirk I know all too well.

That smirk sets my teeth on edge and makes my heart rate kick up as I wait for his next move. He's way too amused, like he knows something I don't. I *hate* him knowing things I don't. And right now, I'm so far out of the loop, I'm not entirely sure what the loop *is*.

Ada leads me to the kitchen table and I set down the pies, but I don't take my eyes off of Callahan. What the heck is he even doing here? It seems doubtful any of these ladies had a bicycle break down on their way to book club and had to call an emergency mechanic. So? What gives?

Ada introduces me to the other women. I nod along, but I

can't pretend I'm memorizing anybody's names. Safe to say I'm too distracted by the Callahan of it all.

Finally, she gestures between the two of us. "I'm guessing introductions aren't necessary here."

He shoves his hand out to me, ready to be properly introduced. I roll my eyes and lightly smack it away, but that's a mistake. Touching him is always a mistake. A zing of awareness lights up a panel somewhere in my nervous system labeled *Inconvenient Attraction.* It's like my body never got the memo that the man's a life-ruiner, and instead gets fixated on useless things like *warm, strong hands.*

He makes a rumbly sound in the back of his throat, as amused with me as ever.

"Fill your plates," Isabel instructs. "We're pretending it's still summer and having our discussion on the back deck."

"The patio warmers are already toasty for us," Ada adds. "And we've got a big stack of blankets if you need an extra layer."

It's only early October, but I still expect some kind of complaint from the group. Nobody seems fazed by the revelation, though. I would have worn more than the light hoodie I've got on if I'd known we'd be hanging around outside for book club.

Right now, the chill in the air isn't my most pressing concern.

Callahan shifts to the back of the crowd around the table, letting everyone else go first as if he's some kind of gentleman. I'm waiting for him to realize he wandered into the wrong house by mistake and sneak out, but my dreams remain dashed.

Rosetta, Sunshine's library director, turns from the food to face me. Her silver-streaked hair is twisted into a braided bun atop her head like an ornate crown. "We're happy to have you with us today, Wren. It'll be good to hear another young person's opinions on our book."

"Who is the other young person in the group?" I ask. Because the obvious answer makes no sense.

"I can't decide if that means you think I'm not in the group or not a young person." Callahan's low voice is like a shiver up my spine, equal parts pleasant and unsettling.

"Only one of us is under thirty." I've still got a year to go. Not even Callahan can take that away from me.

Rosetta chuckles. "We have a more generous definition than that."

"Krause can be a stickler with details," Callahan says, eyes on me.

"That's a relief," the woman next to Rosetta pipes up. Janet, I think. "Most of us forget the finer details of the books before we ever get together to discuss the...ahem...broader aspects."

They'll be sincerely disappointed in me, then, since I was expecting to discuss the *broader aspects*, too. By which I assume we mean the kilt-wearing hero.

But I should probably come up with something a little more specific to say about the actual romance. "Well...I think the hero believing that love is a lie is relatable for most—"

Rosetta raises a hand to stop me. "Oh no, no, no. No literary discussion just yet. Not until we've got our food and are settled in."

"There's a structure to it," Isabel says.

"Oh. Right." I look past them to the table where the other women are piling their plates. Along with the pies I brought, I spot a couple of vegetable dishes, a fruit salad, some kind of spicy chicken, and a hearty loaf of bread.

"Krause is eager to discuss her skepticism about love." Callahan's gaze stays stuck on me as the women titter over their plates.

"Yup. That's me." I grab his hand. *Mistake.* Too late to do anything about it now. "You don't mind if I steal Callahan for a minute, do you?"

Pretty sure fresh laughter rolls around the group as I drag him to the relative privacy of Ada's hallway. It's lined with framed photographs and an old-fashioned travel poster of Mount Bachelor. It's also only about fifteen feet from the crowded table, but shutting ourselves up in a bedroom would be wrong on so many levels.

"How are you here?" I hiss at him.

He smirks down at me. Just a twitch of his lips beneath his short beard, but it's enough. He dips his head, sending locks of his mouth-length dark hair over his forehead.

Mouth-length? No. That's not a thing. Ear-length. Somewhere in the vicinity of his cheekbones. Nowhere near his mouth, which I'm definitely not looking at. Whatever the length, his hair is perpetually windswept and messy, like he just hopped off a motorcycle.

Which isn't really the point right now.

"Rosetta invited me," he says.

"When?"

"A few months ago."

A few months? I've been finagling my way in for at least that long.

"Why?"

He lifts a shoulder. "I enjoy reading. We were in the library. Just in case 'Where?' was going to be your next question."

"You don't even read romances." I have no basis for this assertion but the other option is too absurd to comprehend. Shepherd Callahan, sitting around reading about love and romance and relationships? Never.

"You make a lot of assumptions about me."

He squeezes my hand, and I'm horrified to realize I didn't

let go of him when I dragged him back here. I make up for it now, and drop his hand like it's on fire.

"They don't let anybody into their group," I hiss again. My gaze darts past him, but nobody's followed us into the hall. "They keep it a big secret. It took me forever to get them to invite me."

Isabel tried to pretend ignorance even though she's come into Blackbird's to buy desserts for the book club several times.

His smirk widens. "We're a very exclusive group."

"Ugh." My hard-won invitation doesn't seem so special now. Not if they hand them out to just anybody.

"What? Am I not allowed to read books and discuss them with some of Sunshine's most interesting minds?"

No. Not really. He can join some other book club. Not the one I've been so desperate to get into. I can't believe he's been privy to the inner workings of Ada & Isabel's romance club for actual months.

"But it's *romance.*"

That word seems wrong spoken out loud to him. I don't like having it in the air between us. It's a giant, invisible mosquito I want to swat away.

He purses his lips at me. "Krause." He drags it out slowly, teasing me with my own name. "Judging me for reading romance? That's not very enlightened of you."

I take a step closer to him. My traitor gaze skims up his open flannel shirt and the tight, black T-shirt underneath. Unhelpful. As is the flush of warmth creeping up my neck. But stepping out of his space would count as a win for him. Better to stand my ground.

"Just tell me what you're doing here," I seethe.

He inhales so slowly, I almost think he's breathing in my orange and lavender perfume. Which would be crazy. Obviously. This is Callahan. He's probably trying to suck all the air out of the room before I have a chance to breathe it.

For a fraction of a second, his gaze dips from my eyes to my mouth. The heat on my neck becomes an inferno. He snaps his gaze back up to mine.

"Maybe I need more romance in my life."

I snort. "That wouldn't be hard to achieve."

He quirks his eyebrows at me. "Flattery will get you everywhere."

I make a tiny sound of disgust. Naturally, he would take what I say the opposite of how I mean it.

"Are you two ready?" Ada calls from the kitchen. "Better get your food before there's nothing left to eat."

"That won't happen," he whispers like we're sharing secrets back here. Which I suppose we are. "They always send me home with leftovers."

"Is that why you come here? For the free food?"

"You've figured out my scam, Krause. Brilliant sleuthing. Are we done in the hallway or did you want to hold my hand some more?"

My mouth falls open, but I'm pretty sure anything I want to say would get me kicked out of Ada's house. I storm past him, ignoring the hand he's holding out to me and knocking my shoulder against his in the process. The move is always so perfectly dismissive in the movies, but in real life, it's more like an unintended full-body caress.

Sick burn, Wren.

We're the last to fill our plates. I keep my focus trained on the food, willing my brain to erase the last five minutes of sensory input. I can still salvage this, Callahan notwithstanding. Just because he somehow managed to score an invite to their book club first doesn't mean I can't prove myself to be a valuable part of the group. What would he even have to say about romance books?

I kind of hate how much I want to know.

Outside, I'm in for another unpleasant surprise—the ladies have taken up all available seating except for a snug-looking wicker loveseat. They've thoughtfully draped a blanket over one cushion, as if inviting Callahan and me to share it.

Ha. Never.

He sits, and I can't help but notice his jeans-clad thigh doesn't quite stay on his half of the loveseat. I hover behind him, staring at the sliver of leg that's clearly crossed a boundary.

"Come sit down, Wren," Isabel says amid the low chatter. "Shepherd won't bite."

He looks up at me. Something in his brown eyes promises that yes, he absolutely will bite if I get too close.

But there's nothing I hate more than backing down from one of his challenges, spoken or not. I round the loveseat and sit next to him. I lift my eyebrows at him, lobbing back his little dare. I will sit here and eat this delicious food and talk about a Highlander jaded to love, all with our thighs and arms pressed together on this too-small loveseat, possibly while sharing a blanket.

It doesn't bother me at all.

Keep an eye out for Wren and Shepherd's book, One Small Spark!

ACKNOWLEDGMENTS

Thank you for reading Tess & Ian's book! I hope you enjoyed this story of a guarded single mom finding love with her grumpy neighbor. Sorry, not sorry for all the pirate imagery along the way!

Claire, everybody should have a cheerleader like you! Infinite thank yous for your feedback & support, for listening to me doubt everything, and for straightening me out & helping me make every book better! If we weren't already, we'd be instant BFFs for our shared love of classic Arnold movies!

Amanda, I love how you get me right in your head as you read so I can see in real time what's hitting or not.

Kristy, thank you so much for reading this with the experience of a T1D mom.

Cindy, I'm always grateful for your editing expertise that makes my books shine.

Melody, I'll say it forever—you are talented beyond words. This cover is sooo stinking cute!

And finally, to my family, I love you more than my little heart can express. You're my "why" & my rock & my inspiration. I'm just gonna say it: you complete me.

ALSO BY GENNY CARRICK

The Love in Sunshine series

Cinnamon Roll Set Up

The Loch Effect

The Magnolia Ridge series

ABOUT THE AUTHOR

Genny Carrick is a fool for happily ever afters, especially if there's a whole lot of laughter along the way. She writes rom-coms about sassy women, the cinnamon roll men who fall for them, and swoony moments outdoors whenever she possibly can.

When she's not lost in romantic reads, she's probably up to something crafty or trying to get her dog and two cats to love her.

After a quick detour in Texas, Genny recently returned to her true love, the Pacific Northwest, and lives with her brilliant husband and two hilarious kids.

Stay up to date with book news at gennycarrick.com